The SummerHayes Painting

The Art Curator series: Book Two

KENN WILLIAM

This book is a work of fiction. Names, characters, places, and incidents are either products of the author's imagination or are used fictitiously. Any resemblance to actual persons, living or dead, events, or locales is entirely coincidental.

The SummerHayes Painting

The Art Curator series: Book Two

KENN WILLIAM

PART ONE

A large bird soared over the coastal vegetation on a thermal, its silhouette fifty metres above a clump of moonah trees and tea-tree scrub. Stuart followed the bird's passage against the broad summer sky. *Is that a sea eagle?* The bird gained more height, appearing smaller as it effortlessly rode the warm current of air. It banked and flew beyond the frame of the glass wall through which Stuart was watching its progress. Below the building, at ground level, a green carpet spread around three kidney-shaped areas of creamy sand. A motorised buggy with a blue and white striped canopy, two adults in a child's toy, did a slow circuit of the putting green then took a sandy track into the thick vegetation. *And they were never seen again.* Stuart Williams, senior curator of Australian Art, was replete with too many meetings and too much conference coffee. Activity outside the tinted glass wall of the Victorian Automobile Club's resort conference room was as much a distraction as a means of resting his eyes.

'Okay, enough suspense – the big announcement.' *At long last. Bloody Michael's been sitting on this for the last two days. He's like an expectant parent with a gender reveal.* Stuart returned his attention to the room he shared with twenty colleagues from the National Art Gallery of Australia. It was the third and last day of NAGA's senior management strategy and planning retreat. Acting Director Michael raised his hands in response to non-existent applause. He dropped one arm, emphatically snapping the remote control in his other hand to change the presentation. The screen showed a gilded frame around a plain white surface. In the centre was a large question mark.

'Very soon,' said Michael, 'I will be announcing a major acquisition for NAGA.' *You've already told us that.* 'I can't tell you what it is now, but it will be big, very big. *He's channelling Donald Trump!* It will be the biggest acquisition, from this period of art, of any gallery in Australia for decades. It will be a huge drawcard for the gallery, I can promise you that.' The room was quiet.

Above average in height, Michael could be described as solidly-built, but perhaps for not much longer. His well-fed and lubricated frame was putting a strain on the buttons of his checked shirt. He had to loop his trouser belt lower these days to accommodate his expanding stomach. Jane Hollingway, Audience Attraction Manager, broke the silence.

'Michael, you're teasing us. It will be fabulous to have a new drawcard. It's so exciting!'

'Thanks Jane. You and your team will play a big role in developing a program around this work and its acquisition. I can give everyone one hint, one clue.' Michael held up his finger. *Now he's like a man with the punchline to a dad joke.* 'Remember this – my personal area of expertise lies in the Heidelberg School artists.' There was no response until Dominic Valentini, Assistant Director Finance spoke.

'What acquisition fund will it come from?'

'It will come from the director's discretionary fund, but good point Dom,' said Michael. 'The painting,' Michael gestured to the question mark, 'is a recent discovery. Through a personal contact of mine, NAGA is in the very fortunate position of being given first option. You'll appreciate we have to keep this quiet, but to answer your question – we will be purchasing it through thc dircctor's fund, plus a couple of other avenues which I'm currently exploring.' Michael looked down the conference table, his morning-after puffy eyes undermining his earnest expression. 'The gallery's going to get huge attention out of this, which in turn will flow onto the exhibitions and programs we have been planning over these last couple of days.'

Following their last break, Stuart's friend Alison, NAGA's Research Manager, and fellow curator Kelly Bertolucci brought their cups, and plates of fresh fruit, back to seats next to him at the conference table. The aim of the NAGA retreat was to plan a ten-year program of work for the gallery. While a decade was an ambitious timeframe, the gallery had to plan well ahead to allow for lead times of major acquisitions, overseas exhibitions and coordination with fellow national and international organisations. Four months ago, Michael was promoted from Assistant to Acting Director of the National Art Gallery of Australia. With permanent director Angela

O'Keefe on sick leave, the board had appointed Michael in her position. He had referred to their director in his opening remarks at the retreat.

'Unfortunately, Angela is still unwell and is unlikely to be resuming her duties in the near future.' Michael, hands clasped, paused in respectful silence.

'She hasn't died,' Kelly had whispered to Alison.

'But we can't afford to play a holding game,' said Michael, rallying. 'I know she would want us to crack on with all our programs.' There was no argument that the gallery must set out a schedule of exhibitions, its acquisition plans, a conservation schedule, promotional activities, major events and joint ventures.

On the first morning of the retreat Dominic had given his finance presentation. Until recently, Stuart had not taken a great interest in NAGA's finances, leaving that side of the gallery's operations to the people he thought best equipped to handle the intricacies of ensuring their financial stability. However, Stuart's management of the last blockbuster exhibition, *Masterpieces from the Musée d'Orsay,* had drawn him into a situation of high stakes and personal stress. The success of that exhibition, never a foregone conclusion, had been critical to the gallery getting through a financial crisis known to only a few players.

Dominic's dark suits, short black hair and lugubrious manner contributed to his nickname of Dracula. He had spoken of NAGA's financial plan in his dry, bloodless style, cautioning managers to manage their funds carefully and cut back on resources where they could.

Stuart had some questions, and was looking for reassurance following the just-averted financial crisis. He also wanted to know more about NAGA's dependency on the Sodaspring Beverages Group as a corporate sponsor. Michael had cut off any opening for questions, moving to the next agenda item.

Michael's vocal cords were showing the strain of consecutive days in full conference mode – he sounded like an old-fashioned pack-a-day man. As well as leading discussions, Michael had drunk a lot of wine at dinner the previous evening. He was not the only one. People were in a mood of either celebration or relief at the thought that they had almost completed their program of planning activities. They had all had their fill of presentations, whiteboards with dried-out markers and discussions dominated by the same voices. Stuart accepted a slice of melon, smiling a thank you at Alison. Kelly's subdued mood was evidence that she had been one of the stayers in the resort lounge the previous evening.

Michael had waited following his announcement of the pending acquisition, but there were no more questions.

'I know you have a lot more questions but we'll have to keep it under wraps for now. I will be giving the board a briefing at their next monthly meeting. Please keep this between us.' Michael held his arm in the air, auctioneer-style. 'And on that note,' He slapped the table. 'Let's pack up and head back to Melbourne.'

The handle of Stuart's car was hot to touch. As he opened the driver's door a blast of thick, hot air hit his face. The car had been parked and un-used for the duration of the retreat. The accumulated heat of three thirty-five degree days met the outside air. Kelly put her suitcase in the boot of the car with Stuart and Alison's belongings, opened the door and flung herself onto the back seat. She was wearing large sunglasses and had bottled water in both hands. Alison and Stuart waited a few minutes for some of the stale air to escape before getting in. Stuart drove along the paved road of the resort to its exit. By the time Stuart joined the highway to Melbourne, Kelly was asleep, mouth slightly open, one water bottle on the seat, her grip loose on the other.

'The poor pet,' said Alison.

'Self-inflicted. She did well to keep up with Michael, Jane and the rest last night. But this afternoon must have been a struggle,' said Stuart. Alison looked at the passing parade of holiday homes along the section of highway. The architecture ranged from the displaced suburban to the grandiose statement, with original old-style beach shacks a rarity.

'What did you think of Michael's announcement?'

'A non-event. I don't know what he was expecting,' said Stuart. 'Without telling us what the supposed acquisition is, did he expect us to shower him with praise, break into spontaneous song or something? It was weird.'

'You know Michael, Stuart. It's all about him. He's desperate to make an impression as director while he's acting in the role.'

'He's a very risky choice. I don't trust the man.'

'Well, you've good reason not to.' She was referring to Michael's actions when Stuart managed the *Masterpieces from the Musée d'Orsay* exhibition. Stuart checked his exterior mirror before overtaking a slower moving car. He had taken on the role of staging the last NAGA blockbuster which Michael had initially negotiated with the Musée d'Orsay. Michael's exhibition preparation and planning had been sadly lacking, and his contribution as senior manager next to useless. Somehow, Stuart had got the blockbuster exhibition ready in time, and the audiences that the gallery desperately needed attended in their thousands. He raised his eyes to check on Kelly, remembering how she had rallied NAGA staff to shut down the gallery when Michael tried to take the exhibition manager role off Stuart. She was slumped down in her seat, her head resting against the side panel of the car's interior.

'How are things with you and Lucy, Ali?'

'We're fine. Lucy's enjoying a hectic social life with fifteen of her closest friends from school.'

'And you, still seeing Ben the Banker?'

'He's not a children's character, Mister Jealous. He's okay. We're going to the open-air theatre in the Botanical Gardens this weekend. Though I could sleep for two days. What about you?'

'What about me?' replied Stuart. He increased the car's pace as the highway merged with the freeway and he chose his lane for Melbourne.

'Yes, you Stuart. You're separated, finalising a divorce. You've just shifted into a house with another person. You're closer to forty than thirty. You've got shared custody of Declan. And you're father's seriously ill. How are you?'

Stuart flicked his indicator to change lanes, the view to his left still offering a distant glimpse of the blue water of the bay. He thought back to the ocean swim he had done that morning. He had entered an undulating sea, the sun above the horizon but behind a screen of silky grey clouds. There were only two other swimmers, a hundred metres down the beach. He swam out a little way, treaded water, then set off for the point at one end of the beach's arc. After a few strokes he acclimatised to the temperature of the water, after a few more he settled into his rhythm. In the windless summer morning, he was aided by the absence of any substantial waves, able to turn his head and breathe easily every third stroke. Although he had not joined the big-drinking group after last night's dinner, he had drunk more than usual. There were several people in his group of post-dinners drinkers, but he only recalled talking with Alison. The sharp tang of the sea cleared his head; his strong swimming stroke took him to his turn-around point. He trod water for a few seconds only, then swam back across the small bay. He kept a steady pace until he aligned with the sandy path to their accommodation, then flipped onto his back and floated. The sun broke through the film of early morning cloud. He allowed its searching rays to settle on his face.

'Stuart?'

'Sorry. Yeah, Declan's good. He seems to be coping well with the two-homes arrangement between Leah and I. Dad is not getting better. Mum says he might have to go into a full-time care facility.'

'Must be hard for your family.' Stuart nodded.

'You want to stop for anything? Buy water, stretch your legs?' he asked. Kelly stirred in the back seat, shifting her position, padding her head with a rolled towel.

'Are we there yet?' she mumbled. Alison stage-whispered to Stuart.

'I think we all need to get home.'

'Dad, those people are watching me.'

'That's okay, ignore them.' Stuart and his ten-year old son sat on the warm, splintery timber of a pier, part of the Hobson's Bay marina complex. Their feet dangled a couple of metres over the gently slapping water. The late morning sun danced on the water's surface, causing father and son to squint. Across the water, at some invisible boundary, Hobson's Bay became the larger Port Phillip Bay. Melbourne's skyline of office buildings and residential towers was in distant profile. The light painted the buildings in pastel shades, except for one tall tower with a metallic side, shining brilliantly.

Behind Stuart and Declan people ambled and strolled, drawn by some mysterious power to the end of the pier. They peered over the edge into the water, admired the moored boats, pointed at stingrays, then walked back down the pier. Declan was conscious of people's legs as they paused to see what he and his father were up to. Families strolled with children, toddlers in hand, babies in prams. Young and old couples passed, chatting, eating ice-creams.

'Can I have an ice-cream, Dad?'

'Sure. When we've had enough, we'll go to the shops before we go home.' Stuart glanced across at Declan's drawing pad. They had driven to Williamstown after breakfast to do some sketching. The old port suburb of Melbourne offered great subject matter; a protected harbour, boatyards, cafes and restaurants, a park and playgrounds, bunches of cyclists (helmeted and bearded, pedalled and motored) yachts, open boats, leisure craft and even an ex-World War 2 ship.

'What's that big grey ship, Dad?'

'An old warship, called a corvette. They did a lot of work in the war as mine-sweepers.'

'Does it have guns?'

'It would have – it had to defend itself.'

'Why is it here?'

'They built ships here.' Stuart indicated the boatyard and marine sheds. 'Williamstown was a big boat and shipbuilding place. The ship's been restored so that people can visit and take a tour to see how it operated during the war.'

'How do you know so much about the ship?'

'You know your grandad Evan, my dad. Well, his father, my grandfather, served on corvettes during the war. When we were little, he told us about this ship.'

'Did he tell you about the war?'

'No, he didn't, next to nothing.' Declan's drawing pad had several just-started and half-completed boats. 'Can I show you something?' Stuart angled his own drawing pad towards Declan, pencil poised. 'Can you draw a figure eight? Like this?'

'On its side? Yeah.' Declan copied the elongated figure eight.

'Now, if we do four or five of these, vary their sizes and shapes a little, but keep them in the same direction. Use the pencil really lightly.' Declan had forgotten about the people treading the weathered timbers behind them.

'What we do now is over-draw the figure eight like this, which gives us the curved shape of a small boat.' Stuart drew the hull of a boat, making a pointed bow and cutting off a blunt stern. He added a tilted mast.

'Neat. Can we have an ice-cream now?'

'Good idea.'

*

Six weeks ago, Stuart had moved into a new shared-house arrangement. After the split with his wife Leah, he had lived in an apartment by himself, remaining in the same inner northern suburb. Sometimes Declan stayed with him for a week, on other occasions he had Declan for the weekend only. It appeared to be working. In the car on their return from the sketching trip, Declan had demolished his ice-cream and started exchanging messages on his phone.

'Huh.'

'What are you huh-ing at?' asked Stuart.

'Something from Jupiter. It's nothing.' The boy, with his dark brown hair falling over his eyes, focussed on the phone messages from his best friend at school.

'Jupiter says his parents argued last night. They forgot all about him and he stayed up really late.'

'Do they argue often?'

'All the time.' Declan kept looking downwards. 'Jupiter's dad calls his mum Queen Bitch.'

'To her face?'

'Nah, it's like, Jupiter says … where's my school bag? His dad goes, "ask the Queen Bitch."'

'What do you think about that?' asked Stuart.

'She says to Jupiter, "talk to Knobhead", about his dad.'

'That doesn't make it okay though.' Declan's eyes moved away from his phone screen, sliding briefly up to his father's face. Stuart concentrated on the traffic, letting Declan draw ten-year old conclusions about relationships and marriages.

The shared house, in the suburb adjacent to his family home, had come about through a contact at NAGA. Art handler Matt Keegan's boyfriend Shane worked at one of the Australian football clubs. A newly re-located player had been seeking a housemate, at the time when Stuart had told Matt that he was looking for a more companionable home set-up. The two men had met at a café in the neighbourhood shops near the shared house. Stuart said that he did not follow the football closely.

'Mate, that suits me.' Tarquin Power tucked his long legs under the outdoor café table. 'I've come back from interstate. I'm from Melbourne, but got drafted at eighteen to play in Western Australia.' Stuart thought he had heard Tarquin's name, either on the news or in the context of office chatter, but he couldn't be certain. Tarquin finished the last of his bowl of quinoa salad.

'I had too much of the football world in WA. Melbourne is intense enough as it is without living it 24/7.'

'You renting this house?'

'No, I bought it when my WA contract ended. I always wanted to come home, and my girlfriend and I had split up, too.' Tarquin gave a 'shit happens' shrug. Stuart's first impressions were shaping well.

'I have a ten-year old boy, and – '

'Stuart, if you're interested, let's go and have a look.'

Stuart had liked the house and moved in. He discovered they were both in their thirties, though at opposite ends of the decade. The townhouse, built six years ago, took up most of its block, with space for a side courtyard and minimal backyard. Tarquin had taken over the rear bedroom and bathroom, leaving the front bedroom and ensuite for Stuart. There was a smaller third bedroom. Tarquin had been very generous.

'Here's your son's room. You can set it up so that he can leave his stuff here.' Between their bedrooms at either end of the house, the two men shared kitchen, dining and lounge spaces in the central part of the house. These rooms opened to a paved terrace and small garden with barbeque. In the garage, Tarquin had set up a weights bench and treadmill. He said he did most of his weights at the club so Stuart was welcome to make use of the equipment. It was a domestic relationship which, to date, was working well for all three of them.

*

On return from their outing, Tarquin was standing next to the coffee pod machine on the kitchen bench. His large hands were pushed into the pockets of his loose-fitting tracksuit top.

'Declan-dude! A hot chocolate?'

'Yeah. How's the calf?'

'It's going okay. Coffee, Stuart?'

'No thanks. What calf?'

'Dad,' Declan was mildly disgusted, at least disappointed. 'Tarqs has a calf injury and he's in rehab.'

'I'm running now, building up gradually.' The pre-season was a long grind for Australian football players. In an early get-to-know-you chat, Stuart had learned that Tarquin saw his new club as his last opportunity to play football at the highest level. He was being realistic. Now, in his thirties, he had played almost two hundred games, but also had had too many soft-tissue injuries in recent seasons. He told Stuart he was hoping to eke out another two seasons, at most three. He also told Stuart that he was in the middle of studying a course in sports law. Tarquin had in turn been interested in Stuart's work at NAGA, the country's premier arts institution. He had asked Stuart about the gallery's blockbuster exhibition *Masterpieces from the Musée d'Orsay*, which Tarquin had caught in its last days. Unaware that Stuart had been intimately involved in the exhibition as project manager and curator on the Australian side, he had made some observations.

'The Monet and Renoir were great, but a couple of the graphic works were awesome.'

'Which ones?' Stuart felt a little mean putting out this test.

'The Toulouse-Lautrec figure, even the Gauguin self-portrait. I like the immediacy of drawings.' Stuart made a mental note to watch his prejudices and predetermined opinions in relation to this well-built sportsperson.

'What position are you going to play this year, Tarquin?' Declan accepted his chocolate drink from the footballer.

'Gotta get a game first, dude. But a run-with defender role looks most likely.' Tarquin levered himself from a half-standing, half-leaning position against the kitchen bench and turned to go into the hallway to his part of the house. 'Back to the books for me. Catch you later, Decs.'

Stuart had been checking messages on his phone, but was still aware of the easy exchange between his son and housemate. Leah wanted to know what time he would be returning Declan tomorrow afternoon, ending her message with a smiley-face emoticon. Stuart had observed that his wife seemed more relaxed than had been the case for years – another indication the Williams family may be safely navigating the post-marriage waters. That may have also been due to her new job at the Kalorama Writers' Retreat, a centre based in an old guest house in the Dandenong Ranges.

He read a short message from Alison (just before she was off to the theatre with Ben) that said she had been contacted by Melanie Norman, great grand-daughter of Australian artist Arthur Norman. This message was work-related, and interesting, but Stuart read it again for any personal note. *Anyway, she's busy getting off to the theatre*. The last message was from his mother.

Letting you know your father has moved into the full-time care facility at the Eastside Gardens home. Talk to you soon, love Mum

Stuart waited until Declan had settled into 'the dude's room' before he called his mother. He asked her if it was a good idea to take Declan with him when he visited his father the next day.

It had been a wet start to the year. High summer in south eastern Australian was usually defined by long, hot days, with soaring temperatures that leached all colour from the grasses and made trees angle their leaves away from the sun. If Melbournians were in luck, strings of hot days built up to bruising thunderstorms that brought sudden and dramatic drops in temperature. They could cause flash-flooding in the streets or disappoint with a side-swiping let-down of a shower. On a hot, cloudless morning the bright green lawns and garden beds at Eastside Gardens were holding up well due to the summer rains. Stuart and Declan left the car park and entered the oldest part of the residential aged-care complex.

'Okay, phones away,' said Stuart, sliding his phone into his shorts and watching as his son did likewise. The entrance and registration area was instantly cooling. Stuart felt a tinge of sunburn on his forearms, a souvenir of their outdoor sketching yesterday. He took a large breath as the temperature contrast hit them with force – and to steady his emotions. They had come indoors from a blazing, sun-filled, expansive day. A day of activities and possibilities. Inside the red-brick building, it was quiet and contained. This was where his father now spent all his hours.

'It stinks Dad,' whispered Declan.

'That's only cleaning smells,' said Stuart as they set off to find his father's room.

Evan Williams was propped up in bed, the corners of his pillow making exaggerated ears. Stuart was not sure his father recognised him or Declan until he was next to the bed. To make certain, he leant over, putting his head in front of his father's lop-sided face. A grin in response, and, with effort, a few words.

'Stuart … with Dec … lan.' Stuart's father had been a statutory planner. Retired for some years, he had been active, taking regular walks around the leafy suburb which had been his and his wife's home forever. He maintained the garden, did too many home maintenance jobs when he should have delegated or paid someone, and read biographies for relaxation. He did not follow the football or cricket, or initiate drinks or meals with friends, but did his bit when there were family meals and other milestone occasions. He was a willing participant and companion on his wife's trips to Europe, particularly to France where she had a long-term French friend. Stuart's mother Rosemary said she only saw the demon within the man if she ever had cause to pick him up from his weekly game of tennis.

'The competitive streak breaks through then! And the sulks if Ron and Alan beat him and Jeffrey!' It was not while playing tennis, but on an innocuous shopping trip when Evan tripped on a bluestone gutter, coming down heavily and breaking his hip. He told the story with relish when convalescing.

'Oranges and potatoes rolled everywhere, all over the blessed carpark. I was on the ground trying to stop them rolling away. A nice young man came and helped me up, but my stupid, wonky leg wouldn't support me.' It was possibly the most words he had heard his father say at one time. The broken hip should have been a temporary inconvenience, however four months later he had another fall, this time at home. No-one, not even Evan, knew how the second fall happened. Rosemary came home to find him lying in the middle of the backyard. He was semi-conscious, not dressed warmly enough, with the upturned wheelbarrow and spilt gardening tools around him. Evan's decline had been rapid. Two strokes had propelled him along a rapid pathway from active to non-active, home to facility, husband and father to patient. Declan had been standing back but now edged forward.

'Hello grandpa.' Declan's eyes were large pools of dark chocolate. A thin arm in pyjamas moved a centimetre at a time towards the edge of the bed, eventually reaching Declan's hand resting on the bed clothes.

'Good … boy.' The man's words came from a place deep within his shrinking body, tripping over dry, trembling lips.

'You comfortable, Dad? Do you need a sip of water? Are you sitting okay – can I prop you up more?' Again, the words were effortful.

'Good … boy.' Before his father's decline, Stuart had observed his interaction with Declan with warmth, and a measure of puzzlement. Was the man who romped through improvised children's games really the same person who lived with Stuart when he was at home? And what about the man who three months ago told Declan a bawdy joke – was that Evan Williams or an imposter? Bawdy joke? This from a man who Stuart had never heard utter a swear word. Stuart thought of his father as a constant. Not just any constant, but *the* constant while growing up, and in his life. He was always there, without noise or bluster, without fanfare or ceremony. His mother Rosemary would be planning family events, organising her swimming classes, researching their travels, talking about friends, chasing Stuart and his brother and sister, asking questions, seeking their ideas and opinions, driving them to suburbs near and far, listening to their stories. Stuart had only lately realised his father had been there too, sharing the load, while observing and listening. Had they been guilty of taking him for granted? Probably.

'Dad, has Alexandra visited?' Stuart did not see much of his older sister. She was in a corporate role with one of Melbourne's largest consultancy firms. Something to do with business continuity. They got on well on occasions such as family meals but neither felt the need to seek out each other's company. His father hadn't answered and may have dropped off to sleep.

'Can I play outside?' asked Declan.

'Sure. Say goodbye to grandpa and stay on the big lawn.' Stuart watched Declan's mop of curly hair bounce as if on springs as he left the room. He wondered how, if he was asked, Stuart would describe his relationship with his father. Stuart certainly hadn't talked to his father like he allowed Declan to talk to him. At those times when Stuart defaulted to the dad-joke stereotype, his son responded in a scathing, long-suffering manner. They both played their roles.

Evan and Rosemary had another son, Stuart's younger brother Gareth. After finishing school Gareth took off on a gap year. More than ten years later, he hadn't returned. Or so it seemed to Stuart. Gareth's trips back home to Melbourne were periods of rest between travels. He had travelled solo, and with friends, in Europe, Asia and South America. His family might not hear from him for up to two years at a stretch. Rosemary was relying on his last communication to try to contact him.

'He was working in a bar in a town on Lake Como in Italy,' she told Stuart. 'Just down the lake from George Clooney's place apparently.'

'That's convenient, I'll give George a call and get him to pass on a message to Gareth,' suggested Stuart.

'Very helpful. He's still with that Colombian girlfriend too.'

'What Colombian girlfriend?' For Stuart, Gareth was an irregular apparition of grinning, long-haired images on his phone. Full beard with headband, drink in hand and attractive young woman at his side. 'What's her name?' Rosemary frowned. 'Valencia or something like that. She was a model … and studying at uni. We need to let him know about dad.'

Evan was now definitely asleep. Stuart held his father's hand for a minute, then released it. He talked for five minutes with one of the staff before leaving. On the lawn, Declan was kicking a large seed pod, running to where it stopped, kicking it again. Seeing his father come out of the building and cross to the carpark, he ran to their car. Putting on their seatbelts, he asked the same thing that was preoccupying Stuart.

'Is grandpa going to get better?' The head of nursing who had spoken to Stuart had been unequivocal.

'He may remain as you saw him today, Mr Williams. For quite some time.' Stuart paused from starting the car. 'It's sad for us, Decs, but they don't expect him to get better.'

'That sucks.'

The National Art Gallery of Australia is a mixture of buildings on the northern fringe of Melbourne's central business district. NAGA's different building constructions reflect the architectural styles of their day – these times coinciding with spurts of national prosperity. Set back from the corner of two streets, the buildings containing the country's premier art collection dating back one hundred and fifty years. Some buildings had been reconverted to newer uses; most had been added onto over the years to accommodate the art works or the gallery's operations. Surrounding the buildings were gardens with mature trees. The older European deciduous trees cohabitated with towering eucalypts. Dotted around the grounds were robust sculptures, dating from the nineteenth to twenty-first century. The main gallery building connected to the other buildings and public galleries by doorways in adjoining walls or via a couple of colour-coded walkways. In this way, NAGA resembled a university campus. Like a campus, it was a wayfinding nightmare. No matter what signage system was adopted, at any given time half of NAGA's visitors were either lost or asking for directions from patient gallery staff.

Stuart stood with Marion Dellacourt next to a neat stack of blue-painted crates. Marion was the curator from the Musée d'Orsay with whom he worked on the gallery's recently closed blockbuster exhibition. The same exhibition that Michael had tried to remove Stuart from managing on the eve of its opening. The Director who had over-ruled Michael was now on indefinite sick leave and Michael was Acting Director.

Stuart wondered if other people at NAGA, or the musée, understood or appreciated the work which Marion had put into the exhibition to make it happen. Stuart was more than aware. Given the task of managing the exhibition, then being told the financial future of the gallery was dependent on its success, he was more than grateful for her professional contribution. Marion had accompanied the artworks on their travels to Melbourne, and had now returned for the repacking and return trip.

Stencilled black numerals indicated which precious art works from the *Masterpieces from the Musée d'Orsay* exhibition were contained in each crate. The exhibition of loan works from the famous French museum had proven to be a popular exhibition, attracting thousands of visitors and helping to turn around the precarious financial situation. The responsibility of making the exhibition a success was huge. As well as working closely with Marion, Stuart had developed a good understanding with her Musée d'Orsay colleagues Jean-Paul, known as JP, and the Directuer, Relations Internationale, Tony de Belleville.

'Et maintenant nous disons au revoir, Marion', said Stuart. Marion moved from crate to crate checking code numerals against her laptop. They were in the basement of the main storage area of NAGA. Marion turned to face Stuart.

'Oui, Stuart. L'exhibition s'est bien terminée.' Soon a truck would be arriving and they would supervise its loading for the trip to Melbourne airport.

'Jane Hollingway tells me that the final numbers are very good,' said Stuart. 'Although Jane being Jane, she couldn't resist pointing out that the sale of catalogues and merchandise through the exhibition shop accounted for 52 percent of the revenue.'

'Yes,' Marion let her shoulders dip minutely. 'But that is why when we do these big exhibitions, we have people exit through the shop. A fact of life.' Stuart had many nervous moments, in Melbourne and in Paris, when preparing the blockbuster-style exhibition. It was with Marion's cooperation that he had managed to secure a major attraction for the exhibition while he was at the Musée d'Orsay.

'The Renoir and Monet were the highlights, as we expected. It was marvellous of Tony to pull strings within your bureaucracy and get the Renoir at the last minute. What did you and he decide about our desert paintings?' Stuart was referring to a deal between the two galleries to 'exchange' the Renoir masterpiece for the loan of some central Australian paintings. Marion put her laptop on the top of a crate level with her waist.

'I'll show you.' Marion brought up an image of NAGA's Dreamtime Gallery. 'These ones of the overall room are for our reference. Tony and I will be making a strong presentation to our directorate.' The French curator flicked through full screen images of aboriginal bark paintings, woven textiles and wood-carved sculptural figures. She slowed down her flicking speed when she came to a series of dot paintings. These were paintings done by central Australian aboriginal artists, dating from the 1980s to the current decade. 'This is our shortlist at the moment. We have decided to create our exhibition around only three masterpieces.' The paintings on Marion's screen showed myriads of tiny dots, as well as swirls of sinuous lines and the placement of centuries-old symbols and representations.

'Tony and I have learnt so much in our visit. Only now we realise how little we know, and how your indigenous art is so misinterpreted. So, we have decided on a highly didactic exhibition. Three superb paintings, but supported by much educational material – videos, photographs from central Australia, interviews with the artists. We even hope to bring out two aboriginal artists to Paris during the show.' Stuart was confident Marion's professionalism and enthusiasm would enable her to help European audiences appreciate the art of central Australia, at least to a certain level.

'I'm sure you'll do a great job, Marion.' The truck was due five minutes ago. Stuart suddenly had several things he wanted to say to Marion. A final and heart-felt thank you for working with him on his exhibition. He wanted to wish her success with the central Australian art exhibition. Pass on his greetings to all at the Musée d'Orsay and … Marion's phone beeped.

'Ah, the truck is two minutes away.' She flipped her laptop shut, gathered her notes and a canvas tote bag. Marion faced Stuart, leant towards him and they exchanged two-sided cheek kisses. 'I shall see you next time you are in Paris, Stuart.'

'Definitely.'

On way to his office on the administrative level, Stuart checked his phone messages. There were three of most interest. Acting Director Michael had sent around a request for Stuart, along with other gallery managers, to attend tomorrow's NAGA Board meeting – the agenda item unspecified. His mother had an update saying that she had still not been able to contact his brother Gareth. She added that his sister Alex was pursuing a contact in Italy who may be able to help. The other was from Alison.

Hi Stuart – you okay for a coffee sometime today?

*

In the mid-afternoon, the gallery café was showing the signs of the tail-end of the busy peak period. Two tables were yet to be cleared, there was a paper napkin and the remains of a muffin on the floor, and waiting staff were slowing down as they recouped. Alison and Stuart sat against a wall, beneath an image of Monet's *Blue Waterlilies* - a poster from the *Masterpieces from the Musée d'Orsay* exhibition.

'Did you see Marion off today?' Alison was wearing a pea-green, cashmere cardigan with the top button only fastened. Stuart nodded.

'Yep. The show's all packed up and gone now.'

'Do you think you got to know Marion at all through your working together?'

'Well, I know she is a highly competent curator –'

'You're not giving her a reference. Do you think you know her better as a person?' Stuart turned down the corners of his mouth.

'She's French. You know, they maintain this cool, professional reserve with colleagues, even with their own people –

'Not JP. He was chasing every eligible female in NAGA when he was here.'

'Yes, well. JP is an exception.' The gregarious Jean-Paul was, in Marion's term, a *blageur* or joker. Stuart finished his coffee but wanted to stay in Alison's company. He thought of ordering another but didn't need it. Alison suggested they walk back through the galleries.

They walked at visitor pace past the entrance to the Dreamtime Gallery, choosing a route down a long, narrow gallery that was more of a corridor than exhibition room. It displayed a selection of Australian photography from the permanent collection.

'Isn't this cute?' Alison inclined her head towards a colonial-era photo of a forested gully with extravagantly fanned tree-ferns. Under the large fronds a pipe-smoking man with an abundant white beard and battered hat impishly stared out at the nineteenth century photographer. They looked closer at the black and white photograph, Stuart admiring a fine network of lines at the corner of Alison's eyes. He thought impish was also a good word to describe Alison's smile.

'They loved those ferny gullies, the white settlers,' he said. Moving further down the gallery, Stuart asked, 'Do you know what Michael wants us for at the board meeting tomorrow?'

'It's to do with his big announcement, I've heard. But that may be a rumour. How was your father, last visit?' They stopped at the end of the gallery. They were in front of a large contemporary photograph, a tableau of decaying fruit, broken children's' toys, torn books, used clothes and much more.

'Looks like washing day at my place,' said Stuart. 'Dad's not going to get any better. He may hang on for … who knows? We're trying to get my younger brother back from overseas … in time.' Alison put her hand on his arm.

'Such a hard time for you all. How is Declan coping?' Stuart was unclear if the question was solely about Declan coping with the seriousness of his grandfather's illness. It could also be about how he was dealing with the separation of his parents.

'Declan is doing okay, I think. He's delighted that I'm sharing a house with Tarquin Power.' They left the photography exhibition and went to the lifts.

'It's my mother's 70th next month,' said Alison. 'Would you like to come to Canberra for the weekend? Be my date for the party?'

'A 70th party?' Stuart held the lift door for Alison to enter. 'What about Ben?'

'I can invite whoever I like. Do you want to have a weekend in Canberra with me or not?'

'I'd love to. Have to check that Leah can look after Declan.' After he had the date for the party and seen Alison to her workspace, Stuart walked to his office. He had a strong step and a grin on his face.

As Stuart got to the door of the NAGA boardroom Matt Keegan called out to him.

'Hey Stu! Hold the door will you, mate?' Matt, NAGA's Lead Art Handler, was holding one side of a rolling easel. The other was held by Christina-Rose Woolton, NAGA Conservation Manager. Stuart held the door open as the two staff members wheeled the easel and its load into the boardroom. A rigid rectangle, white cloth completely covering it, rested on the easel ledge. It was secured at the top by a wooden bracket. Matt and Christina entered the boardroom to a chorus of comments and exclamations.

'Hello, hello.'… 'Here it is!'… 'Michael, what have you got for us?' The noise, attention and expectation resembled the arrival of a cake at a milestone celebration. Matt and Christina-Rose positioned the easel in the furthest corner of the boardroom. Michael hovered, tugging at the cloth to make sure it was not revealing anything. Stuart saw his fellow managers mingling with the eight board members. Most were standing with tea or coffee. Stuart watched Michael fuss over the angle of the easel, directing its orientation to be just so. When Michael turned his back Matt moved the easel ten centimetres back again. Board Chairman Russell Dalton-Smith broke away from a conversation to talk in a low voice to Michael. The chairman placed a hand on Michael's shoulder. Christina adjusted the goose-neck lamps attached to the top of the easel. Stuart joined Alison at the refreshments side table that was set out for the late afternoon break.

The NAGA Board meeting followed a regular format; an agenda of business items, an after-meeting tour of the latest exhibition in the gallery (conducted by the relevant curator), a break for board members to check messages, make calls and attend to other matters, then pre-dinner drinks. The monthly dinner for board members, and a limited number of guests, was always a gastronomic highlight. This month an unveiling by Michael was taking the place of the guided tour.

'Have you heard what Michael's big announcement is, under there?' asked Alison, looking in the direction of the easel. She dipped her head as if she could see what was beneath the obscuring cloth.

'No, I haven't,' said Stuart. 'You?'

'I would have told you. Not keep it to myself.' Michael raised his voice over the chatter.

'Please take your seats everybody.' Michael was wearing a deep charcoal suit, teamed with a crumpled-look, pale orange shirt with a button-down collar. Stuart thought the suit was new and the shirt was a winner.

'We won't have to wait long now,' he said to Alison. Michael sat at the top of the table with the chairman. His voice filled the room.

'New attendees, please use the chairs around the walls if there is no more room at the table. Thank you. Russell?' The chairman had the sort of moon-face that would always look over fed, if not pampered. He swivelled in his seat to better take in the room of attendees, gesturing with his hand at the easel.

'So. Here it is. I bet you're wondering what's under that cloth?' He beamed at his own statement, milking the moment. 'But first, Michael will give us a bit of background.'

'Thank you Mr Chairman. In a couple of minutes, Russell will unveil a major acquisition for the National Art Gallery of Australia. This is a fantastic occasion for NAGA, one which will help to keep us up there as the country's premier art gallery. I'm confident that our new acquisition will be that rare prize in the art world – a critical success and a public favourite.' Dalton-Smith was moving in his seat, edging towards the easel. 'Two more things for everyone here today. One, and the chairman and I can't stress this strongly enough, is that the details of this acquisition must stay within the knowledge of this room and today's attendees. That is, until we make a major public announcement in due course. Therefore, keep the painting and artist to yourself, as hard as that might be. And secondly, the painting's provenance, also to be kept to yourself. It has come to us through a contact in Victoria, through a collection which I have had close, personal knowledge.' Michael tilted his chin up, and drew a breath which made his chest rise. 'Through my association, I can tell you that this painting has never been seen by anyone outside the owner's family and circle, nor has it been sold or exhibited. Let's do the honours, Russell.'

The chairman and Michael rose from their chairs and positioned themselves at either side of the easel. People tilted in their seats or shifted their chairs to get better views. Jane Hollingway had a camera in her hands, raised to take a photo. A couple of other people held up phones.

'Sorry!' Michael made a traffic policeman's stopping gesture. 'Only Jane to take photos please. For the internal record, not for distribution.' The chairman had picked up a cord attached to the covering cloth. Michael and he looked at each other. Michael said 'on the count of three – one, two, three!'

Dalton-Smith pulled the cord and the cloth parted in the middle. A third of the painting was still covered at either side. The two men drew the cloth away and over the top of the painting. Jane had taken several photos in succession and now led the chorus.

'Hooray!' She clapped her hands, still clasping the camera, as others spoke.

'It's an Australian landscape, by –' 'Lovely painting.'… 'What a grand scene, looks turn of the century?'… 'It looks familiar –' 'Who's it by?'
Stuart leant against Alison's shoulder.

'Who do you think the artist is?' Before she could answer, Michael stood in front of the landscape painting, cutting off the reactions and commentary. With both hands in the air, palms out, he stood with feet apart.

'Ladies and gentlemen, you are looking at … a newly-discovered painting by … the Heidelberg School and great Australian artist … Arthur Streeton. It's *Wooreen, on the Grange Burn*.' He pointed to the many-chimneyed, stone house set in the farming landscape. 'This is the *Wooreen* Homestead, painted by Sir Arthur Streeton in 1924.'

'I thought it looked like a Streeton.'… 'A late career one.'… 'It's one of those pastorals.' 'Didn't he do the

Golden Fleece painting in that district?' Michael again raised his voice to speak over the meeting.

'I can understand your excitement. I know you must be bursting with questions. Let's take them one at a time.' The chairman and Michael sat down, Michael pointed to Jane to prompt her question.

'Where did you discover it, Michael?' It was clear to all that Jane knew exactly where it had been found.

'In the proverbial old shed on a farm, Jane. Well, not really, but close enough. The Streeton was painted for the SummerHayes family, from Victoria's Western District. It has been in their possession since – never left their property until it came here.' Next to him, Stuart sensed Kelly Bertolucci's arm raise.

'Why has the art world not known about it?' Michael allowed a silence before answering.

'The painting was a private commission. It was then put on open display at *Wooreen* for many years. There was no secret about it. Then over the years it seems to have been relegated within the homestead from one room to another. It got forgotten as part of the family history.' Jane interjected, all but fluttering her eyelashes.

'Michael, you have a personal connection to *Wooreen*, don't you?'

'I do. I have been friends with the SummerHayes family for many years. It was through my friendship with the current owner, Andrew SummerHayes, that he made me aware of the painting.' The story of the painting was a good one. Michael had privately rehearsed his telling of it. Today was his premiere performance. He appeared to reflect, gazing into the upper far corner of the meeting room.

'As a curator, you dream of those moments. Those times when all the years of hard work, research and study pay off.' Michael let the image of their hard-working, but insightful, acting director linger in the room. 'Through Andrew, I had visited and stayed at *Wooreen* many times. We were schoolfriends, lived in the same boarding house. On holidays at the farm, I had seen this painting a few times, and I always thought – there's something about this painting. Even at a young age I knew it was special, a cut above the other artworks at *Wooreen*. Which are lovely.' Again, Michael threatened to get lost in the mists of time and the far-away homestead, but brought himself back to the present. 'Anyway, as you know, the years race by. Andy and I kept in contact. It wasn't until quite recently that circumstances meant I got an opportunity to get re-acquainted with the painting. To have a really good look at it. And that's when I realised what I had discovered.' Michael was about to continue but the chairman interjected.

'Michael, we should talk about the funding arrangements for the Streeton.'

'Of course. I did flag at our staff retreat that I would be using my director's discretionary fund, as well as a proportion of the Australian art allocation, but Russell, please, you add to that.'

'Okay,' said Dalton-Smith. 'Part two of today's announcement is that we will be launching a public purchasing fund to support the acquisition of the

Streeton. The SummerHayes family have been generous in granting us first option on the painting, but we will have to raise fifty percent of the purchase funds through our benefactors, sponsors and supporters. I can say, between us again, that the Sodaspring Beverages Group will be contributing in a significant way to the acquisition fund. More details about that at a later date. That's why we ask you to keep this to yourself, for only a short time, before we go to the public.'

'The public will love it.' Jane's declaration gave the public no option.

As the meeting broke up a few attendees pressed close to the Streeton to better admire the painting. Stuart and Alison peered over shoulders, then edged closer to join Kelly and Matt in front of the canvas. Stuart's eye was immediately drawn to a place left and below centre of the canvas. This was where Streeton had positioned the two-storey, bluestone, towered homestead.

'That's a great diagonal,' said Matt. He indicated the tree-lined road leading to the homestead which came in from the lower left of the painting, taking the viewer to *Wooreen*. 'And then there's the sweep of clouds in the upper right which draw your eye to the home too.' Kelly nodded, pointing to the mountains in the distance.

'Is this where the Grange Burn rises? Such a Scottish name for an Australian creek.'

'It is,' agreed Alison. 'So typical of that those Scottish Presbyterian settlers to choose a name like that.' Stuart waved his hand over the space surrounding the homestead.

'Look at all the scattered farm and outbuildings Streeton's shown. The family did alright for themselves.'

'They did. Love those rolling paddocks here. They balance the composition too.' Kelly slowly drew her hand across the area in the lower right quarter, ending at the painter's signature, *A. Streeton.* Stuart bent down to look more closely at a section of the painting, but he felt a new presence behind him. Michael touched Stuart on the elbow.

'Need to see you, Stu, and you too Alison, first thing tomorrow.' Michael had moved on before either of them had a chance to do more than acknowledge their boss. Stuart looked back to the painting.

'Let's have a drink at the Northern,' said Matt.

'Twenty minutes. You have achieved your goal'
The electronic voice on Tarquin's treadmill told Stuart he had completed his warm-up run. He pressed the red button and the treadmill mat slowed, stopped. He read the screen message.

'You exercised for 20 minutes. You reached a distance of 3.6 kilometres. Well done!'

The double car space at Tarquin's home was free of vehicles. Unless you counted bicycles, which both men kept there. Tarquin parked his car in the driveway, Stuart found a spot for his ten-year old car in the street, usually a few houses down. In his six weeks residence it had already been broken into: luckily, they had not driven it away. The parking arrangements made room for a weights bench, hand weights, treadmill and stationary bicycle – a more than adequate home gym which Stuart had been using three times a week. Tarquin had helped him customise an online fitness program, which he was now doing before going to work.

Stuart loaded up the bench press with a weighted barbell. Wriggling onto his back he breathed in, and then out, raising the weight on his out-breath. The previous evening, he had stayed at the Northern Railway Hotel for a few drinks, enough to be unsure of the exact number, but not so much that he was suffering from after-affects this morning. Still, he appreciated his usual practice of keeping a water bottle close by for regular sipping. His workmates at the Northern had discussed Michael's announcement about the Streeton. Kelly was onto her second glass of wine.

'After Michael's big build-up the announcement could only have been an anti-climax.'

'It is a big deal though, to find a new Streeton after all these years,' said Stuart.

'It's a big deal for Michael,' said Matt. 'Really, I don't think I can survive if he is permanently appointed as director.' Kelly groaned.

'I'll be an alcoholic if he is.'

Stuart finished his bench press set and picked up two dumbbell weights. Turning over to lay face down on the bench he extended his arms and slowly raised the weights to horizontal. In the bar of the Northern, Matt had taken them through his concept for his next set of paintings. His last exhibition had been at the gallery in Ballarat, where Alison had bought one of the paintings. At about the same time as Matt's exhibition, Kelly had curated an exhibition of paintings at NAGA by the Australian artist Ben Quilty. The subject matter of Quilty's series was the devastating 2019 bushfires, executed in his trademark, lavish impasto technique.

'I suppose your new paintings are going to be inches thick in paint then, Matt?' Alison had teased the artist, knowing Matt and Stuart were both big fans of Quilty's work. Matt had laughed.

'I'm a lowly paid art handler. I couldn't afford that much fucking paint.'

Stuart moved onto his next exercise. He had done his program enough times to know the sequence without having to refer to the program on his laptop. *Triceps extensions. Knee on bench, into crouch position, extend arm backwards.* Alison had to leave the pub after one drink to pick up Lucy, but not before she had given her verdict on the new play she had recently seen with Ben. Alison had said that the play had been a bit 'shouty' for her. She said the two main leads had long scenes of serious discussion and debate, which too closely resembled argument. Stuart didn't care about the play. He had listened with attention to try to pick up any nuance when Alison referred to Ben the Banker. *Did Alison's evening out with Ben compensate for the so-so play? Had she said anything about Ben at the pub? Did she say why she hadn't invited Ben to the party in Canberra, or if he was unable to make it? Pathetic. I'm carrying on like a teenager.* Stuart rolled his shoulders, flexed his fingers to pump blood into his hands and picked up the barbell again.

Stuart finished his exercise program, working through the series of stretches which Tarquin had recommended. As he did a calf stretch, he realised he could actually feel the benefit of the program. His muscles had gone past the burning, hurting stage and he thought he was definitely better toned. His regular lap-swimming and commuting by bicycle had kept him reasonably fit, but now he had to look more than respectable if he was to be in the same room as a footballer.

Stuart was in no hurry this morning. He could do his exercise program, shower and ride into work and still be confident of being at NAGA to see Michael 'first thing'. He and Alison had conferred last night, agreeing that from experience it would be reasonable, the morning after a board meeting dinner, to expect Michael in no earlier than eleven o'clock.

*

At NAGA, Stuart checked with Alison that Michael had not arrived. In his office he sat down, but didn't immediately set to work. There was plenty he could do, but he figured Michael would be in at any moment. He also admitted to feeling at a loose end after the closure of the blockbuster exhibition. He had ample work to go with; potential acquisitions, other galleries exhibitions to view, lines of research to follow, planning for future exhibitions. His recent promotion at NAGA also meant more administration duties in his week.

He called his sister Alexandra. She started talking, telling him she was stepping out of a meeting.

'Stuart, I've got two minutes. Some good news. I've got through to my contact in Italy. She works out of our Milan office, she's in our – '

'And?'

'And she said she will ask around her circle if any of them had come across Gareth. Though she did add that people around that Lake Como area may remember his Colombian model girlfriend more readily.'

'Or, he may contact us out of the blue as usual,' said Stuart.

'The bars and restaurants on the lake are a popular destination for Violetta's friends, who go for weekends etcetera so you never know. Stuart, I'm going back into the meeting but you do know our dad is really bad, don't you?'

'I saw him on the weekend. Has he got worse?'

'No, I haven't had any news. I merely want you to be prepared, and to remember to look after mum, too.'

'Okay, big sister.' Alison had appeared outside his door and indicated upwards with her finger.

Stuart had not quite adjusted to seeing Michael in the director's office. In all Stuart's time at the gallery Angela O'Keefe had been NAGA's Director. He admired her as a knowledgeable art person and a highly competent administrator. She had steered NAGA through its latest crisis, though at some cost to her personal health it would seem. The latest gossip was that her period of indefinite leave would not see her return to her position at all.

Michael was sitting in a chair behind the director's desk. As Stuart and Alison entered, he waved them to the informal lounge setting. They all sat down, Stuart looking around the office at the art works on the wall or any other signs of Michael's occupancy.

'I haven't re-painted the place, you know.' Not for the first time, Stuart questioned whether Michael had the ability to read his thoughts. Self-centred, self-serving, cunning and perceptive, Michael was not to be under-estimated. Michael sat forward to engage his two staff. 'What do you think about the Streeton painting? Stu?'

'It's a fine example of its type and time.'

'It's more than that,' said Michael. 'It's an iconic Australian painting which will be an absolute crowd-puller. And this is where you come in, Alison.' Alison tilted her head.

'I want you to do some research around the Streeton. Actually, not around the Streeton itself, I've got all I need on it, but look into the SummerHayes collection. Talk to the family, find out what they have in their collection, and yes, be good to flesh out the story behind the Streeton.'

'You want any correspondence around Arthur Streeton visiting *Wooreen,* photos, contemporary accounts, that sort of thing?' said Alison.

'Exactly. When we go public with the Streeton I want to have the story there for us to tell.' Michael narrowed his eyes, suggesting a deeper emotion. 'I want the romance of the story, that's it. The painting has been in the family, in the homestead, in Western Victoria.' Michael was warming to his theme. 'Now it's able to be seen by all Australians … a newly discovered iconic painting.'

'And you want me to work on the Streeton, too?' asked Stuart. 'Actually, there was something about the painting I wanted to ask you.' Michael sat back, frowning as if Stuart had made a comment in bad taste.

'No. I've got something else for you. In a minute.' Michael directed his attention back to Alison. 'You'll get all the information from the background file on the Streeton. But that's just reading the file. I'll arrange with the family for you to visit *Wooreen*. It's on their property and in the homestead where you're going to turn up the sort of material needed. And this is important … the SummerHayes family must come out of this looking good. There's not going to any bullshit about them locking away the painting, or being country bumpkins too thick to know what's hanging over their fireplace.' Stuart couldn't stop himself from smiling at Michael's imagery.

'Back to you, Stu. You're going to work on the Rodin drawings for me.'

'That's your project, isn't it?' Stuart and Michael had both travelled to Paris as part of developing the *Masterpieces from the Musée d'Orsay* exhibition. While Stuart had worked with Marion, JP and other staff at the Musée, Michael had done little for the exhibition, pursuing his own objectives. An opportunity arose from Michael's visit to the Rodin Museum that tied in with NAGA's ownership of six Rodin drawings. The drawings were done by Rodin in preparation for his book *Cathedrals of France*. It was as much a surprise to Jean Lehni, Director at the Rodin Institute, attached to the Rodin Museum, that an Australian gallery held some Rodin drawings as it was to Stuart that Michael wanted him to work on the project. 'Michael, you set this up with Monsieur Lehni in Paris, I had nothing to do with it.'

'Stuart, you're a senior curator now, you've got to be more flexible in your thinking. I promised the Rodin people that we would welcome their collaboration with research on the drawings, plus other mutually beneficial programs.'

'I have my work program to pick up after the Musée show and – '

'Jean Lehni is going to be coming out here for this project. You're the French expert, as we all know.'

Michael was referring to Stuart's affinity for the French language and her people, which had been so critical in making the Musée exhibition a success. 'Stu, in my role as director, it's not realistic to expect me to spend time on the Rodin drawings. Don't worry, I'll be here to help you as back-up.' This was hardly comforting information for Stuart. He had suffered before from Michael's version of back-up assistance.

'I might be better off by myself, or with Alison's help.' Michael took his own inference from Stuart's remark.

'Good, then that's settled.'

On their way back to their offices Stuart, preoccupied with his thoughts, did not register Alison's comment.

'Aren't you interested?'

'What? Sorry, Michael threw me a bit there.'

'I said that I'm going to contact the Norman family. Remember I had to call Melanie Norman?'

'Yes, of course, I'm really interested.' The gallery had an Arthur Norman landscape painting which last year had caught Stuart's attention. Norman was a minor figure in Australian art history, active for some years in the early part of the twentieth century. In delving into Norman's history, Alison's research added to the scant information on record about the artist. A brochure about Arthur's brother Walter, a successful businessman and local politician, had provided some references to his artist brother. Alison was able to make contact with an elderly family member, Lynette (or Netty) Norman, who did the original family history research. Netty's research recorded the story of the distinguished Walter, rather than her black sheep artist, grandfather Arthur. In recent years Netty's daughter Melanie had picked up the family history story. She had been revising the brochure about Walter, wanting to make it more about both brothers. It was Melanie who had contacted Alison last year, and now wanted to talk to her again.

During some stressful moments in Paris, working on the Musée exhibition, Stuart had heard from Alison that Arthur (who as an art student had travelled to Europe and France) returned to Paris in his later years and was buried there. Stuart had taken a short break from his work at the Musée d'Orsay and discovered Arthur Norman's grave in the Montparnasse Cemetery. He enjoyed that memory, including having Alison share the discovery.

'I wonder what it's all about?'

'I'll let you know after I've spoken to Melanie.'

The summer evening retained the heat of the day. Stuart took his pasta dinner out to the terrace. A glass of water and laptop on the outdoor table, he was scrolling through the online news when he heard Tarquin's car pull into the driveway of the house. Shortly after Stuart could hear Tarquin in the kitchen. He called out to his housemate.

'There's pasta in the saucepan if you're interested.' Tarquin came through the opening and joined Stuart, pulling out a chair and splaying his legs to full extension.

'I'm right Stu. Had a big feed at the club.'

'How was training?' Stuart was learning about the routines and lifestyle of an elite athlete.

'Good. We had a strategy session after our weights program.' Tarquin had a sip from his water bottle. 'Actually, that does look good. I don't think the club dietician will object if I have a small bowl.' Tarquin went into the kitchen. Stuart finished his dinner as his phone alerted him to a message from Alison. He could hear the beep of the microwave before Tarquin returned with a bowl of pasta.

'Was the strategy meeting useful?'

'It was actually.' Tarquin waited while he ate a forkful of rigatoni. 'Back in WA I'd been there for so long those sessions were a drag. I knew the script off by heart and had to work hard to stay awake.' Stuart laughed. 'No seriously, you get so buggered from training and then they feed you, sit you down and talk at you. It was funny to watch others drop off, but not if the coach has the grumps.'

'Is it different at the new club?'

'Yes and no. A lot is so similar, across all the clubs, but there are a couple of differences here. I reckon a change was long overdue for me.' Tarquin flexed his leg as he dug his fork in and loaded pasta and sauce together.

'The calf still okay?' Tarquin gave his lower leg a reflexive rub as Stuart's phone sounded. He saw who it was and mouthed a 'sorry'.

The light was fading in the terrace courtyard, the warmth now easing out of the day. Stuart took his phone into the lounge and dropped himself into an armchair that was more a collection of cushions than an upholstered chair.

'Melanie Norman and I have chatted,' said Alison.

'About Arthur or Walter?'

'Both, I suppose. You know Netty is living with Mel and her family at *Conquest*.' This was the home built by Walter Norman in the well-tended suburb of Kew. 'Netty is almost eighty I think, anyway the family is setting up the home so that she can have her own self-contained part of the house, while Mel and her lot have the run of the place.'

'Planning for the future, I guess.' Stuart reached across and flicked on a table lamp.

'Yes, Netty's fine with it though, but guess why Mel rang?'

'More information about Arthur's life as an artist? In Paris?' Stuart and Alison were both enjoying the pleasure of slowly revealing exciting news.

'Better. As part of the work on the house, they have got renovations on the go – '

'Yes –'

'And have discovered a stash of Arthur's artwork.' Stuart sat up. Tarquin came to the lounge entrance.

'Coffee, mate?' Stuart nodded a quick affirmative before speaking to Alison.

'What have they found? Paintings, drawings, did Walt get Arthur to do some murals?'

'They don't know. Mel was so nice. She said when the builder demolished the wall and turned up the art work she said she didn't want to touch it, but to give us a call. They want us to look at it.'

Stuart had come across Arthur Norman's 1903 painting, *Evening at Beech Forest*, one day at NAGA. He had admired it immensely. It was modest, but he had liked it for its lack of pretension. He appreciated the artist's skill (Norman had professional training at the Melbourne Art School) and wondered why Norman had not had a more illustrious career. Norman had paintings in a couple of regional galleries, but was by any measure a minor figure. Still, the painting, and its painter, touched Stuart. And now it appeared there was more of Norman's work than anyone knew. From experience, Stuart and Alison spoke cautiously.

'Could be a load of crap that Walter or Arthur had stored there,' said Stuart.

'And, it could be in any old condition too. Imagine how it's been stored for, what, a hundred years?'

'We don't know, do we. Mice could have been feasting.' They were both working hard to not get their hopes up too much. Alison's voice betrayed her.

'Still, it is exciting, isn't it?'

'It is, what's next?'

'I'll talk to Mel and we'll arrange a time for you and I to visit. It needs to be soon because the builder is on hold, in the meantime working on another part of the renos.' They talked for a bit longer, about their families, Arthur Norman, and the projects which Michael had assigned to them earlier in the day. In finishing the call, Alison was unable to resist some final speculation.

'Wouldn't it be funny if we turned up a new Australian masterpiece? Can you imagine Michael's reaction?'

Tarquin placed a coffee on the table next to Stuart. He had ended the call with Alison but still held his phone.

'Thanks for that.'

'Everything okay with your dad?' asked Tarquin.

'Still the same.'

Tarquin took his coffee to his half of the house, leaving Stuart sitting, looking at his phone. He sipped the warm drink. He should visit his dad again, soon. He should send something to Declan, now – some funny video, a photo or something. He tried to send at least a text to his son every day. His sister had reminded him today that he needed to be mindful of the stress and worry that their mother must be undergoing. He should call her too. What about Gareth? Will the happy wanderer be found with his arms around a tanned model in Lake Como? *Was life simpler when it was just him, Declan and Leah?* He finished his coffee, took a selfie of himself with coffee cup, sent it to Declan ('*Cheers big-ears')* and got up to retrieve his laptop from the terrace. He wanted to see if he could turn up more information about Arthur and Walter Norman.

His online research did not reveal anything he or Alison had not already seen. To refresh his memory, he looked up the information on the two Norman works held by regional galleries. The Ballarat Art Gallery had a painting, untitled but referred to as *Farm scene* by the gallery, showing a rural courtyard at the back of an unnamed property. On the other side of the state, the Gippsland Gallery had a painting thought to be of South Melbourne market. Norman had lived in South Melbourne, not far from the market. It was painted when the market was closed, neighbourhood children using the shuttered doors and alleys for games. Both galleries displayed their painting occasionally, usually as part of a selection of twentieth century Australian works. He sent the relevant links for the paintings to Alison before closing his laptop.

The next weekend Stuart and Alison drove to the strip of local shops nearest to the Norman's house. The day was sunny, the sky clear but a sneaky breeze rattled around the shoulders of people at the café's outdoor tables. Alison wore a red cardigan with pale blue jeans, plus black-framed sunglasses in which Stuart could see his reflection. He was in jeans, t-shirt and sneakers, banking on the temperature increasing while they had a coffee-and-something. The shops were set back along a service street parallel to the local road, the footpath broad enough to cater for clusters of tables and chairs from several outlets. Stuart had swung into a parking spot two seconds before another car had the same idea. He and Alison walked past a hairdresser, florist, yoga studio, café number one ('no, not this one'), Asian bakery, Italian restaurant (open for lunch and dinner), another hairdresser, women's clothing, children's toys and gifts (sustainable), beauty and day spa, finally taking places at a table outside café number two.

'Melanie said this was the good one,' explained Alison. 'They have the best cannoli.' Stuart was still putting keys and phone on the table when the waitress greeted them and took their order. Alison resisted the cannoli, having coffee only, while Stuart asked for coffee and a roasted vegetable focaccia.

'I think all this weight program of Tarquin's is increasing my appetite.'

'The house-sharing could be good for you.' Alison removed her sunglasses. 'Mel is expecting us on the hour. I hope it's worth it.' She gave a shiver of excitement for extra emphasis. 'Or it could be a real let-down.' Coffees and the focaccia were placed in front of them, with the customary 'enjoy.' Stuart sliced a portion of his brunch for Alison.

'When do you get to do your field trip to *Wooreen*?'

'Be good to get out of the office. Michael has given me the contact details of the owner, his mate Andrew SummerHayes, and we're sorting out a time for the day trip. I got the usual Michael-standard file too, so I don't know much about the SummerHayes collection until I get there.' Alison ate her mouthful of focaccia. 'Andrew mentioned that his daughter Charlotte had more of an idea of what they had at the homestead than anyone else in the family.'

'Is there a Mrs SummerHayes?'

'Andrew talked about Annabel.' Alison grabbed a stray half-olive off Stuart's plate. 'You're not happy about having to take on the Rodin drawings, are you?' Stuart shrugged.

'I don't mind. I've got enough stuff to do in my Australian art portfolio, but once I thought about it, it could be an interesting project.' He wiped his lips with a paper napkin. 'Michael always seems to railroad me into doing what he wants me to do. And unfortunately, he is acting director so I can't say 'get stuffed, I'd rather do my own thing'. Have you finished?'

At their car, an SUV stopped in the service street, prepared to wait while Stuart backed out.

'Popular spot.'

The street for the Norman house was only two minutes' drive. They cruised down the street reading house numbers, passing a line of parked cars, progressing through an avenue crowned with mature plane trees in full leaf.

'This is the definitive leafy suburb,' declared Stuart, leaning forward and across to read house numbers. 'Ah, fifty-three, here we are.' He swung the car into a driveway marked by two-metre tall brick pillars. The curved, asphalted drive was edged with brick kerbing for water run-off. Alison checked out the grounds on either side of the car. Stuart registered large, fully-grown trees, firs, oaks and lemon-scented eucalypts, spaced in expanses of recently-mown lawn. Ahead was the solid red-brick home, *Conquest,* built by Walter Norman in 1909. Stuart and Alison knew a little about the home through their reading of the brochure, '*Walter Norman and the Gardens of Kew'* by Lynette O'Brien. The family had provided this to Alison when she made contact seeking more information about Arthur. The author explained that her title referred to the work which Walter did as an early 20th century councillor to establish the formal gardens and parks in the City of Kew.

The home sat in its park-like setting, partly in sunlight and partly shaded by the established trees. It was on a generous block of about four regular suburban homes, although it was likely that sections of Walter's original block had been sold off over the years. If so, the carving off of the original holding was done so that the neighbours' dwellings did not impact on the outlook or amenity of *Conquest*. Once again, Stuart shook his head at Walter's droll naming of the home. The driveway had taken them to the house, offering drivers the option of parking in front of the entrance steps to the house, or taking the drive to the side of the house where there was a multi-vehicle carport. Stuart made a quick calculation that his car would be happier parked to the side of the house. The other car under the shelter was a standard family sedan. The garden side of the carport was protected by a thick, vigorous wisteria vine. Their arrival had been heard or observed. By the time they got to the entrance steps a woman was walking down the steps, hand extended.

'Hello, you must be Alison and Stuart from the gallery. Welcome, I'm Melanie Widdicombe.' The woman was in her early fifties, guessed Stuart. She was wearing a cotton dress with a subtle floral pattern, her grey-blonde hair held back by a dazzling white headband. 'Come in please. So good of you to come.'

The russet-red bricks of the house had mellowed with age. The dwelling was a horizontal line, its presence exuding stability and respectability. It looked as if the building's walls, masonry, tiling and plumbing had not altered in the hundred plus years since completion. As they went up the stairs Stuart noticed the green paint work, in very good condition, on the window frames and around the doorway. He was trying to find the right word to describe the restful green, his thought broken when Melanie asked if he and Alison would like to have tea or coffee.

'No thank you,' said Alison. 'We don't want to take too much of your time.'

'Oh, but I hope you have time for a little tour before we show you our discovery.'

'That would be lovely, replied Stuart. 'Very kind of you.' He had not seen any evidence of building works on their arrival – perhaps it was at the back. Melanie led them from the entrance hall into a dining room – polished table and upholstered chairs in the middle of the room, bookshelves and cabinets against the walls. Stuart could see some original artwork on the walls, though framed family photographs outnumbered the paintings and drawings.

'Do you have any of other Arthur's paintings in the home?' he asked. 'We know from your family story that Walter brought home some of his brother's work from Arthur's home in South Melbourne.'

'Then he and his housekeeper destroyed a good lot of them. We have two paintings by Arthur; they're in the study.'

Double glass doors led through to a lounge room, at that time of the day its orientation channelling beams of sunlight through its windows. The heat was kept at a distance by layers of window furnishings. Off this room was the study. From the doorway Stuart could see a diamond-shaped leadlight window, a design element employed throughout *Conquest's* formal rooms.

In the study the two visitors were immediately drawn to the two paintings hung over a flat-top desk. These were two of the paintings by Arthur Norman which Walter had retained. They were both landscape studies. The same qualities which appealed to Stuart in NAGA's *Evening at Beech Forest* were present in the late afternoon painting *Bridge on the Darebin.* It showed an arched red brick bridge over the gently flowing waters of the Melbourne creek. The artist's technique was assured and relaxed.

'Was this done around Alphington, Ivanhoe perhaps?' asked Alison.

'We think it's out the back of Thornbury actually. The bridge is still there, Bell Street or Darebin Road … I'm not sure.' The paintings each had small bronze plates screwed onto the bottom of the wooden frame, telling them that the bridge was painted in 1919. The other plate carried the title and date *Summer Morning 1923*. It showed a girl or young woman sitting in a courtyard, the morning light striking her hair and making a handspan of it, for a moment in time, golden. The subject was perched on a stool, the toe of one shoe almost touching the ground. Stuart and Alison were shoulder to shoulder peering at the enclosed courtyard of an inner-city terrace. The subject was lost in concentration, focussed on her task.

'Is she sewing?' asked Stuart.

'Darning or mending possibly. We think this one was done in Arthur's home at South Melbourne. In the backyard of his own little terrace.'

'This could be one of his family then?' asked Alison.

'Quite possibly. Too young for his wife, but they had a daughter,' said Melanie.

'And Arthur probably couldn't afford a model either,' said Stuart. 'Like many artists, the family members get roped in to serve their purpose.' Stuart thought the painting was two things in one – a study capturing the effect of the morning light and a tender portrait. His appreciation of Arthur Norman increased the more work he saw by the artist. He shared a smile with Alison. Their trip today was already worth it, just to see these two enchanting paintings.

'Walter must have liked the two paintings because they go so well together,' said Melanie. 'Not just because they're a similar size, but the contrast between a calm evening and a sunny morning.' Stuart took out his phone.

'I think you're absolutely right. They do go well together. May I take a photo of each?'

'These two paintings, plus the one at NAGA, are the best preserved of Arthur's works,' said Melanie. 'As well as the two in regional galleries, of course.' Melanie was referring to the two paintings that Stuart had mentioned to Alison the previous evening.

Melanie took them to a door, through which Stuart could hear someone talking. They went on to the back of the house.

'Alison says you're the gallery expert on Arthur's paintings, Stuart.'

'Hardly an expert, but very interested in his work, and keen to know more.' They entered an open plan part of the house, containing a kitchen, family room and less formal dining area. Two girls sprawled across a fabric sofa, all legs and long hair. Their heads were touching as they read the same screen, both wearing headphones. The light-flooded rooms had multi-paned glass and white woodwork.

'This is a lovely space Melanie,' said Alison. 'So much light, with a view to the garden.'

‘Call me Mel please. We spend most of our time here. I’ll get the girls to say hello.’ She leant over the sofa and removed the headphones, causing the girls to look over the back of the sofa. ‘Dottie and Willow, this is Stuart and Alison from the gallery.’ Greetings over, the girls resumed their listening. ‘We have a son, Scott, who’s on a Bunnings run with my husband Rob.’ Melanie continued her tour. Off the living area there were several doors.

‘There’s a study there, a mud-room, laundry and toilet through there.’

‘Is this area more recently built?’ asked Stuart.

‘No, it’s actually original, which is incredible. We have done a little bit of interior work to open up the kitchen but the external is all 1909. I’ll take you through to the reno bit … it was quite a rabbit warren of rooms off here.’ Stuart could see more lawn and garden, as well as cream flagstone terracing. From the living area Mel did not take them outside to a separate dwelling, as he expected, but through another side-door which opened into a room. To Stuart it looked like a classic utility room.

‘We think this room has been used as a pantry at some stage. It connects to the set of rooms which we’re setting up for my mother.’

‘Your mother was a Norman?’ asked Alison.

‘Yes, her married name is O’Brien. She was the daughter of Albert, who was Arthur and Elsie’s third child. I’ll tell you more later, but I wanted to show you how we made our find.’ They were now at the site of the building renovations. The builder’s brief was part renovation, part extension. The room they stood in, about the size of the floorplan of Alison's townhouse, had been completely stripped back to its original brick walls and floorboards. It had a worktable in the middle, ladders against a wall, lengths of coiled electrical cord, tins of glue, sealant and other building paraphernalia. The light from a set of casement windows highlighted a fine covering of plaster and sawdust on every flat surface.

'Our builder is using this room as his workshop, as you can see. This will be my mother's personal lounge and dining room. It gets lovely evening light. Off this room will be a kitchenette, through there, bedroom and ensuite.' Melanie raised her step over a stack of timber architrave, making her way to the furthest corner. Alison and Stuart followed. 'But this is what you've come for. All this is still part of the original structure …' Melanie opened a door to a smaller and darker area. They were further away from the light. The skeleton frame of a partly-demolished wall drew their attention. It was clear that work had stopped mid-job – plumbing pipes were disconnected and went nowhere, sheets of fibrous plaster were stripped off a section of the wall and there was an open-air gap in the floorboards where some large object had been removed. In a corner was a dinted metal trunk, once painted a khaki colour.

'Watch your footing there,' said Melanie. 'It's in this old shipping trunk.' Melanie indicated the cramped space they were occupying. 'On the 1909 plans, the smaller part of this area was labelled as the 'Housekeeper's Room'. It must have been a personal space for her to have a single bed, a chest of drawers … no window as far as we can tell. It was when the builders demolished this wall that this space was found. There were mostly dust and droppings, but also this trunk.' It was a story Melanie was refining, knowing it was going to be told and re-told. 'I waited until Rob and the kids were all home, and then we crammed in the doorway while the builder prised open the lid. The kids were positive it was going to be full of treasure, but it was all junk – old tennis racquets, a rotten tennis net, some books, a set of wooden skittles … and this.' Melanie lifted the lid and revealed a rectangle of weathered leather, resting on dusty cardboard boxes.

'It looks like an old school satchel, though it's more of a shallow box,' said Stuart.

'This is bigger than those old school bags,' said Alison. 'Perhaps a postal bag or delivery box of some sort? It looks like something you might see in a 1920s office.' Stuart carried the container to the worktable in the main room, while Alison took some location photographs. She recorded the space which the builders had exposed, the shipping trunk and its interior. The table was cleared of builders' items and some clean cardboard spread on the surface.

'We did lift it out, of course. You can imagine the kids' curiosity, but put it back because we thought you may want to see it exactly as we did. Those corner straps prise back.' All eyes were on Stuart as he eased the short, diagonal leather strips off on each corner. One of the corner straps was already rotten, one broke as he levered it off. A voice broke into the silence.

'What are you doing there?' A small woman with a bob of white hair and wearing a purple wrap entered the room. It was Netty, grand-daughter of the artist Arthur Norman. 'Are you going through the paintings and drawings?' Melanie took charge.

'Mum, these are the people from the gallery. Do put something on your feet.' Introductions were made; Netty ignored her lack of footwear.

'Carry on, I want to see what the experts say too.' Netty perched on a stool, folding her hands together in front of her. She commenced to educate the visitors about her family, starting with a statement. 'Walter hated Arthur. Could not abide him. Thought he was a degenerate wastrel … is that the word? Anyway, he had no time for him, nor his work as an artist.' Stuart and Alison wanted to hear a lot more of this, but Melanie intervened.

'Mum, let Stuart and Alison see what we found first.'

'We would love to hear all about your grandfather, especially your research into him and his brother,' said Alison.

'Walter was an old stick-in-the-mud. I can remember when I was a girl – '

'Mum.'

'I wish I had written more about Arthur than Walter, perhaps the experts – '

'Mum.' Stuart extracted a package from the satchel with two hands. It was a bundle with heavy cardboard sheets on the top and bottom. It had been unwrapped and then wrapped again, so it was not difficult for Stuart to unfold the packing paper. The package was about the size of a poster, or in modern terms A2. It was, surprisingly to Stuart, not that dusty. Due to the protection of the leather container, the wrapping paper was in reasonable condition. The tight-fitting shipping trunk and the stable environment of the concealed space had been quite effective in preserving the object. Netty continued her reflection.

'Walter never supported his brother. He had all the money from his business … he and Marigold only had the one daughter. That was Lydie, or Lydia, very musical she was too. But she went to Europe and never came back – died in her twenties. You'd think Walter and Marigold never got over it, I don't know. I remember them living here as an old, cold couple.' Netty gave a little shiver. Alison and Stuart were listening and attending to the package. Alison mentally vowed to capture Netty's oral history at the next opportunity. Netty was playing with two rings on her finger, drawing on memories from the 1950s when she was a young girl. Her relatives must have seemed distant, ancient characters.

'Walter left Arthur and Elsie to make the best of it in their little South Melbourne house. It must have annoyed the hell out of Walt to leave his home to my father. That was Albert, Arthur and Elsie's third child. The older of the two boys. He owned Norman's Menswear in Elizabeth Street –'

'Mum. Let them concentrate on their work and you can tell them more later.' Stuart had revealed some sheets of paper, pieces of cardboard and it looked like several small unframed canvasses.

'Actually, I would love a cup of tea, Melanie? If you don't mind?' Stuart asked.

'Not at all. Mum and I will set it up outside, under the fir tree.'

'Excellent. Alison and I will make an inventory and bring it out to you.' Melanie made to leave, but Netty remained on the stool.

'I'm staying here to watch the experts,' she said. Melanie left, saying that she would also put out some food as the children would be hungry. Stuart and Alison continued, turning over each sheet of paper and artwork as Netty observed. They used a NAGA form to list each item. Netty was content for a while to prop and watch.

After a few minutes, as Stuart slowly turned over a pencil landscape sketch, she had to speak.

'I'm resisting the temptation to pass comments on these, or ask questions.' Stuart and Alison said nothing. 'It's a big effort.'

'Mmm,' said Stuart.

'Albert and Irene, my parents, had four children. I was their third. Of my two older brothers Ivan went to New Zealand, ran a farm or something and died over there years ago. Edward, the eldest, inherited *Conquest* and lived here with his family. Edward took over our father's menswear store, also had two newsagencies, both down on the Mornington Peninsula. I worked at Norman's … learnt the accounts and admin books. This was at the same time I was raising a family. Later I did book-keeping and managed a community centre for years. Anyway, Edward lived in *Conquest* with his family, but when he retired … in 1984 or 86, he lived in the Sorrento home, oh that's a lovely big place, and my husband and I moved into *Conquest.* Now Melanie and Rob are here, which is as it should be. There was another sister Meg, younger than me but she was killed in a car accident in the seventies.' Netty paused. Alison glanced at her but Netty was drawing breath. 'All Edward's family congregated around Sorrento, so it was only natural that when he went into aged care down there his family took up that property. The main house was big enough to divide into two homes, and build two more new ones on the same block. Francis, that's Edward's son, he could show you some of the Heidelberg School paintings they have down there.'

This was almost too much for Stuart and Alison to absorb, however they did not want to stop Netty's stream of information. They had both read the family history about Walter which Netty had compiled, but were hearing new information almost every sentence Netty spoke. But at that moment they needed to record today's discovery as a priority. They came to the last item, one of several small rectangles of canvas. This one was an oil painting, probably done on location, showing farmland and a distant mountain range. Stuart had studied NAGA's Arthur Norman painting *Evening at Beech Forest* at close quarters. He appreciated Norman's deft handling of the late evening light and the way he had captured the elements of nature in one crystallised moment. Now he wanted to pore over these new canvasses and sort through the drawings, but patience was necessary.

'That's it,' said Alison, making a last note to complete their list. With good timing, or either she had been waiting in the wings, Melanie returned, her husband and son with her.

'This is Rob and Scott, Stuart and Alison. Let's go outside for refreshments.'

The temperature had climbed with the hours, while the earlier breeze was more subdued in *Conquest's* lawn and garden setting. On the table was a spread of cut sandwiches, a baked slice, tea and coffee options. Netty had detoured on the way to the table and was now dressed in slacks and a top, set off by tennis shoes.

'Will you take Arthur's drawings and so on with you?' asked Netty. The family and visitors sat around the table on outdoor chairs, shaded by the fir tree. Stuart returned his gaze from the luncheon spread to answer.

'Yes. That's what Alison and Melanie have discussed. It's better for the works to be in our storage rooms while we make a detailed report.'

'Mel says you're a bit surprised by how well they've weathered the years,' said Rob.

'Oh, they could be heaps worse,' said Stuart. Alison leaned forward to place her cup and saucer on the table. Stuart was going to elaborate on the process they intended to follow but Netty made a shrewd face.

'How do we know what you are taking?'

'Mum.'

'It's fine,' said Alison. 'The list we made this morning is a preliminary inventory. One of the first things we do back at the gallery is to make a detailed list, which we'll send to Mel. Today we'll leave you with a copy of this inventory – '

'That's like a summary?' said Rob.

'Yes, so it says …' Alison picked up their form. '… the package has been stored in bundles, but these have been mixed up at some time in the past. What we have recorded is; 37 pencil drawings, 7 paintings on canvas, 25 watercolours on paper, 13 original etchings, 8 lithographs, French prints, ephemera.'

'What are the French prints?' Mel asked as she offered the slice to Stuart.

'They appear to be commercial prints, leaflets, small posters even,' replied Alison. 'Stuart will have a closer look but they are not limited edition works. But there are some of those, the etchings and lithographs.'

'And ephemera?'

'That's a term we use to cover a multitude of material. Theatre programs, advertising flyers, gallery invitations, bread-and-butter thank you notes – '

'People don't write those any more,' declared Netty. 'I thought there might have been more paintings in that trunk. Walter did bring some back from South Melbourne after Arthur went back to Paris.' Netty turned to Alison and Stuart, her eyes cornflower blue. 'You have seen the two we have in the house, the courtyard one and the *Bridge on the Darebin*?'

The children left the table and the adults had had enough to eat and drink. Melanie went into the house and returned carrying a photograph album.

'Would you like to see a photo of Arthur Norman? We only have a couple.'

'We would love to. There is not a lot of documentation in our gallery material,' said Alison. Stuart could recall one image reproduced from a newspaper photograph. He thought it showed the artist at the Ballarat Regional Gallery. Melanie had marked the page with a slip of paper. She opened the album and let the visitors lean in.

'This is Arthur Norman with his family … in these grounds.' The caption read: Arthur Norman, Elsie, Millie, Albert and William. The daughter was standing in front her mother, the two boys looked the same height and age.

'When was this, Mel?'

'They're not dated but I think the 1920s judging by the size of the trees. And what they are wearing.' Mel pointed to two smaller and less professional photos. 'That's Arthur in the backyard of the Dorcas Street home, with the boys Albert and William.' Arthur was toasting the photographer with a mug of something, perhaps beer, while the boys were beaming at some unknown joke. 'That one is earlier … the boys are younger.' Stuart was fascinated by this photo of Arthur. He asked permission then used his phone camera to copy the photos from the album. He zoomed in to get the best image of Arthur's face. There were several other photos, one which Alison noted.

'This is beautiful. That's Arthur with his daughter, isn't it?' The picture had been taken in a park. Mature palm trees lined a broad sealed path. Stones, cemented together, edged the path and in the distance was an empty band rotunda. This did not appear to be a posed photo. It showed Arthur paused in the middle of the path, bending at the waist and angling his head towards the young woman. It was an unusually natural scene compared to other photographs – an eternally private moment caught forever.

'I think that may be Lydia, Walter's daughter,' said Melanie. 'Going by the other photographs in the album.' Stuart captured this image too. Alison spoke for them both.

'These are so precious. Thank you so much for letting us know of your find. And for letting us take the work away for further research. Stuart and I have loved meeting you, and getting to know about *Conquest* – '

'Are you a couple? You two married?'

'Mum!'

'I can ask.'

'We're not married, nor a couple. Just good friends and colleagues,' said Alison.

After saying goodbye, Stuart drove down the drive from the house. The Arthur Norman discovery was on the back seat, wrapped in a clean cotton sheet.

'It's all been very well looked after.' Stuart indicated the house and grounds in general.

'*Conquest* has been in the Norman family since it was built – that must help. Are you excited by the discovery?' Alison asked. Stuart peered down the treed street, exited the driveway and turned right.

'Yes and no. As a curator you always get a buzz out of finds like this, but you always hope for more. I liked the two paintings we saw, and I'll have to follow up about those supposed Heidelberg School paintings in the Sorrento home. Perhaps with Mel.'

'I marvelled at your restraint there,' smiled Alison. 'Michael is a Heidelberg School expert; you could let him follow up.' They both knew this was never going to happen. They merged onto the main road to the city's north.

'Netty is a hoot, said Stuart. 'You blushed when she asked if we were a couple.'

'I did not.' Alison kept her head down as she continued reviewing the photographs she had taken at *Conquest.*

Stuart drove from the eastern suburb of Kew to the National Art Gallery of Australia on the north of Melbourne's central business district. He and Alison checked in the *Conquest* art found, recording its status as 'temporary loan – for research and study purposes.' After dropping off Alison, Stuart went eastwards again to his parent's home. He had arranged to pick up his mother and accompany her to see his father. While waiting for his mother to gather her things and lock up, he sent some photos and a message to Declan.

Hey Declan. Went to an old house today to look at some treasure they found! When they were pulling down the wall (in the pic) they discovered a secret room which the family did not even know about. They found a lot of dusty old stuff but also this mysterious trunk. What do you think was inside?

Rosemary had a tote bag with things to take to her husband's care home; some plastic containers of cut-up fruit, pyjamas and replacement toiletries.

'Thanks for coming with me, Stuart. The nurse said this morning that he had a comfortable night.' When Stuart pulled up at Eastside Gardens he checked his phone. Declan had replied,

A pile of junk? A dead body!!!!

Stuart asked his mother for a minute so he could deflate Declan's expectations in the next set of pictures.

This old box, which contained the artist's drawings, prints and paintings in these photos.

Ten seconds later:

Boring, no skeleton.

Rosemary went to the side of her husband's bed. He appeared to be sleeping.

'It's me and Stuart, Evan.' The man did not stir. He reclined in the same position Stuart had left him, arms outside a mustard-coloured blanket, mouth agape. Rosemary busied herself with the items in her tote bag, also giving the room a quality control inspection.

'Stuart, you could empty that vase, those flowers are past it. I should have brought in fresh ones. I will next visit.' Stuart welcomed being able to do something useful. He took the vase down the hallway, a staff member helping him with directions. When he returned, his mother had pulled up two vinyl chairs close to the bed. She finished storing items in the tall cupboard and sat down, patting the other seat.

'Come here Stuart.' As if he was the one who had been bustling around. 'Have you said hello to your father? It's never really obvious when he is asleep and when he is still aware of what we're saying.'

'I had better be careful what I say about him then.' Rosemary placed her hand over her husband's, then looked sideways.

'You would only have good things to say of your father, wouldn't you?' Rosemary asked with a drawing together of her brows.

'Of course. Hospitals and places like this bring out the stupid in me.' The comment made Stuart think of something Alison had asked him in the car. She had enquired after his father, then followed up a couple of beats later.

'Are you close to your dad?'

'Of course,' said Stuart. He said this as in, isn't everyone? But, if he answered after giving the question more time and deeper reflection, how would he respond? Was he close to his father? He knew he wasn't … distant. He didn't feel estranged or alienated, as he knew happened in some families. It wasn't as if he didn't know his father at all. Though, once again, he found it hard to reconcile his father with the man who had told Declan a dirty joke. He decided his mother didn't need to know this bit of secret men's business.

'Dad is a great dad,' Stuart declared to his mother. 'You don't have to go to the pub and drink beers together, or play chess in the evening in front of the fire.'

'I didn't say you did,' said Rosemary. She gently squeezed Stuart's arm, but spoke to her husband.

'Evan. Gareth is coming home. He's on his way back from Europe. Alexandra had a friend get in touch with him and he's making travel arrangements. We don't know when to expect him yet.' Rosemary had told Stuart this news on their way to Eastside Gardens.

'Is he bringing Miss Colombia?'

A b-double truck passed in the opposite direction, buffeting Alison's hire-car with its invisible force. There were mostly trucks on the highway, fast-moving billboards for supermarkets or transport companies. There were also numerous UWVs – her pet name for the ubiquitous white vans delivering their anonymous cargo. Today's drive to the SummerHayes property of *Wooreen* in Western Victoria was a day out of the ordinary for the NAGA research manager. She was dressed in jeans, a black, round-neck jumper and sturdy sneakers. Her rural destination and the forecast of occasional showers meant her overnight bag contained an additional change of shoes, beanie, sleeveless puffer jacket and lightweight scarf. It was summer, but a colleague had warned her of the perils of getting caught in a Western District paddock when an 'occasional shower' caught up with you.

As the bitumen road thrummed its rhythm, she went over Michael's instructions for her visit to *Wooreen*. She was going there to do further research around the creation of the Arthur Streeton painting. Alison had, with an effort, avoided commenting on the extent and quality of research in the Streeton file which Michael had passed over. She was also tasked with casting her eye over the other art works at *Wooreen*, to establish what they had in their collection – acquired and stored in the homestead since the 1850s. Her background reading told her that the original SummerHayes family had brought out some artwork to Australia. They had also had shipped out homewares and décor pieces from England when the forebears took up their grazing land.

Alison had set out early from Melbourne, the city roads already clogged with commuters and freight trucks. Four hours later, studiously taking a break after two hours, she took the turn-off at Hamilton and crossed the Grange Burn. Sneaking a look down at the watercourse she saw a creek which may or may not have been flowing. Now she needed to be on the lookout as she would be leaving this road and taking another leading to the homestead. She slowed down as an intersection came into view, but it was Harrigan's Road, whoever Harrigan was. The next turn-off was Grange Creek Road, a narrow, sealed road which was her route.

Alison drove down the middle of the patched road, paddocks outside every car window. Dark clouds had gathered over the hills, at a guess to the west, thought Alison. There were cows, glossy brown and doleful. Flocks of sheep spread themselves through other paddocks. The land was undulating, dotted with dams, the breeze rippling the water's surface. Alison admired the many gum trees which had survived the land clearing. They were either lone survivors, or small groupings, a tangle of fallen, broken and dead branches marking their presence. Alison braked. A faded, painted sign on the fence announced the *Wooreen* property. Next to the entrance was a cut-down metal drum fixed horizontally to serve as a roadside mail box. She turned, feeling a little foolish using her indicator. The gates were double entrance wide, with a metal grid set into the ground on one side and the other closed to entry with a wire mesh gate.

Alison rumbled over the metal grid, passing by a tumbled down timber shelter outside the gate, most likely a shelter for children waiting for the school bus.

Inside the gate, Alison had a choice of two compacted gravel roads. A sign-post in the middle of the fork told her the right-hand side was for 'All trucks & deliveries.' She rolled down the left road to '*Wooreen* Homestead'. It had gotten darker over the last few minutes and now the clouds which had masked the sun scudded across the farmland. The breeze picked up, parting around Alison's car as a rattle of rain assaulted its side. The shower had come and gone before Alison could find the control for the windscreen wipers. More paddocks on either side, more up and down undulations, more animals, fencing and dams. Close to the fence Alison drove past two sheds, one with unpainted weatherboards and one clad with rust-brown corrugated iron. The sheds were in the lee of massive pine trees. Looking further afield Alison could see long lines of continuous pines, defences against the wind, black against the sky. *Where is this homestead? Surely, I must be there soon.*

Alison rounded a bend and topped a rise. There were structures on either side of this rise, their purpose not clear, but below, unmistakeably, was the homestead. Alison stopped the car. She had seen photographs of the heritage listed homestead – in the gallery file as well as multiple images found online. The clouds had sped across the sky and ultra-bright sunshine fell on the bluestone building. *Where's the fanfare of trumpets?* From where Alison had paused, she could see an array of buildings; timber, brick, bluestone, large, small, multi-storied, low and humble. In the middle of its own village was *Wooreen*. Built in 1857 by the colonial settler Gordon M. L. Summer Hayes, in the days when a home could be established a long distance from the access road, proximity to power and services not a prime need. Alison also wanted to believe that the first Mr Summer Hayes (subsequent generations spelt the two names as one) had more than practical considerations in mind when he chose the location for the homestead. The rectangular, two storey building faced east, a formal entrance in the geometric centre. Above the two storeys, built of the same bluestone, rose a tower, a turret from which to survey the property and the world. To the east was the farm land which Alison had driven through. To the north paddocks stretched as far as she could see. Similar farm land stretched to the south, the sun now illuminating prime agricultural land before a range of mountains sat on the horizon. These were Gariwerd, also the Grampians Ranges, a rugged outcrop forming a long escarpment from where the Grange Burn began its meandering journey. Alison did not know how much of this land belonged to the SummerHayes family; however, she could not see another farmhouse. Beyond the homestead and its tower, a line of dark trees and vegetation tracked the course of the Grange Burn. Alison resumed her drive and, in few minutes, had parked on the light gravel forecourt at the front of the homestead.

Alison walked to the large wooden doors, thickly panelled and darkly varnished. The lower walls of the house were edged in garden beds, a profusion of roses in white, red and pink. Large swathes of the bluestone walls were covered in ivy, in places encroaching across the outer edges of the windows. The front doors were bracketed by smooth stone columns, pale grey, reached by climbing a flight of similarly coloured stone steps. Her knock on the door seemed ridiculous to her own ears. She soon gave up on the idea that the front door would open and walked around the sunnier, north side of the house. As she did so, she could hear small machinery in operation, a mower or something.

On the west side of the house a paved brick courtyard dominated the area. It extended from the rear entrance of the home to a series of buildings fanning out in a rough semi-circle. Pestering leaves, twigs and dust from the bricks was a man in jeans with a hand blower. He wore a check shirt and broad-brimmed hat. Alison veered into the man's line of sight.

'Ah, you must be Alison,' he shouted, then cut the motor. 'From the gallery.' He brushed his hands on his jeans and offered his hand. 'Andrew SummerHayes.'

'Alison Bennett.'

In ten minutes, Alison was sitting down at the kitchen table, a cup of tea and plate of biscuits in front of her. Andrew explained that his wife Annabel was in Hamilton attending a committee meeting, but that they would come across his daughter Charlotte 'somewhere on our travels'. The owner, and current SummerHayes senior male, was keen to show Alison around the property. She was torn, happy to have an explore of the farm, but itching to get into her research and auditing job. They left the kitchen and crossed the brick courtyard, Andrew's arms waving.

'That's the original laundry and washhouse. Two-person privy next to it … still usable. That was the dairy, where we made our own butter and cream. That's a toolshed, then garden shed – that's Annabel's domain, another toolshed … the big one with an open side is the main machinery shed. The old brick building was a kitchen, additional to the house one. That's just a woodshed.' Alison was trying to take this in and keep up with Andrew's long strides as they walked to a roofed structure which could accommodate several vehicles.

'This lot are the homestead out-buildings. We'll drive past other farm buildings, some used today and others from when *Wooreen* was a village in itself.'

'I've read a bit about your property and home.'

'We'll jump into the ute. In winter you might have to use the four wheel-drive to get around.'

Andrew drove the utility away from the house, through an opening then after a few metres came to a closed gate with paddocks behind.

'Your job, passenger.' Alison got out of the car, hoping the chain and lock would be easy to manage. The property tour commenced near the stables – Alison saw two horses, then around a confusing cluster of farm buildings that served the homestead and its farming operations. In the nineteenth century the farm was self-sufficient to such an extent that it had its own dairy, butcher, bakery and church. *Wooreen* was unusual in that many of the buildings constructed to serve the needs of its community still stood. From the driver's seat Andrew indicated the shearing shed with its stone foundations and timber upper level. It was possibly the biggest of the farm's buildings. He pointed to the butchery, old schoolhouse ('been a junk room for ages'), grain storage facility made of beautiful red, weather-softened bricks, a plain timber chapel, shearers' quarters which were still in good condition ('we use this for B and S Balls') rundown workers' quarters, and other buildings and structures that Andrew didn't bother to label.

'They're gravestones, Andrew?' Alison had seen weathered headstones, dry grass and iron railings – the unmistakeable signs of a cemetery. Andrew stopped the ute.

'Yeah. We had our own cemetery till the last century, but haven't used it for years now. The rules and regulations around burials have changed.' They drove on, the ute rocking from side to side. 'It's political correctness gone mad.'

Andrew drove with one hand and dangled the other out the driver's window. He explained the uses of different paddocks and what he called the business side of running the farm. Alison understood some of what he described, guessed at more through the context, and was content to remain ignorant of other matters. The paddocks were large areas of grass, some with trees, some without, some with dams. She closed yet another gate, threaded the wire clasp to secure it shut, climbed into the ute again, and looked out the windscreen. The vehicle now left the farm track and struck uphill across a faint sheep trail, rounded rocks jolting the uphill journey. They arrived at a vantage point. Andrew kept the engine idling.

'This is my favourite view,' said Andrew. Then, he seemed to react to an impulse. 'Let's get out and have a look.' The rise on which Andrew and Alison stood gave them a view of the homestead, garden and its outbuildings. It also overlooked, from a distance, the Grange Burn. Beyond the valley of the watercourse, farmland stretched all the way to the Grampians Ranges. In their exposed location, Alison felt that the sun and wind were barely on the right side of comfortable.

'I reckon this is where it was painted from,' said Andrew.

'What was? Sorry?' Alison was lost in the distance but then realised before Andrew elaborated. 'Oh, the Streeton of course.'

'Yeah, I've lined up the sight lines, and when you look at the painting …' Andrew indicated the small rise where lichen-covered, rounded rocks broke through the ground. 'I reckon Streeton would have sat on that rounded rock, setting up his easel exactly here.' Alison looked from rock to view.

'That's some thought. I'll take a couple of photos.'

The view was absorbing. Andrew stood immobile, weight on one leg.

'So peaceful, and still resembling a village,' said Alison. 'The Grange Burn looks lovely too. I suppose your family swam in the creek?'

'Sure. We've got photos of family picnics on its banks, fishing outings, mucking around in boats. My grandfather Alexander dug out a swimming hole with a raft and diving board. Donny, my father, said they used to net the Burn and get a heap of fish.'

'Did the aboriginal people live on the Burn or in Gariwerd?' Andrew pursed his lips as if it was a trick question. He delayed so long, Alison wondered if he had heard her question.

'The aborigines kept to the Grampians. There're a few rock paintings there, not much chop to be honest. They didn't come here.' Andrew gave the tail gate a shake. Reassured it was secure he went to the driver's door.

'Better get you back to the house. You must be wanting to see the paintings and other stuff.'

It was well into the afternoon by the time Alison had dusted her sneakers and was in the high-ceilinged rooms of the mid-nineteenth century home. She guessed Charlotte was about twenty. She was as tall as her father, with long, light brown hair gathered at the nape. She wore a men's style, loose cotton shirt over a t-shirt top and jeans. Charlotte had met Alison in the kitchen, then took her through to the entrance hall. They were standing on the other side of the heavy varnished entrance doors. From the inside the doors looked just as un-used. There was one problem. After her early start, Alison had not eaten anything for some hours. Breakfast was a distant memory and one homemade biscuit was all that was sustaining her.

'This is silky oak panelling on the walls.' Charlotte referred to the chest high timber cladding, glowing in the afternoon sun. 'It's used in the all the formal areas downstairs like the lounge, library, dining room, sitting room, Dad's study.' Charlotte walked through a door to a formal dining room. 'Obviously we don't have our meals here. Have a look at the paintings.' Alison needed to crane her neck upwards as most of the art works; oil paintings, watercolours, prints, photographs of people and farm scenes, were hung above her eye height. Even the domestic-scale sculptures on the mantelpiece and sideboard required her to raise her heels.

'I'll get you a little step-stool for tomorrow, said Charlotte, letting Alison make her way around the room. 'There's a lot to see. Why don't we do this?' Alison paused to hear Charlotte's suggestion. 'I'll take you on a quick tour of all the rooms where the artworks are, then we set ourselves up in the sitting room. That's the most comfortable. I'll take you through the list artworks I've put together. And we'll grab something to eat with tea or coffee.' Alison could have kissed her.

*

The sitting room had a maroon sofa and matching lounge chairs, much faded and much sat upon. Alison was finding Charlotte a well-informed family art guide. They perched on the edge of the lounge, leaning forward to eat and drink off a chunky, wooden coffee table. Charlotte had reached into the family-sized refrigerator and the booty was now on the table. Alison had a choice of warmed zucchini slice, a mushroom and feta tart, homemade muffins and biscuits, and a selection from the fruit bowl. Alison wondered if Charlotte had heard her stomach protesting or if the young woman was naturally perceptive or empathetic.

‘Is your father joining us?’ asked Alison.

‘He might, I texted him. But he could be out doing anything for the next few hours.’ Charlotte placed a printout on the table, suggesting they go through her list as they ate. Alison held the spreadsheet in one hand and the last of the tart in the other.

‘When did you put this together, Charlotte?’

‘It was during COVID–19 in 2020. We were in isolation here, which was pretty much business as usual, but for a while I couldn’t see my friends or go into town to a café or pub. I’ve always taken the most interest of anyone in our family in our art collection. I did art in year 12, and I wanted to set myself a project while in lockdown. So, I got out all the old typed up and hand-written notes from the cupboard.’

‘We should get you a job at NAGA. This is fabulous.’

‘Better finish my psych degree at Ballarat first.’ The sun had moved off the mullioned window in the sitting room where it had magnified the mottled glass panes. The temperature in the room had gone down several degrees. Charlotte did up the buttons on her over-shirt as she explained the spreadsheet.

‘I’ve set everything out according to type, whether it’s a painting, drawing, photo and so on. But in the sheets you’ll see I’ve cross-referenced them by location, so they go sitting room, main bedroom, upstairs hallway … like we saw as I took around the house.’

‘Where did you have the Streeton hanging again?’

'On the return of the landing. One story goes that grandfather liked to see the painting of *Wooreen* as the last thing he viewed at the end of the day. And another goes that the family didn't want any random visitors to the house to know that we had a Streeton.'

'Family folklore is funny,' said Alison. 'You know I'm staying in Hamilton tonight? I'll go through these pages and then I'll start my audit first thing tomorrow.' Alison was feeling more refreshed in body and mind. 'Can you tell me what *Wooreen* means?'

'Two versions again. The official family line says it's an aboriginal word for enclosure or settlement.' Charlotte grinned. 'But I've spoken to local aboriginal families in Hamilton. They told me it translates as 'don't know, don't bother me, bugger off' which was like their standard response to our forefathers' queries.'

Alison's overnight accommodation in Hamilton, the commercial centre of the Western District, meant she had to retrace a short part of her morning's drive. In the evening, her arms were a dead weight on the steering wheel. All her energy had disappeared and she felt she could hardly lift her small suitcase. Her room was one of eight in a row – the motel attached as an afterthought to the older, original Caledonian Hotel. As she used her passcard, sunlight struck the lock in the orange painted door. She thought the evening hours had extended for an unreasonably long time.

In the bathroom, after showering off the dust of the day and some of her lethargy, Alison changed into tracksuit pants and pulled her jumper over a short-sleeved top. Facing the mirror, she leaned forward, inspecting a small red spot on her jaw. No make-up. She broadened the inspection, seeing a fine maze of lines under her eyes. The same micro-creases were on her upper lip. Her eyes were red-rimmed. An early start, long drive and long day will do that. Alison reached behind her neck and gathered her pale honey hair, scrunched it, then let it loose. In planning her trip to *Wooreen* Alison had anticipated her task would need more than one day. She had also envisaged an evening meal in the town, finding a quiet restaurant, or even sitting at a table by herself with a pub meal. As it turned out, the hours in the car and late afternoon meal had taken its toll and removed her motivation.

Alison went to the foot of the double bed, sat down and surveyed her room. Standard motel furnishings and décor, nothing to distinguish it from thousands of others.

She had called her daughter Lucy before showering, most of the call taken up with her thirteen-year old daughter's complaint about her homework. Lucy was staying with Alison's ex-husband Craig, so there was also a comment about the new woman in his life, and the couple's fondness for showing affection in front of Lucy. Situation normal. Alison had also written a summary email about her day at *Wooreen* for Michael. She assured him she was still on the trail of Streeton material. Alison turned on the motel room's television, adjusting the volume of a digital music channel. She called Stuart with *Noir Café Music* in the background.

'Hi, what are you up to?' she asked.

'Tarquin and I have demolished a baked zucchini slice he made. The club dietician gives the players recipes but didn't say how much is a serve. We had half each, but it's mostly water, isn't it? How was *Wooreen* today?' Alison rolled onto her back and crossed one leg over in the air.

'It really is a village unto itself. I've never been on a rural property with so many outbuildings. And, I struck gold this afternoon. The SummerHayes daughter, Charlotte, is very switched on. She's a uni student but during COVID–19 she set herself a project of bringing up to date the listing for their art collection.'

'Bless her.'

'Yes. There were lists in different documents and old brochures, but this afternoon we went through a consolidated spreadsheet she had pulled together.'

'Find any other gems in the collection?' There was a sharp noise on Stuart's end of the phone. 'Sorry, I'm opening a post-dinner beer here.'

'The collection has its highlights. Other Australian artists like Norman Lindsay, and Carl Hampel –'

'Let me guess, a gum tree painting?'

'And a pastoral scene. There's a Blamire Young, a lovely family portrait of one of the SummerHayes women by Nora Heysen, and some watercolours by R.W. Sturgess – do you know him?

'Rings a bell, sort of Clarice Beckett-y?'

'Mmm. Plus, there's glassware, sculptures and ceramics, and of course lots of photographs where I need to sort out the family snaps from the odd art-photo.'

'It is a big job, Alison.'

'I'll know more about the scope of it tomorrow. They have a family portrait which is supposed to be by Sir Henry Raeburn, but it's dubious.'

'You'll sort it out.' Stuart considered. 'It's quite possible the Scottish painter could have painted one of their be-whiskered ancestors. Have you found any correspondence about the Streeton?'

'Not yet, more for tomorrow. How's your dad?'

'Still hanging in there, but hey, Gareth is expected back in a day or two.'

'The prodigal son. Your mother will be pleased to have him home.'

'Yeah. I also had a look at the works we picked up from *Conquest.* They're in good-ish condition. As well as those two nice paintings of Arthur's in the study, there's more rural scenes and some urban landscapes, pencil or charcoal studies he did around the market and wharves, also what looks like a country railway station, mostly domestic subject watercolours –'

'You sound more enthusiastic about the discovery today.'

'I think I am. The prints are possibly the most interesting. The etchings and lithographs have unusual subject matter for that time in Australia. They show slum-like homes in the streets of Fitzroy, Port Melbourne and Collingwood, including the service lanes and woodsheds backing onto the alleys. I can't think of another Australian artist doing this subject matter at that time.'

'Do you think our man Arthur may have been highlighting the difference in living conditions around his home in South Melbourne and his brother's place in Kew?'

'Be fun for us to find out,' said Stuart, inserting the plural intentionally. Alison rolled onto her side, her eyes falling on the SummerHayes collection spreadsheets.

'Stuart, I have to review Charlotte's documentation again and do some more research –'

'That's okay. You'll need to be well-rested tomorrow for the audit and research, then the drive home.'

'That's true. One last thing, Stuart. You are okay for Mum's 70th in Canberra? I should let them know and we also need to book flights and accommodation … car hire.'

'I am, I am,' said Stuart. 'When you get back let me know what you want me to book.' They ended the call. Stuart drained the rest of his beer. He had never experienced looking forward to a 70th birthday party before.

On her second day at *Wooreen* Alison met up with Charlotte again. The owner's daughter provided a light stool to take from room to room, as well as more documentation on the family art collection. The boxes of papers, cuttings, brochures and other printed material were spread across one half of the polished wood dining table. Charlotte was sorting them into a rough chronology while Alison was on the top step of the stool, taking a close inspection of a group of three, framed watercolours by R.W. Sturgess.

'We don't know much about that Sturgess chap.' The new voice in the room was that of Annabel SummerHayes, Charlotte's mother. Alison stepped down for introductions. Annabel was in very tight denim jeans, polished boots, and a sleeveless quilted jacket over an aqua polo shirt.

'We're so pleased to have the gallery here to assess our collection.' Annabel re-adjusted some of the papers on the table as she spoke. 'Andrew wanted to flog off the whole collection but really, you can't do that, not after all the years and all the family connections to it all.' She rested one hand on the table surface and waved the other to include all the artworks in the SummerHayes Collection. 'In the end I said to Andrew he could sell one painting, and of course it had to be the Streeton. We would love to keep it here but it deserves to have a wider audience. I'm always fascinated by how many people seem surprised that Streeton did a pastoral of *Wooreen*.'

'That would be because we never told anyone mum, especially the Hamilton City art gallery. Because the last thing you and dad wanted was to have them sniffing around our collection, wanting to borrow this and that.' Charlotte's comment was a perfect blend of barb and jest. Annabel was all business.

'So, Sturgess, Alison. Aren't they lovely watercolours?'

'Yes. He loved coastlines. He must have been very patient to capture the coast at Portland in such quiet moments.' Alison was speaking with the benefit of online research from the previous night. 'And his gentle washes and soft touch make the Grange Burn look idyllic.'

'Have you got to our Raeburn yet? Is it, or isn't it?' Annabel had a habit of making every second sentence a challenge.

'I really can't say anything. It's obviously a portrait of the period, but I understand that it's not signed by Sir Henry –'

'That's always been the problem,' said Annabel. 'But who else would have painted Dugald Summer Hayes in 1815, but the most important Scottish portrait painter of the day?'

'Therefore, it must have come out here to Australia after being painted … in Scotland?'

'Old man Gordon could have brought it out,' said Charlotte. 'Gordon Summer Hayes, the man who established *Wooreen* and the last to spell our surname as two words.'

'If that means anything,' said Annabel. Alison was pouring over the papers on the table as she talked with the two women. She was grateful for the assistance which Charlotte was providing on her visit, but thought that one more assistant may be counter-productive. Possibly reading the situation, Annabel declared she had places to be, things to do.

'I'll leave you in Charlotte's capable hands, Alison. I do hope you find more information around the Streeton painting. There's a wealth of correspondence and stacks of photos kept in those cupboards.'

Charlotte did indeed look after Alison, helping her sift through the letters, printed material and photographs; while ensuring they took companionable mini-breaks. Alison took photographs of items in the SummerHayes Collection as part of her audit. She had a good list of the paintings, drawings, and domestic sculptures. The glassware, ceramics and photographs would need many more hours.

Some hours later Alison sighed, moving a box of SummerHayes family photographs closer to her. The photos were desperately in need of organisation. Alison counted the number of cartons of photographs under her breath. She lifted the flaps from one carton. Photographs were stored in albums, folders and scattered throughout the container. She lifted out the top layer.

'Here's another plague-time job for you Charlotte – sorting out all these photos.' The photographs were a rich pre-digital record of Wooreen and the lives of the SummerHayes families. They were a family history and a history of the district – from the perspective of a white family that assumed land over which no contract or treaty with its custodians ever operated. Alison continued to ponder the vast number of brown and grey photographs, her eye roaming across people in military uniforms, sporting teams, bumper crops and new babies – only a few with writing on the back. *'Esme, 7 months'*... *'Grange Burn FC – runners up'*. Alison knew that photo repositories such as these revealed something of a family's history, but very often concealed just as much.

'Yuk.' Charlotte had joined Alison and fanned out a selection of black and white images. Among shots of a car with ten or more passengers, and floodwaters over *Wooreen*'s lower paddocks, were shots of triumphant men, proudly displaying their handiwork. In one, three men were in front of a string of dead foxes, another showed a man in a broad-brimmed hat holding up a dead snake taller than himself, another with four men and three youths posing with guns behind a spread of twenty or so ducks.

'We're good at killing things.'

In the middle of the afternoon, Alison and Charlotte were again in *Wooreen's* sitting room. This time they were both reclining after working all day. They shared a pot of Earl Grey tea. Alison replaced her tea cup and pivoted sideways on the maroon sofa to face the younger woman.

'Charlotte, you've been brilliant, a great help.'

'I've enjoyed it. Mum loves to talk about our art works but has never done any real work on the collection. Dad is usually against me showing any interest in 'that old stuff'. As if it's a waste of time, or an unnecessary indulgence which doesn't pay the bills.' She smiled. 'I'm happy to keep auditing the glassware and other items if you like?'

'That's a very welcome offer.' Alison frowned. 'The thing which would be really great is if you manage to turn up any correspondence or references to the Streeton.' As they had been working in the house and reading old letters and papers, Alison had explained the importance of any context to the painting by Streeton. 'Anything at all about the Streeton would be a find. Something to help us tell the story around its painting. Anything about his visit here, where he stayed, what other paintings he may have done, that would be gold.'

*

Alison packed her notes and laptop into her hire-car, preparing for the drive back to Melbourne. Annabel had gone to visit a neighbour, but Andrew appeared in the brick-paved courtyard. He had been in one of the sheds, the purpose of which she had been told but had forgotten.

'You're off, then?' Andrew's voice carried across the courtyard as he whacked his thighs and shoulders. He left a cloud of dust behind as he paced towards Alison.

'Thank you very much Andrew,' said Alison. 'Please pass on my thanks to Annabel too, and Charlotte has been magnificent.'

'I'm pleased. I hope you got plenty of good info about the collection.' Andrew rested his weight on one leg, folding his arms, settling in for a chat. 'You know, we should have you stay and have a meal and drink next time. I can tell you some great stories about Michael and I when we were students.' Alison thought Andrew may not have spoken to anyone all day. 'Geez, the things we used to get up to when we had a few drinks. Michael is Mr Gallery now, but we –'

'That would be lovely, Andrew. I may have to do further research so another visit is a real possibility.' Alison was not sure if she wanted to hear about Michael's exploits as a younger man. 'But it is a long drive.'

'Of course, don't let me hold you up.' Andrew unfolded his arms and turned towards the gate. 'Now don't forget, at the fork in the Hamilton Road you need to take the road to the right, then go to the T–intersection, take a left there past Harrigan's place, and that'll get you to the highway.'

*

While Alison activated the car's route navigation system in Western Victoria, in Melbourne Stuart entered the main room of NAGA's conservation department. He had received a text summons from Michael asking him to meet there.

The head of conservation, Christina-Rose, was in her glass-walled office, but there was no sign of Michael. Christina-Rose, always called her full name, resembled a school principal far too much for Stuart's comfort. She was a good colleague and excellent conservator, but whether it was her studied way of speaking, or the way she peered over her bifocal glasses, Stuart had to resist the feeling of being called to the principal's office. Outside Christina-Rose's door, Stuart saw the Streeton painting propped on an easel, portable study lights directed at it, but turned off. Two low-set chairs were arranged in front of the Streeton, an odd set-up for the conservation area which made Stuart think of an old-fashioned drive-in cinema. *Showing tonight, Streeton's Wooreen painting.* He went to the painting and leant forward to look at the surface.

'Michael said he would be here in a couple of minutes, Stuart.'

'Not a problem. I'll wait.' Taking out his phone Stuart left the Streeton and walked to a vacant bench, parked on a stool. As he brought up his messages, he noted the conservation staff doing their usual quiet work. There were two people in their cubicles, both with dual-computer screens in front of them and both tapping at keyboards. On a workbench two conservators were side by side, bent forward over a work on paper which Stuart could not see. He could hear murmurs of their conversation as he read a message from Declan.

dad, Tarq's gonna take me to the football. When he plays and I might be able to go in the clubrooms after the game.

Sounds good Declan. Do you know where and when? And am I invited?

Not sure.

Stuart was prevented from continuing by Michael's arrival. His big voice was unnaturally loud for the conservation area.

'At ease, team,' he announced to the room of technical experts. They had not moved from their work areas, only raising and turning their heads at his voice, then resuming their tasks. Christina-Rose met Michael, who greeted her and sat down in front of the Streeton.

'Christina-Rose, sit down here.' Michael patted the other black and chrome lounge chair. 'You too, Stu. Pull up a seat.'

'Did you see this, Stu?' Michael was indicating the Streeton which the three of them were now all facing. 'Christina-Rose's team have done a preliminary clean. Can you see the difference? See how well it came up? It didn't need much did it?' Michael looked to his head of conservation for confirmation.

'No, it was quite good really. Thank goodness it hadn't been hanging above a smoky fireplace or in direct sunlight for all those years.' Michael sat back, tucking his chin into his chest, gazing at the Streeton.

'In the 1920s Arthur Streeton was at the top of his game, Stu. A master in full control of his skills. See the sweep of the land, the solidity of the ranges in the background ... and the way he shows *Wooreen* itself, you can tell it's a grand home, but he doesn't let it dominate.' Michael now sat up, while the other two silently wondered why Michael had brought them together. They both knew from experience that Michael would get around to it, leaving you in no doubt what he was after, this time. For now, he was still in casual lecture mode.

Stuart peered at the painting, trying to ignore the subject matter and concentrate on Streeton's technique, his brushwork and palette work.

'Michael, I think the particular way he's used the palette knife –'

'Yes. You know, art historians always say Streeton's did his best work as a young man, in the 1890s as a young buck, out painting in those artists camps with Tom Roberts and his mates. But this gem …' Michael pointed at the painting. 'This is his mature work. Here you see him in full control of his art. It's not a bloody sketch dashed off before he could knock off and boil the billy, or roll a smoke.'

'We still have a little work to do before the announcement. Do you have a date for that?' said Christina-Rose.

'Soon, that I do know. We need to get out there and make the public aware of this major acquisition. Jane's doing a PR campaign around the launch of our funds appeal, which will be huge. I'll talk to Jane and let you know what her timing is.' Michael clasped his hands together.

'Alison will be back tomorrow. She tells me she had a good time at *Wooreen*. She's very impressed with the place of course, but also what's in the SummerHayes Collection. The family look after their art and have heaps of documentation, so what Alison finds about Arthur Streeton's visit there will give context to this acquisition.' Michael was in such a talkative and expansive mood, Stuart thought the Acting Director was going to stay there all afternoon. Stuart opted to prompt him.

‘What did you want me for, Michael?’ Michael reacted in mock surprise.

‘To enjoy this master painting in front of you, Stu. Isn’t that enough?’ Stuart waited. ‘Actually, now you’re here, how have you got on with the Rodin drawings?’

‘You know Tony from the Musée d’Orsay ticked off on their authenticity and –’

‘That was never in question.’

‘– and Christina-Rose’s team have updated their condition report, so we –’

‘Stu, Jean Lehni from the Rodin Museum will be out here soon. Huong will have the exact date. You need to work out the program between the two of you. I’ll be too busy on the Streeton announcement. Just make it happen.’

As Christina-Rose explained the remaining, minor conservation work to be done on the Streeton, Stuart took the opportunity to leave. He would see Huong, Michael’s assistant, on the way back to his office.

Stuart returned to the conservation workshop the following day. He had set up a time to meet with Christina-Rose and her team member Astrid. The Streeton painting had been moved from yesterday's position and was not in sight. The chairs had also been taken away.

'I half-expected Michael to be still sitting here in his lounge chair gloating over the Streeton,' said Stuart. Christina-Rose did not comment, save for a pursing of lips. Her eyes were on Astrid who approached carrying a Solander box ahead of her. These specially designed containers, made of acid-free materials, were standard in galleries and museums since their invention. They protect and preserve artworks and prints from the threat of dampness and exposure to light. Stuart and Christina-Rose stood back for Astrid to put the flat, rectangular box on the workbench. She removed the top, exposing sheets of protective paper, the two managers at her side. Wearing thin protective gloves, Astrid picked up a folded piece of card from the workbench. Using the card as a lifter, she peeled back the top layer to expose the first of six drawings.

During a lifetime of artistic achievement, the French master Auguste Rodin only ever published one book. A labour of love, *Cathedrals of France* was published in 1914 when the artist was seventy-four. Over many years the great sculptor visited the grand churches of France and recorded the buildings in drawings and watercolour washes. He dedicated himself to drawing the cathedrals of Paris and other French cities to ensure their rich architectural tradition would always be appreciated.

Rodin had witnessed the arrival of the industrial revolution and like other writers and artists, anticipated the risks of a fast-modernising world. The studies of the cathedrals were never meant to be architectural treatises, but faithful depictions of the buildings' Romanesque and Gothic heritage. Rodin once wrote, 'as all Greece is epitomised by the Parthenon, the whole of France is in her cathedrals.'

Stuart watched as Astrid lifted the first of the drawings from the Solander box. His reading of NAGA's file had told him the story behind the gallery having six on-site drawings by Rodin in its possession. A Melbourne antique and fine arts dealer had owned the set of drawings since he acquired them in the 1960s. The dealer had been in contact with the gallery about the drawings since the 1970s, and around 1988 (according to the file) had offered to donate the drawings to NAGA. Eventually the gallery acquired the Rodin drawings as a donation (with a financial consideration) from the family estate when the dealer died in 2009. It was an internal embarrassment to NAGA that a series of staff members never took the antique dealer seriously, for nearly fifty years not accepting that they were in fact sketches by Rodin. It was only when the gallery accepted the estate that sufficient scholarship was done to establish their authenticity. Even then, the rogue-ish reputation of the dealer made NAGA tread cautiously. No major announcement, special exhibition or other activity has focused on the drawings. Through a succession of directors and senior curators, their presence in the collection was kept low-key. If Acting Director Michael had his way, this was about to change.

The first drawing in front of Stuart and the two conservators was of Reims Cathedral, or the Cathedral of Notre-Dame at Reims. It was a pencil sketch, with an overlay of black pen, showing the entire frontage of the 13th century cathedral's imposing entrance. The second drawing was of the same cathedral, also in pencil and pen, but from a low and off-centre perspective. Rodin had sought to capture the detail of one of the cathedral's twin towers. The next three drawings were all of Notre-Dame d'Chartres. This cathedral contains an immense number of sculptures, particularly figures, from miniatures to large columns. The attraction to Rodin the sculptor was obvious and was reflected in his drawing of the Royal Portals, and two studies – one of angels and one of grotesque figures.

'It's only in the two studies of detailed sculptures, the angels and monsters, where our drawings have Rodin using watercolour washes,' said Astrid. 'This last one of Notre Dame in Paris completes the set and is in the worst condition, or should I say, least good. They're in very good condition overall.'

'What's going to happen with these, Stuart?' asked Christina-Rose.

'Monsieur Lehni will be coming here next week. I would like you to meet and talk with him. He's the Directeur of the foundation at the Rodin Museum, so he will want to have a very close inspection. Then I have to talk to him about a program around the drawings; further research, a seminar program, some sort of exhibition.'

'Do you have all the provenance you need?' asked Christina-Rose.

'Not prior to the 1960s when they were in the possession of the dealer. I'm going to see what I can dig up before M. Lehni's visit.' The gallery file records the deceased antique and fine arts dealer as Herbert Hillier. This man had run a successful store and auction business in Melbourne for almost forty years. In the file there were a couple of references in correspondence to a J. Hillier, with a Melbourne phone number. It was not clear if this person, presumably a relative, was a son, grand-daughter or whatever. At Stuart's request Alison had also reviewed the Rodin file. She had made some suggestions about further research, stressing that contact needed to be re-established with the donor family. She and Stuart had both called the mystery number, for no response. Stuart had also called a couple of Hillier's based on directory information, receiving a polite response, and a very impolite response, in each case letting him know it was not the lead he was seeking.

*

Stuart left the gallery to meet with his mother and brother at Eastside Gardens. As he got out of his car he tried to work out how many months it was since he had seen his younger brother. Gareth was certainly not at the Christmas dinner this summer, nor the previous year.

'Stu!' A sun-tanned Gareth stood on the steps of the reception building, his white-teethed smile and ear to ear grin complemented by extended arms.

'Gareth.' The brothers hugged. 'You're so skinny. Haven't you been eating in Europe?' In some of his irregular photos sent to Stuart's phone, Gareth's hair had been very long. Today it covered his ears and neck, cropped before it could be mistaken for a ponytail.

'Mum's inside. I've already seen Dad.' They went inside the building and saw their mother talking with one of the home's administrative staff. Rosemary finished her conversation and turned to her sons.

'Hi Stuart.' She started to walk towards the room where her husband was in the last weeks of his life. After a few steps she stopped in the empty corridor, taking a hand of each of her sons. 'Be aware Stuart, he has got a little worse. He is comfortable. I was talking –' Cutting herself short, she drew the two men into a tight embrace. She held them, then heaved a sigh and then a torrent of tears, now seeming to be holding on for support.

'Mum, mum … mum.' Gareth and Stuart held their mother, then helped her into a seat in the corridor. Rosemary fished tissues from her bag, simultaneously talking.

'I'm sorry boys. I've been so good holding it in, but having the two of you here together, and your dad is –' Again she couldn't finish her sentence.

At the end of the visit, Stuart arranged to get together with his brother and have a drink. Gareth was staying with his mother at the family home, the Colombian girlfriend remaining in Italy. It would have to be after Stuart's weekend in Canberra. His mother and brother urged him to go despite his father's poor state. It was only a weekend.

Stuart and Alison arrived at Woden City centre in Canberra in the early afternoon. The nation's capital was Alison's home town, where she was brought up and studied, so she would be 'head chef' for the weekend. Stuart, appointed 'sous chef', was content to let Alison decide how they would allocate their time around the party for her mother's milestone birthday.

After checking in, Alison confirmed with her Canberra friend where they would meet for their coffee catch-up. She was looking forward to seeing Harumi, someone with whom she had kept in touch since their secondary school days. On her way to the lakeside café, she would drop Stuart off at his chosen destination, the sobering Australian War Memorial. It was a shorts and short-sleeve shirt summer weekend in Canberra.

Alison drove up Anzac Parade towards the memorial, its imposing façade framed by Mount Ainslie in the background. The wide road, designed for symbolic occasion and daily commuting, formed part of the triangular axis of Canberra's layout. Stuart's head swivelled from side to side, finding interest through his and Alison's car windows.

'Are these all war commemoration sculptures?' He was looking at the series of sculptures and monuments that occurred at regular intervals on either side of the broad parade.

'Yes, you can walk the length of the strip visiting various memorials to service people who've fought and died in wars.'

'Too many.'

'Yep. There's a couple of lovely touches to the design of this area. The red gravel path was made from crushed Canberra house bricks, to give a crunch sound as you walk – an echo of military boots on the ground. And the vegetation is both Australian and New Zealand native plants.' Alison pulled into the drive for the memorial. 'I'll give you a call late this afternoon and pick you up from wherever.' Stuart thanked her. She leant across and kissed him on the cheek. He hooked his small backpack over his shoulder and waved her off.

'Have a great afternoon.' He stood and watched the rear of the hire car as it pulled away, took a left turn and disappeared from sight.

Stuart was spoilt for choice as to how to spend his afternoon as a Canberra tourist. He had wanted to see what was on display in the National Portrait Gallery, which he could have done together with a visit to the National Library. But as he went into the War Memorial's entrance and picked up a guide brochure, family connections were forefront in his mind.

Earlier that morning, he had cleared up his and Declan's breakfast remains and taken his son to the nearby park. They had tennis racquets and were going to the local tennis courts, but found the gate padlocked.

'Sorry Declan. It's usually open and anyone can wander in.'

'Doesn't matter, Dad. We can have a hit in the park.' They took their racquets to an open grass area where Declan invented a new ball game. The aim was to hit the ball to each other, starting a few paces apart and then gradually increase the distance with every third hit. They were making great progress, whacking high soaring shots that caused the other person to scurry and try to retrieve the shot to the other player. It was surprisingly strenuous, and their efforts to retrieve impossible shots made them laugh. They only stopped when a couple's border collie dog decided to join in, snatching the tennis ball before they could reach it. They rested on the trunk of a long-dead tree, kept in the park as wildlife habitat. Father and son used it as a casual seat, Declan doing controlled bounces with a tennis ball on his racquet. They had been talking about Stuart's flight to Canberra in a few hours.

'Are you going with Alison, Dad?'

'I am Declan. We're going to a party for her mother's 70th.'

'Is she your girlfriend?' Declan was watching the bounce of his tennis ball on the strings of his racquet.

'We're good friends. Like you and Jupiter.' As he said it, Stuart thought it was a stupid analogy, comparing an adult relationship with the dynamic of a primary school best friend. Jupiter was the boy whose parents had split up in a most non-amicable manner. Declan stopped bouncing the ball.

'You and mum are not going to make up though, are you? And get back together.'

'No buddy, mum and I agree that's not going to happen.' The border collie came up to the tree trunk, his mascara eyes pleading with Declan to hit the tennis ball. Stuart wondered if he should say something else. Declan balanced the ball on horizontal racquet strings; the dog sat on its haunches.

'Is grandpa going to die?' The question hit Stuart in the chest. He took a heartbeat to gain control of his breathing before answering.

'He is, and perhaps soon. No-one knows when but we have to get used to the idea. I have to get used to the idea.' The border collie's owners were calling their pet.

'Sniffy, Sniffy, come boy, come here.' As Stuart and Declan watched, the dog responded by walking the length of the fallen tree, then cocking its leg against the smooth log for a territorial pee.

'That's what I reckon too,' said Declan.

*

Harumi's chosen café was part of a development which took advantage of a waterfront aspect. It was in Kingston, and on this sunny Saturday was humming with customers. Alison paused at the door, peering into the depths of the café for her friend. From just inside the door a person on a stool called out and signalled.

'Alison!' Harumi stood up and the two friends embraced, holding the embrace while they talked.

'Harumi! Love your hair. How are you? Thanks for getting this spot.' Harumi, red-orange hair secured by a black headband, stuffed the thick novel she had been reading into her bag, then led the way to a table.

'You're looking good Ali, so great to see you. I'm ordering a big mug as we've gonna have a massive catch-up.'

Harumi and Alison went to the same co-educational secondary college in Canberra. They were in the same year level. Alison parents were both public servants, one in the ACT government and one in the Commonwealth Government. Harumi had an Australian father in the country's foreign affairs diplomatic service. Her mother was born to Japanese parents – who had been long-term residents of Western Australia. At secondary school both girls were quiet and studious, achieving good marks in their subjects. They applied themselves to musical instruments – piano for Harumi, cello for Alison, as well as sporting endeavours – hockey for Harumi, soccer for Alison. In the early years of secondary school, they knew each other, but were not close friends.

After the summer break between years ten to eleven, this changed. Over those weeks Harumi had sat in the backyard of her hot home in suburban Hughes, reading book after book. She thought about her family, her two brothers, school, her friends, and by the end of the holidays had made a decision. The quiet (timid), well-behaved (intimidated), neatly-presented (conformist) Australian / Japanese student from previous years did not return. Harumi entered the last two years of her secondary school with a capital A attitude. She dyed blonde streaks into her hair, she decided to answer *every* question in class which she could, she would ask questions if she was not clear on the teacher's instructions, she would question the teacher's opinions and statements, and when the boys turned their necks, she would answer their gaze – what the fuck are you looking at?'

In the first English class of year eleven, Alison found herself sitting next to the new Harumi. She had long forgotten what the class discussion was about, but remembers the exciting energy which Harumi exuded. Later, Alison came to understand that it took Harumi's lead for her to feel more adventurous, more emboldened. Alison followed the blazing trail which Harumi established and maintained, the two creating a friendship for the final years of college, into university and through to their professional lives. Alison knew that she would never be as fierce a blaze as Harumi, whereas Harumi understood that Alison was the vital other side of the coin she needed in her life.

'How is Riku? He's eight now?' asked Alison. Harumi had a son, from her marriage to a man who was in the former band where she had played electronic keyboard.

'He's great, playing with friends today. What about Lucy?' Alison was going to say something about her growing into a Princess, or indulging in teenage terrors, but stopped herself. It wasn't true, and her best friend deserved her best answer.

'I love her, more and more.' Harumi placed her hand on top of Alison's for a few seconds.

'What about that filthy rich man you were going out with?'

'Ben? He's not that rich, although –'

'He is a merchant banker –'

'Yes, but he's … I'm with my friend from the gallery, Stuart, this weekend.'

'Oh, so he's the one to meet the folks.'

'It's not like that. Though I do like him, a lot. It's very sweet, but I need to be careful.' Alison picked up the menu card. Harumi dropped her shoulders to meet her friend's eyes.

'Take him to bed tonight, Ali. That will help him make up his mind.'

'Done that, it's just that … I don't know. I'm investing a lot in my relationship with Stuart. And that's scary – for both of us I suppose.' Alison put the menu card back on the table. 'I don't need anything to eat. Let's walk along the waterfront after coffee?'

The two women strolled past outside tables and chairs, following the timber bulwarks defining the edge of the lake. They each checked their timing. Alison had to arrange when to pick up Stuart and Harumi had to pick up her son from her friend's place.

'How's your work, Harumi?'

'Ugh, absolutely horrible. I don't want to talk about the Department of InHuman Services. Your work is more interesting. What are you working on?'

'I do have some interesting stuff at present. I had a trip to the wilds of Western Victoria about a new acquisition, which is top secret. I've been doing research on a private collection at a heritage property. And, I had a lovely time with Stuart at a home in Melbourne where they were doing renovations. We found some old artworks by an early twentieth century Australian artist.'

'With Stuart?'

'Yes, it was a lovely morning, we –' Harumi extended an arm to stop her friend.

'Your face always gave you away, Ali. No wonder you couldn't get away with the mischief I got up to.' They had reached a white painted railing marking the end of the waterfront walk.

*

At the Australian War Memorial Stuart found the section he wanted. He took his time getting there, following the brochure's floor plan while allowing himself to be diverted by displays and objects; the compressed diary writing of a Gallipoli soldier, a photo of Australian soldiers goofing it up with coconuts and grass skirts under a palm tree, and the black and white television footage which brought the Vietnam War into Australian homes.

He stood in front of a photograph of the light cruiser HMAS Sydney. In the official portrait photograph, the flagship of the Australian World War 2 naval fleet was sitting serenely on a calm sea in the Pacific Ocean. Tucked away midships, or somewhere on the ship presumed Stuart, was his grandfather, Evan's father Rex Williams. In a few months, the HMAS Sydney would be lost at sea with all 645 crew, sunk off the Western Australian coast by a German raider, HSK Kormoran. Rex had been transferred to serve on a corvette class ship, only ten weeks before the Sydney was sunk. Able Seaman Rex was to go on and serve three more years on corvettes, undertaking escort and minesweeping duties till the end of the war.

'Look at the raft, cool.' A boy had trotted in and zeroed in on the large object on a low plinth in the centre of the room. It was a Carley life raft. While it bore no name, researchers at the War Memorial believe it was recovered in the right time and place to have come from HMAS Sydney. Stuart had been brought up to know about his grandfather's time in the navy and his war record. The story was told many times how his grandfather was so lucky to have been transferred off the HMAS Sydney before its tragic end. That was the beginning, but also the end of the stories. There must have been a lot more to tell about the exploits of the corvettes and the subsequent three years, but grandfather Rex never spoke about them to his family, nor to anyone as far as Stuart knew.

Stuart checked the time. He wanted to meet up with Alison and allow themselves time to get ready for her mother's party. He felt empty but unsettled in his stomach. Must have been the early start and plane trip.

The evening party was at Alison's parents' home in Torrens.

'Did we have a Prime Minister called Torrens?' asked Stuart.

'Don't act thick. He was a South Australian premier, one of the many DWMs who get perpetuated.'

'Dead White Males?' Alison steered around the curving road, peering at the houses.

'It's a middle-level suburb befitting a middle-level couple.' Alison's mother was an executive with a newly established division of the Commonwealth Government. Alison had trouble keeping up with her mother's changing positions, roles, promotions, restructured departments and new divisions. In contrast, her father had been in the same part of the ACT government, in housing policy, since she was at college. They parked in the street and walked to the front door.

'15 Bradbury Drive wasn't the home I was brought up in. Mum and dad bought this place after the one in Chapman burnt down in the bushfire.'

'In … 2000?'asked Stuart. Alison paused on the concrete porch. It was still light and they could see and hear people inside.

'January 2003, the day my Primary School and family home were burned down. It was like taking away, erasing, my childhood.'

'A lot of homes were lost, weren't there?'

'About 500, but also schools, petrol stations and other buildings as well as people's homes. It was a miracle only four lives were lost.' Alison took a big breath, steeling herself. 'Let's join the party.'

Alison's parents Judy and Ryan invited a mixed crowd to celebrate Judy's 70th birthday. Immediate family was represented by Alison's only sibling, sister Rachel, her husband and two children. Joining them was a cluster of Judy's brothers and sisters, most with spouses. On Ryan's side there was his brother Aaron and his family. Swelling the numbers were neighbours and friends picked up from work, book club or art class.

As soon as they entered the lounge room, a wild-eyed, six-year old girl ran up to Alison, thrust her arms skyward, and was rewarded by being lifted off the ground and kissed on her neck.

'Aunty Ali, don't,' squealed Mia, the younger child of Rachel and Licardo. Rachel had the hand of their son Lincoln, two years older, solemn and holding back. Introductions were made between Alison and Stuart and her sister and her family. Where Alison was fair, Rachel was dark. The younger sister had an olive complexion, whereas Alison never tanned. Rachel's dark hair was cut in an impish mode. Her figure was clear to see in petite-range jeans and a V-neck knitted top. Stuart was drawn to Rachel's deep brown eyes – she had impossibly long lashes and was fox-pretty.

In ten minutes, Alison and Stuart assimilated into the gathering as if they had been there for hours. Alison chatted with her sister and mother, while Stuart was introduced to one of Judy's siblings. Alison referred to her mother's family as The Aunts and Uncles. Judy was the middle child of seven, so with their husbands, wives, partners and children, the roll call could very easily get confused. Alison had not bothered to brief Stuart before they went to the party on who was who.

'You'll work it out.' Neville, an uncle, handed Stuart a glass of prosecco.

'You're not from Canberra, Stuart?' Neville decided Stuart was in need of education. 'You know over fifty per cent of Canberrans were born here?' Stuart didn't, but wasn't given a chance to answer. 'That's right, and less than fifty per cent of Canberrans work in the public service. It's not a public service town and hasn't been for a long time.' Neville had quickly got on a roll. 'It's the pollies who fly in here, live in some subsidised flat as cheaply as they can, then bag the place to everyone back wherever they came from. The same place that provides them with all the perks and lurks they love to take up.' This defensiveness about the nation's capital was something which, to a lesser extent, Stuart had also heard Alison express. Surely not everyone in Canberra had a chip on their shoulder. Neville put Stuart on hold while he looked up an online news story.

'Listen to this crap I read this morning. *Canberra operates in a bubble removed from reality. Life is easy for its residents – no traffic jams or queues at the supermarket. Everyone is on such a good wage that they can all afford cleaners and send their children to private school. Canberra is a community of affluent, middle–class people totally removed from the lives of ordinary Australians who –'*

'What's the context for the story?' Neville had become distracted by something else on his phone.

'Stuart, come and meet my parents.' Alison took Stuart by the elbow, wanting to introduce him before too much time had elapsed. She had caught the direction of Alison's mother's glance across the lounge room, checking out this man Alison had talked about and brought up from Melbourne. Her father saw Alison with Stuart. He left the people he was talking with, offering his hand.

'Ha, you're Ben. Welcome mate, make yourself at home.'

'This is Stuart, Dad.' Alison looked panicky, Stuart smiled.

'Pleased to meet you, Ryan. Alison tells me you moved into this home after the bushfire.' Ryan gestured dismissively with his non-drinking hand.

'That's history now, ancient history. Alison always did live in the past. That's why she loves researching as a job. You're in banking though aren't you, Ben?'

'Dad! Stuart works at the gallery with me,' said Alison.

'Well, why didn't you tell me?'

Later in the evening, most guests had had a couple of drinks, and were pacing themselves according to habit. Younger children with limitless energy ran in and out of the house, three teenagers took themselves to the base of a tree in the most remote corner of the backyard: they stayed there, un-noticed for four hours. A group of three were drinking more than most; Adele, one of Judy's sisters, with Neville and Aaron. They made a boisterous corner of the large family room. Food was served buffet-style, music was out-volumed by the conversations. Ryan had made a brief speech and the party had self-consciously sung happy birthday.

'Ridiculous for a seventy-year old,' said Judy to Stuart. 'Alison tells me you did a marvellous job on the blockbuster at the gallery. We didn't get down there to see it, but she said you were the one who managed it, and it wasn't easy.'

'Did she say that?' Stuart felt a pleasant tremor at the thought of Alison talking about him to her mother. 'Alison was a great help to me on that show. She's a terrific researcher. NAGA is lucky to have her.' He supposed his comments to Judy about Alison would get back to her.

A voice called for Judy from the adjacent room. Rachel was trying to find something in the kitchen. Stuart avoided the rowdy corner on his way to the drinks table, poured himself a glass of red wine, telling himself it was his last. He went over to a non-functioning wood heater, drawn by an assembly of family photos on the mantlepiece. Stuart discovered from the framed photos that Alison played soccer at representative level, with some success as the presentation photographs illustrated. Alison joined him, sipping tea.

'Here's the soccer star. You never told me you played at the senior level, or any level if it comes to that.'

'You never asked.'

'What sort of player were you? I bet you were fast and nippy.'

'I'll show you in the park one day. Mum and dad lost their photo albums in the fire. They had to get out in such a hurry. These few were ones taken by the aunts and uncles I think, except my soccer team ones.'

'Was your friend Harumi in the soccer team?' Stuart scanned the faces – rows of braces-revealing smiles, ponytails whipped by the wind across faces distorted by squinting into the sun.

'No, she wasn't part of the soccer scene. She was playing with her band in clubs.' Stuart held the edge of a rounded wooden frame. The photo was of Alison and her sister.

'How old were you in this?' asked Stuart.

'I was in year twelve, so we're eighteen and sixteen. The smart one and the pretty one. That's its title.'

'It's not.' Stuart looked closer to see if there was an inscription.

'It's not the official title, but it's what it is.' Stuart frowned, inviting an explanation. 'When we were growing up together, as soon as we could understand, we were known as the pretty one – that's Rachel, you may have noticed. And I was the smart one. I was the one who did well at school. I had to go on to university.'

'But surely your parents didn't talk to you like that. They're lovely people –'

'They didn't have to say it, although dad did quite often, as if he was being even-handed in recognising admirable qualities in both of us.' Alison finished her drink and licked her lips, the tip of her pink tongue exposed. 'It's how we were brought up.' Stuart was interested in knowing more but Alison said she wanted to say their thank-yous and farewells. She held his hand.

‘I don’t want us to hang around until the conga-line dance starts up.’ Stuart’s face expressed alarm and a question.

‘It’s been known to happen. Let’s go back to our room.’

In the morning, head-chef Alison told Stuart how the second day of their Canberra weekend would unfold. She was going to do some shopping, then drop in on her parents on her own before their flight back to Melbourne. Sous-chef Stuart was to choose his destination and she would drop him off and pick him up. It was another clear and bright summer’s day in the capital.

Stuart sat on a low concrete wall in the Parliamentary Triangle. In front of him the blue-black water of Lake Burley Griffin peaked and rippled, never forming enough momentum to create waves. Stuart sketched in his drawing pad; legs extended straight out towards the water. Behind Stuart was the High Court building, much further back was Old Parliament House, and if he stood up and looked west, he would see new Parliament House. Straight across the water was Anzac Parade with its commemorative sculptures and installations leading to the War Memorial and Mt Ainslie.

Stuart was onto drawing three from this vantage point. His first drawing was a pencil sketch with the lake in the foreground, Anzac Parade almost in the centre, then the War Memorial and mountain. First doing some tentative placement lines to put everything in position, he had included much of the detailed vegetation and other buildings. It had plenty of shading, different textures, the movement of water. He decided to omit the Captain Cook fountain, because he could.

Stuart did the second drawing by placing the first underneath the semi-transparent drawing pad paper. He also thought back to last night's party. The thing he recalled most vividly was the photo of the two sisters 'the smart one and the pretty one'. He traced the key lines from his first drawing, referring to the landscape in front of him, slowly shaking his head.

His subsequent drawing was lines only, no light and dark, no textural detail. Another moment from the party came to him. He was talking to Licardo, sharing their kid's school information, when he overheard the conversation of two of the aunts.

'… Alison … divorced a few years ago … at NAGA in Melbourne, in admin something … a new chap. Alison has high hopes for him, according to Rachel.'

Repeating his process for the third drawing, he slid the line drawing underneath the next sheet in his drawing pad. He paused, staring at the scene in front of him – from water to mountain and mountain back to water, from trees on the left to parkland on the right and back again. He sharpened his pencil, recomposed his sitting position and concentrated on the view. In his third and final drawing, his aim was to draw the scene in the most minimalist style. It would be a few lines only, the absolute bare minimum necessary to capture the essence of the landscape. With a steady hand he drew five lines across the paper, aiming to capture the shores of the lake, the mass of the mountain, the outline of the memorial building. Next, he used the least number of lines to show the thoroughfare running from lake to memorial, the trees and parkland. He stopped after drawing these lines. He packed up his things, putting pencils and pad into his backpack. It was time for Alison to pick him up for their return flight home.

Back in Melbourne that night, he unpacked his overnight bag onto his bed. He also emptied his backpack. He had enjoyed the weekend with Alison, accepting the intimacy she offered by inviting him to view her life pre-Melbourne and pre-NAGA. He took out the minimalist-style third drawing he had done at the edge of Lake Burley Griffin. He held it at arm's length.

It wasn't very good.

In the director's office at the National Art Gallery of Australia, Alison waited for Michael Maher to return. They had only got to pre-meeting greetings before he excused himself 'for two minutes' to respond to an urgent issue. From where she was sitting, she could see him, in the anterior office area, conferring with his assistant Huong. Alison could see evidence of Michael's occupation of the office in his Acting Director role; the concrete gnome in Essendon Football Club colours, his timber frame ergonomic chair, a sideboard stacked with papers, books, coffee-making equipment and a ripped-open packet of chocolate teddy-bear biscuits. As Michael's voice level rose outside, Alison thought how odd it was that the director's office, with Angela on sick leave and Michael in her place, had reduced its own dimensions.

'O.M.G. That Huong can be hard going. What have you got for me, Alison?' Michael sat down in his ergonomic chair, wheeling it around his desk to be nearer her lounge chair.

'The trip was interesting –'

'He's a great guy, Andy, isn't it he? You met Annabel as well? Lovely couple.' Michael stood up, rolled his chair away with a hefty push. 'I can't sit in that thing. Makes my back bloody worse.' He sat down in the matching lounge chair. 'What did you find out there? *Wooreen's* a lovely homestead.'

'It is. Their collection has some highlights. Apart from the glassware and some ceramics, amongst the paintings there's some strong Australian works. I particularly liked a portrait by Nora Heysen of one of the SummerHayes women.'

'Haven't they got a Raeburn portrait?'

'It's not substantiated. It's the right time and right place, but it's not signed.'

'Tell 'em they're dreaming. But what about the Streeton? What else can we say about it, or about the old boy?'

'I saw where it had been hung and Andrew took me to where he thinks it was painted from. That will be handy context for writing about the Streeton.' Alison knew what was coming next.

'Did you find letters from Streeton to the SummerHayes, or an old photo of him painting in the paddocks?'

'No. There is so much material to wade through in their home.'

'You have to keep looking, Alison. There will be stuff there, you just need to find it.'

'I felt that Charlotte may be able to help us out. She said she will do further searching through their … archives.' Alison had a researcher's reluctance to label the stacks of letters, notes, photos, newspapers and other material an archive.

'Who's Charlotte?' asked Michael.

'Their daughter, she was very helpful –'

'Charlotte!' Michael was taken aback. 'Their little girl? She's like ten years old or something, isn't she?'

While Michael came to terms with how quickly the children of friends grew up, in his office on NAGA's curatorial row, Stuart was surrounded by art books about Auguste Rodin. He felt he had done as much research as he could about Rodin's sketches for the *Cathedrals of France* publication. Jean Lehni from the Rodin Institute would be in Australia next week. Stuart had called the French director, confirmed the arrangements and was preparing for the visit. Obviously, M. Lehni would want to see the drawings. He was confident that Christina-Rose and Astrid had the drawings in good condition for the Frenchman. They would also discuss a program around these drawings, which is where Stuart needed to do some work. He had to draft a program of activities and opportunities for Michael to sign off before he put it in front of M. Lehni. It would have to contain a seminar format, a student exchange perhaps, certainly an exhibition but where and when? Stuart would also have to work with Jane Hollingway on a promotional program for the Rodin drawings. This was something the gallery had shied away from, but now, Michael's choice phrase was reverberating, 'we have to milk this fucking thing for all its worth Stu.'

Stuart scrolled through NAGA's internal database on the Rodin drawings. This is where all the information was recorded about a work of art's accession, registration and other details. M. Lehni would be interested in this as well. Stuart read, again, about the Rodin drawings coming into the gallery's possession via the family estate. He lingered on one reference to 'the Melbourne antique dealer who had owned the set of drawings since he acquired them in the 1960s.' This is what intrigued Stuart – how did Herbert Hillier acquire the drawings, from who, where and when? Stuart called the file phone number for J. Hillier for the third time that day for the same result – no answer.

*

Stuart had driven to his family home where Gareth was cleaning up after dinner with his mother.

'Gareth makes a wonderful ragu, Stuart. Melt in your mouth,' said Rosemary.

'I got the chef at the place in Menaggio on Lake Como to show me how he does it.' Gareth picked up his phone and wallet, then led the way to the front door.

The brothers walked the five minutes to the establishment in the local shops, Stuart and his brother at last having their catch-up.

'I can't believe this place, whatever it is.' Gareth swept his arm to encompass the bar's folded back bi-fold doors, showing a stripped back warehouse-style interior, as well as the outdoor seating space where they were enjoying the mild evening. *Ren & Mia*'s was in a strip of shops on one side of the street. 'A bar like this in Heathmont? It used to be a Chinese take-away, didn't it?' They both looked away from the buzzing terrace, as if seeing the shops for the first time. Stuart pointed to the buildings. 'There was a crappy no-name supermarket in the middle, a post office next to that – that's gone, wasn't there a petrol station on that end?'

'It's a delicatessen cum café, open for breakfasts and lunch. I took mum there the other morning,' said Gareth.

'How was mum?' asked Stuart.

'She was fine. She had their big breakfast and loved it.'

When they arrived, Gareth reviewed the craft beer list, wanting to try them all. As they sat down at the terrace table, Stuart registered Gareth's sideways glance at the two women on the next table.

'Hi. Hey, can you help me out? What's the best of these craft beers?' The two young women responded to Gareth's engaging enthusiasm. They both wore sleeveless tops showing late-summer tans. 'The Pale Ale? Is that what you're drinking? Thanks, let us try that then. Stu?' Stuart detected the trace of an Italian accent in his brother's voice.

Despite Stuart's intention, the catch-up chat had turned into that, and something more. The beers went down far too easily. Gareth mined a strong vein of nostalgia, recalling their childhood, the neighbourhood, schoolfriends. Stuart was tempted to ask Gareth if he loved their old neighbourhood so much, why was he never there? Then again, Lake Como and Miss Colombia might have an appeal as well.

Stuart ordered a cheese and fruit plate for them to share, Gareth insisting on 'one last beer'. Stuart knew he would not be driving home that evening. Over the course of their catch-up Stuart learned that Gareth was 'moderately serious about Clara from Colombia, and that he had no intention of altering his European-based lifestyle. Stuart wanted to ask his brother if his underweight frame was due to drug-taking. He didn't know how to broach the subject. After the third beer he found a way. Gareth was gazing at the two women adjacent as he raised his glass.

'Are you doing drugs?' Gareth put down his drink.

'No Stu, fucking Christ, man. Say what's on your mind, why don't you?' The objection appeared genuine to Stuart and the two brothers soon smoothed things over. Stuart apologised, said he was concerned. Gareth accepted the apology, asked a question of his own.

'How's your divorce? I always found Leah a dry stick to be honest.'

Over the evening the number of café and bar patrons increased, requiring some table amalgamation and chair sifting to accommodate arrivals. Gareth had periodically engaged with the young women on the next table. His Italian accent was getting stronger. They had shared first names and Gareth had put out the idea that they meet up with him in Italy next northern summer.

'We should all four sit at the one table,' he said. They were about to raise themselves from their seats when a figure loomed over them. Alex, Stuart and Gareth's older sister, blocked the light.

'Stuart, Gareth.'

'Hi Alex! Sis, have a seat. I'll get you a drink. This is –' Alex's sombre expression and immobility arrested Gareth's flow of words. Alex angled her body so that her back was to the two women who faced each other and resumed their one-on-one talk.

'We've got to go to Eastside. Dad is in his last hours.'

PART TWO: 1924

Arthur and Walter Norman

Walter Norman (1875–959) Melbourne businessman, councillor of *Conquest, Kew*

m. Marigold

Lydia (1905–31)

Arthur Norman (1879-1938) Australian artist of *Dorcas Street, South Melbourne*

m. Elsie Tatlock

Kate (1906–09)

Millie (1908–?)

William (1913–?)

Albert (1912–1989) of *Fairwind, Sorrento*

m. Irene Fairclough

Edward (1938–2004)

m?

Francis (1976–)

Ivan (1940–?)

Meg (1947–1973)

Lynette/Netty (1942–)

m. William/Bill O'Brien

Melanie

m. Rob Widdicombe

Willow

Dottie

Scott

It was smoko for the afternoon shift. A group of about twenty men were in the weatherboard shed, a short walk from the brick factory. The sweet and sour smells of the food production buildings followed them. Most of the men were sitting on the low wooden benches that ran along both sides of the shed, and most were smoking or rolling cigarettes. They had trooped in the door, each going straight to their spot in the shed to his allocated double peg on the wall. Their jackets hung on the lower half of the peg, their hats or cloth caps above. Below each peg, underneath the slat bench, they stored their workbags. The Gladstone bag, made of stiff leather with a metal opening lip, was the workbag of choice. Some of the workers finished their smokes then foraged in their bags. They extracted paper-wrapped sandwiches – thick, buttered white bread, cold meat in the middle with either tomato sauce or pickles.

'Move ya bloody wooden leg, Archie,' said a large man half-way down the room. 'Give a bloke some space to park his arse.'

Archie moved a few inches and the man sat down with a grunt. Archie often shared his views about his wooden leg with his workmates.

'Fair dinkum, they've given me the worst wooden leg in the whole war. This one's got woodworm and hurts to look at it.' His mates chided him at every opportunity. But in subtle ways they made sure his workload on the shift was not excessive, in return for his black humour and cheekiness.

The twenty-minute smoko was the only break over twelve hours for the bottling line of Ockwell's Sauce & Pickle factory in Port Melbourne. The men were eating, talking, coughing, blowing their noses, farting, and again, smoking.

Women also worked at Ockwells. There were about a dozen women from this part of the factory who were taking their shift's smoko. They were making the most of their brief respite in the women's shed. This area was not technically a shed at all, but a covered verandah which ran along the furthest side of the shed, closed off at one end but open to the elements on two sides. The women had a similar wooden bench and peg arrangement. They were all sitting down along their wooden bench, smoking and talking quietly, when Sarge came up to them.

'Got an announcement girls,' said the Ockwell's foreman. 'New line starting next week, so any mates wanting work show up at the gates at seven.'

'Righto Sarge.' Sarge was in his early thirties, the three buttons of his grey dustcoat just meeting their corresponding button-holes. He was younger than most of the women, who ignored him as he walked with a slightly backwards tilt into the men's shed.

'Okay you lot,' he announced into the thick soup of smoke and sweat. He was about to pass on his brief message, but on the spur of the moment, decided to make a point – this time they would show him the respect befitting his position. Usually, it suited both Sarge and the workers, male and female, for him to keep his orders and messages brief, say what he had to, and leave them to their only break from the factory's production lines.

It was the workers who had named him Sarge. He had served in the war, but as he tired of telling them, 'I was only ever a Private, ya galoots.' It was most likely the sly sarcasm that came with every use of the pumped-up manager's nickname that made it stick so firmly. Sarge turned to the door through which he had entered and did something he never did – he shut the door to the men's shed behind him. The men nearest the door tried to prevent him.

'Too warm for that Sarge.'… 'Leave it open Sarge, Archie's farted again.' Sarge closed the door despite the groans and catcalls of protest. The reason the men wanted the door open, for its interior to face the wall, was now clear. The back of the door was a gallery of drawings, from its top almost down to the floor. There were sketches of Ockwell workers, done on pieces of paper of various sizes. Many were done on the white reverse of the paper labels for the Ockwells range of table condiments. These were recognisable portraits of men who were now part of that shift and in that very shed. A shed that had gone uncharacteristically quiet. Sarge was transfixed by the drawings. All the men knew about the drawings, and the artist was in their midst.

The men now looked in every direction but at Arthur Norman, who sat on the bench, his hands clasped together, resting between his knees. He was an unremarkable man of medium height and build. His jaw came to a point, as did his nose. A nose more refined than those of the men either side of him (although to be fair one of those was an ex-boxer). The corners of his mouth were more inclined to rise than turn down. His eyes were a deep-sea blue. His voice was light, more mellow than his workmates. Norman's straight dark hair was receding, but still plentiful on the sides. One worker made a hopeful suggestion.

'Back to work, hey Sarge?' Norman had not stopped watching Sarge as the foreman's head moved from drawing to drawing. He knew what was going to happen next and what the outcome was going to be. His eyes crinkled at the thought.

'What have we got here? said Sarge, as if he was in a Gilbert and Sullivan production.

Work at Ockwell's Sauce & Pickle factory was a continuous slog. For the men and women on the product line it meant lifting heavy cartons and boxes, enduring potent smells and rotting odours, putting up with pounding, hissing, ringing noises that rarely ceased, spending monotonous hours at the same task of filling, capping, labelling, packing or cleaning. Accidents were frequent – a foot crushed by a box of packed pickles, a hand cut to the bone from a smashed sauce bottle, an arm broken in the labelling machine.

The company, established in Melbourne in the late 19th century, was very successful. It sold a lot of green tomato pickles, jars of cucumbers, pots of mustard and other foods to Victorian homes. Trucks with the Ockwell's label – a boomerang in the top left and lower right corners bracketing the content description, rolled out of their loading dock every morning. The company slogan '*You'll come back – for more*' was on the doors of trucks that delivered all around Melbourne, to Victoria's regional cities and as far as the New South Wales Riverina district and Mt Gambier in South Australia.

Each year Ockwell's Port Melbourne plant and machinery produced more goods and made greater profits for its owners. The original Ockwell brothers had been bought out by the current owners many years ago, but the name was kept in the minds of the public. Not least through a radio jingle which was heard on thousands of family radiograms. Ockwell's sponsored radio programs; a popular morning serial, a half-hour comedy program and *Newsabout* – an evening news bulletin. They advertised in newspapers, had posters on railway hoardings, and plastered their name outside grocery stores.

When visiting neighbours for a game of Friday night cards, it was common for people to knock on the door to the tune of the Ockwell's jingle, *Ockwells, Ockwells! Ockwells!!* (knock–knock, knock–knock, knock–knock with a rising inflection). If the homeowner had seen the visitors coming through the front curtains, it was a great lark to time it such that you opened the door, answering '*The home of sauce and pickles!*'

The second couplet of the jingle had the same rhythm, ending with the '*You'll come back – for more*' tag line. Bands of rag-tag children playing hopscotch or ball games in the back lanes of Melbourne or paddocks of rural Victoria parodied the jingle.

Ockwells, Ockwells! Ockwells!!

The home of sauce and pickles,
Ockwells, Ockwells! Ockwells!!
You'll spew up – for sure.

*

Arthur Norman had worked at Ockwells on and off for four years, mixed with other jobs in places near his South Melbourne home. Since the war he had been a factory storeman, worked on the wharves and helped deliver bread with a horse and cart man. He was fitter and healthier than most men in their forties. There were many of the war-damaged in the suburbs – poor souls with limbs missing, faces disfigured and uncontrollable coughs. At Ockwells there were workers older than him, but not many. The work wore a person down.

Arthur was born in the Victorian regional town of Ararat. His father died in a railway accident before Arthur, his second son, could walk. He had trained as an artist. With no artistic forebears, Arthur surprised yet delighted his mother by showing a precocious talent in drawing the town's draught horses. Young Artie could capture the stoic power and endurance of the work-horses, drawing on whatever was available. He would use scraps of charcoal on wood off-cuts, his mother propping them on the mantlepiece, after a few days throwing them on the fire.

'Ah well, another masterpiece to keep us warm.'

At the local school his drawing ability was also recognised. It was recommended that he go to the School of Mines in Ballarat. He gained a technical education there, then in 1897 went to the Melbourne Art School. At eighteen he boarded in the city, taking classes in classical drawing, figure drawing, history painting, anatomy and sculpture. Arthur was a willing student and quick learner, making excellent progress under his teachers. Like many, the next step in his artistic career was travel to Europe. In the company of Art School mate Tomasso, or Tommy Ferraro, they sailed to London, also spending many months in Paris. Tommy and Arthur parted ways in Europe, his mate keen to travel to Italy to meet a string of relatives. Arthur would have gone to Italy as well, but modest funds meant he contented himself with visiting the great galleries and museums of London and Paris. He learnt much from studying the Old Masters up close, but he also sought out the ideas and work of contemporary European artists.

Arthur's mother, who supported his art education with unconditional love, died when he was overseas. His only sibling, older brother Walter, wrote to inform him that their mother had died a peaceful death after a short illness. There was no need for Arthur to hastily return home from Europe – Walter would manage the small amount of funds from his parents' estate, which was their mother's wish. When, months later, Arthur returned to Australia in 1903, he and Walter visited their parents' graves in the Ararat Cemetery and then went back to the family home in Ararat. Walter had arranged for a man representing the Catholic Church to meet with them in the small brick home on a large block of land. The churchman thought the location of the Norman property on the side of a hill made it potentially suitable for the church's future needs.

'But these big 'ouse blocks, they're not worth much compared to good farming land,' he told the two brothers.

'Of course,' agreed Walter.

'The church would have to knock down your 'ome 'ere, an' then …' The man frowned, one eye closing as he explored a rotten tooth with his tongue. 'Tell you what. I'll come back to you Mr Norman with a fair offer.' He was addressing Walter only. 'G'day to you.'

Some weeks later, Arthur was undertaking part-time study at the Melbourne Art School, while teaching a couple of the beginner classes. Walter, executor of his parents' estate, arranged the transfer of a sum to Arthur's bank account. With his own proceeds, which included a sum for 'executor's fees,' Walter set about establishing himself in business in Melbourne. He ran a dye and stain workshop, supplying Melbourne's many shoe and boot manufacturers, as well as the flourishing rag trade behind the clothing industry. Within two years the business outgrew the original premises and Walter purchased a larger factory in Abbotsford.

Arthur's art drew on his learning in Europe, which was reflected in his sketches of lively scenes at the South Melbourne market, or oil studies done on the banks of the Yarra River. Norman painted in and around Melbourne, completing landscapes featuring the more picturesque stretches of the rubbish dump and weed-strangled stream that was Merri Creek, and the marginally better Darebin Creek. He did studies of workers' cottages. He took train trips out of Melbourne, and painted coastal scenes and rural properties beyond the rural fringe of Melbourne.

By 1910 he was married to Elsie Tatlock and the couple had two small girls. They lived in a worker's cottage in South Melbourne. Their first child, Kate, had a short life, dying at age three. Elsie was an ex-showgirl. She was from a well-off family in Geelong, with a passion for songs and dancing. She joined J.C. Williamson, the large and successful theatre production company. Elsie was in a few productions; a couple of musicals, a light opera, and was part of a back-up dancing group which entertained between comedic performers. But she found, like many before her, that in the big city she was one of many. Elsie never formally retired as a performer – she just stopped getting work. She was canny enough to see the writing on the wall and turned her talents to sewing and clothes-making. J.C. Williamson had a need for many different types of costumes for their productions. Through her contacts at the company, she took on the repair and modification of some of the sweaty and stained costumes. New costumes were especially made for new productions, but there was a steady stream of remedial sewing work for Elsie at their South Melbourne home.

Norman sold a few of his works through the art school, but never quite enough to establish himself as an artist. His work was praised but he lacked a well-connected champion for his art. The Melbourne Art School teachers looked after themselves first and teaching work for Norman dried up. Two more children, both boys, were born before the First World War. Norman was now a family man of thirty-five. While he was prepared to do his bit, fighting in Europe in countries he had recently experienced, the Australian Army had a better idea for a man with his training. Norman enlisted, did his initial training, then reported to an army depot in West Melbourne. The depot building, converted from a grain and livestock storage facility, was a lofty brick building with no ceiling but a metal roof high above beams, pipes and girders. Here he was to make his mark for Australia and the mother country, painting camouflage patterns on equipment and vehicles.

His boss in the army was a commercial artist who used to run the art department at Myer, the Melbourne department store which had recently established its flagship premises in Bourke Street. Clarrie L. Stephens had supervised a flourishing art department and workshop at Myer. He now directed a team of men in painting field camouflage on war necessities from ammunition boxes and food storage tins, to horse carts and large heavy-duty canvas tarpaulins. Clarrie was brought up in England where he completed his commercial art training. It was in rural Sussex with the English Army where he learnt about field camouflage techniques. It was an increasingly important part of military tactics brought about by developments in the war such as long-range artillery and the increased use of aircraft. Clarrie and his men were kept busy in their converted granary, but in between deliveries of stock to be painted, Arthur enjoyed talking with the head man about his art interests. Clarrie had a passion for the art of the English-born, Australian Heidelberg School artist Charles Conder. It did not take too much encouragement for Arthur to get Clarrie talking about Conder's lyrical landscapes. Clarrie would inevitably work himself into admiration for his hero's lightness of touch and deftness with the brush.

'Mind you, Artie. If you or I applied ourselves we could knock up something approximate to Conder's style. I'll show you.' The next hour or two would be very absorbing for Arthur as Clarrie rolled out a short length of canvas and set to work illustrating the handcraft of another artist. Arthur, always quick to learn, soaked up the other man's knowledge, turning his own hand to some of the painting techniques Clarrie demonstrated. The two artists amused themselves in this way while others smoked and yarned away the dead hours.

After the war, the work at the art school dried up completely for Arthur. He and Elsie, with children Millie, Albert and William, continued to live in the South Melbourne home. Elsie brought in money with her sewing work for the theatre, while Arthur found work where he could on the wharves, in factories or stores at Fisherman's Bend, at the Spencer Street railway goods yards, or at the sauce and pickles factory in Port Melbourne.

The production lines at Ockwells were insatiable, but it happened that occasionally the vat of sauce or pickles was not at the correct temperature, or the jars were not in position, or they had to get labels or tops from the storeroom. For whatever reason, there was sometimes an order to halt production, and get cleaning. If the pause dragged, the workers could treat themselves to a welcome downtime. Late one afternoon, Arthur Norman picked up a label and turned it over. Using the unprinted white surface, he took a pencil out of his overalls and did a side-on portrait sketch of his workmate. The likeness was captured – a big-eared man with a half-closed eye. The subject proudly tacked his portrait onto the back of the door of the men's shed. Other workmates asked Arthur for him to 'have their drawing done'. The gallery soon grew in size, most men wanting to be part of the fun, then it developed into something else.

'Artie, could ya draw one of the bosses, d' ya reckon?'

'Yeah, draw the Big Boss, or Sarge p'raps?' Arthur took up the artistic challenge. For these two portraits, Arthur required large sheets of wrapping paper. It took several smokos and work breaks to do them justice. The resulting, much-admired drawings now draped down the back of the door. The Big Boss and Sarge were shown naked, except for headwear. The Big Boss was drawn with an aristocratic expression, looking down a lumpish nose. He was wearing a top-hat, whereas Sarge had been drawn in an army sergeant's peaked hat. Norman had excelled himself with his below-the-waist imagination. The Big Boss was given a massive cucumber penis, an absurdly long and thick vegetable which ran down and around the man's leg, then along the ground to the foreground of the drawing. Sarge's penis was a stub of a thing, a truncated cauliflower floweret. The artist had added a small ribbon and bow around it.

During the smoko, it was possibly the comparison with the Big Boss that caused Sarge to redden like Ockwell's beetroot slices, drawing himself so far backwards as to be in danger of falling over.

'Who's the smart alec artist then, Norman?' he jeered. 'Take that grin off your face. You're bloody fired. Git your things off your peg now.'

'Ar Sarge, come on.'… 'It's only a drawing Sarge.'… 'Be fair.' The return-to-work whistle sounded.

'You lot get to work. Norman, take yourself orf.' The men had no option but to return to the production line. Sarge ripped down the portraits of himself and the Big Boss, leaving tacked corners and half-pulling down several other drawings. He glared as the men left to resume their shift, saving his best for the sacked worker.

'One of the sheilas can finish your shift,' he said with a curled lip. Arthur collected his bag, pulled on a thin cardigan, tugged a soft cap on his head. His pace was not slow enough to be insolent, not fast enough to show intimidation.

On his way through the iron gates, Arthur's path was blocked by a truck turning into the factory. The truck's flat tray was loaded with hessian bags of some fruit or vegetable to be turned into an Ockwells sauce or pickle.

Arthur recognised the driver who stopped mid-turn – it was his mate, Tenny, an Ockwells' driver.

'You crook, Artie?' Tenny took a limp cigarette from his mouth and held it delicately.

'Nah, Sarge turned art critic and didn't like my drawings … gave me the sack.'

'Shit, Artie. I've gotta drop this lot off.' He changed into first gear, talking out the window as he drove into the factory. 'I'll have a look around for you, see what –' The rest was lost in engine noise.

Arthur looked at the evening sky and sniffed the air. He set out from Ockwells to his home in the next suburb. There was a breeze which would die down with sunset. For now, it was clearing the smoke and other odours which the factories and home fires sent into the atmosphere. The afternoon shift took its smoko at six, so his familiar journey along the asphalt footpath found many families, if they weren't still eating, out the front of their homes. Arthur nodded or touched his cap to people as he passed their single-fronted terrace homes. They were either sitting on small sheltered verandahs, having a post-meal smoke or leaning across a shared fence chatting with neighbours.

A group of boys was playing cricket in the grassed median strip of Dorcas Street. They had a roughly-shaped fence paling as a bat and the stumps were someone's rubbish bin. The ball was an evil-looking black thing. A cross-bat hit made the ball come his way. He scooped up the ball and lobbed it to the nearest fielder.

'Thanks mister.' The small boy was wearing an out-of-season jumper with the red V of the South Melbourne football team. It had a frayed neck and looked as if it hadn't been washed since the team's 1918 premiership. In the colder months, this clutch of boys played football out the front of the homes with a wrapped newspaper package substituting for an Aussie Rules football. The boys made their football by tightly rolling a newspaper, then binding it by cutting sections of an old bicycle tube into bands. It was an improvement on the coarse kids of the suburb of Collingwood who were said to use old jam tins as their football.

Arthur's wife Elsie was sitting on the wooden chair on the front porch of their rented home in Dorcas Street. He passed two boys of about the same age who were sitting on the gutter playing with bent wire, swung aside the front gate and made the four paces to greet his wife. She looked up from her knitting which she dropped and rested in her lap, her face a question.

'Got the sack, love. Sarge didn't even let me finish the shift.' He tried to smile to soften the news, but knew he could not make light of the event. Elsie stared into the street where their two boys, Albert and William, were bickering over something. She sat up straighter but couldn't identify the source of their argument.

'Albert and Willy, play properly or you can come inside.'

Elsie had to stop and think, to work out how long they had been married. Millie, their daughter, was now a young woman (who would believe it), having turned sixteen. But she was not their first, that was Katie, born in 1906 and died of meningitis in 1909 (the poor infant). And she and Arthur were married a year before she was born so that means it was eighteen years. Four of them were war years too – they must count as double, like you did for dogs.

Arthur propped on the chair next to Elsie to ease his boots off, then went inside, turning left from the corridor to dump his boots and workbag behind their bedroom door. Down the corridor the next room was Millie's, currently unoccupied as Elsie had said she was at a neighbour's house. He went through the main family room which in a more formal house would function as a lounge and dining room. It had a cast-iron wood heater set in a brick fireplace with two compact armchairs either side. On the opposite side was a wooden table, a wire cradle with one orange and a lemon in the middle, six wooden chairs set around the table. Arthur went through a door and down a step past a kitchen tacked onto the side, and outside to the rear of their home. A door to the right belonged to the boys' room, the next door was a laundry, bathroom, store and everything else room. The toilet was a few paces further in the small, brick-paved backyard, next to a neat woodpile. Arthur dodged the washing on the cord strung across the yard and went into the laundry to wash. After washing he reached under a zinc-metal bench into a wooden crate, picking up a lone, amber beer bottle by the neck.

'Better make this one last.' Back in the house, Arthur moved the kettle across to position it over the heat from the woodstove. He got the makings of a pot of tea from a shelf, levered the top off the beer bottle and poured himself a glass. The glass had insignia on it, stating ownership by *The Cricketers Arms Hotel*.

The sun had set but many of the residents of Dorcas Street stayed outside. Albert and Willy had joined up with some other boys and girls and were now playing some rolling, skipping, wrestling, tag game on the median strip. Arthur and Elsie watched from the porch. She had finished her tea and Arthur had poured a second beer. He had told the story of his sacking at smoko, including a description of his drawings and Sarge's reaction.

'You never told me you did drawings at work,' said Elsie. She looked at him over her shoulder, aiming for disapproving but unable to suppress a grin. 'But that's a good one on Sarge.'

'Don't worry I'll get another job, love.' Arthur took the merest sip of beer required to moisten his mouth.

'I s'pose I can ask for more work from Williamsons. They're doing plenty of shows.' Elsie had learnt sewing as part of her schooling in Geelong. Every year, Arthur and Elsie took the kids on the train to Geelong and spent a week with her relatives at their home near Eastern Beach. She was very close to her aunt and uncle, even closer to her cousin Ivy. There was only a year's difference in their ages. She wondered if they were going to be able to afford it this year.

'There's jobs and then there's jobs,' she told her husband. 'I don't want you working on the wharves again.' The couple exchanged a knowing look.

The first step in finding work was for Arthur to ask around the traps. The next day, after toast and tea for breakfast, he lugged the heavy, treadle sewing machine from the laundry store into the lounge room. Before Elsie started her sewing job they sat down at the table, pouring the last of the tea from the pot. Arthur measured his teaspoon of sugar into his cup. They had discussed which pubs to go to, and to whom Arthur would talk to about finding employment – it had worked before.

'Millie spoke to me about going to Geelong again. Now she's sixteen,' said Elsie. She was not changing the subject, which had revolved around their home finances.

'What do you reckon?' asked Arthur. 'She doesn't have to go. I'll get another job soon enough.'

'It might be best anyway. She's not going to do any good out the back of that grocery shop.'

'That bastard Croft's not trying something on Millie, is he?' Arthur was instantly on alert.

'No, he's alright.' Elsie dismissed his well-placed concern. 'It's just that she will get more opportunities … have a better life with Ivy's family.' Last holiday in Geelong, Elsie's cousin had suggested, again, that there was a good position for a smart young girl like Millie in her aunt and uncle's large home. She could do domestic duties, help out in the kitchen and dining room, also clean and sew. The two-storey Eastern Beach house and its gardens would be her home. Millie would be paid a little, on top of her board and keep. Arthur gave his cup a stir to dissolve the last of the sugar.

'I s'pose it's alright.' Arthur stroked his chin with forefinger and thumb. 'You know, Millie has some art ability … she can draw really well. I was hoping she might take more of an interest … Albert has a bit of flair too. More than a bit for his age.'

'I might be able to get Albie something through Williamsons,' said Elsie. 'They use Faircloughs for some costumes. I could ask if they have any apprenticeships open.'

'As a tailor? He could knock me up a good-looking suit.'

'What about asking to take classes at the Art School again?' Elsie was determined to keep it serious. She moved to set up her sewing machine, lifting the varnished timber flap.

'I think I'm done-for there. I like helping the students with their drawings and paintings but I can't do what they want me to. Old Fritz always wants me to get the students to draw and paint exactly like him. I could do it, but it kills me to see students having to hobble their own style and churn out little-Fritzes.'

Elsie had threaded her bobbin and activated the treadle. He left her to her job and went back to the laundry, both hands in pockets. His daughter Millie was in the courtyard, positioning a long three-legged kitchen stool so it was stable on the bricks.

'No work today?'

'I'm going in later. Mr Croft said to skip the morning 'cause he was getting the man to gas the rats in the back of the shop.' Millie had inherited her mother's fine wheat-coloured hair which she brushed aside from her face. She was facing the sun and had to squint because she wanted to see her father's response. 'Did mum say about me going to Geelong?'

'She did. I'll miss my Millie but I reckon it's a good chance for you.' Arthur saw his daughter's smile and knew he had said the right thing. 'What are you doing with that?' He gestured at the stool.

'Sitting in the sun to darn me stockings, that's all.'

'My stockings.'

'No, they're mine not yours, dad.'

'Ha-bloody-ha. You'll have to speak properly down at Geelong.' Millie frowned, sat on the stool and pulled several stockings from the pocket of her pinafore. Arthur went into the laundry and opened a tall cupboard door to expose some shelves. He rummaged at the top, moving things around to find some art materials, pulling out a drawing pad and a canvas. Reaching on top of the cupboard he brought down a folding easel. Back in the yard he took himself to one corner of the bricked area, putting his few items on top of the woodpile. Satisfied, he set up his easel, propping the canvas on it. He put the drawing pad in front of the canvas, turning to a fresh page.

'Are you drawing me, Dad?'

'Yeah, but stay exactly as you are on that stool. Don't move. Except for your darning.' Facing away from her father, Millie flicked her hair and wriggled her shoulders, settling into her pose.

'Are you sketching or painting, Dad?' She looked over her shoulder to check his setup.

'Both. Couple of quick drawings, then I want to get something on canvas this morning.'

'Cripes. I'm gonna have to sit here all morning.'

'Don't slump your shoulders!'

The vendors of the South Melbourne Market were in full voice in front of their stalls, cajoling shoppers to buy their produce.

'Bag of spuds. Me last bag of spuds, goin' cheap.'

'Apples! Shilling a box, red and rosy apples, missus.'

As the bustling market neared the end of its operating hours, the tired traders sold off the most perishable produce at their lowest price. The meat and seafood stallholders had already sold off some, but not all, of their wares. These men were also packing up, giving orders to youths, getting their stock wrapped in paper and packed into hessian or calico bags. There was still a market to be found for lamb chops and skinned rabbits in any number of pubs around Melbourne. And, given a pass on the sniff test, un-sold fillets of fish would be sold at the back door of pubs, hospitals and the better class boarding houses.

Arthur had tagged along with Elsie to one of Melbourne's biggest markets to help her carry home a few items. She was holding a bulging string bag in each hand, and Arthur had slung a sewn hessian bag, which Elsie had made, breaking two machine needles in the process, over his shoulder. He saw Archie from Ockwells coming out of the tobacconists, favouring his wooden leg as he opened a tin of tobacco. Archie had only a minute as he had snuck off from his missus – he talked at his staccato pace.

'Hear about ya mate Tenny? He and his missus gone bush. Got a farm job out Woop Woop, so took off coupla weeks after you got the sack.' Archie rapidly passed on more Ockwells gossip, before saying cheerio. 'Eh, Tenny's coming into the city soon, 'e said, if you want to say g'day to him.' Archie explained that Tenny would be staying with his sister-in-law. 'You know, new set of three 'ouses on the Coventry Street corner?'

This was enough information for Arthur, the day after, to firstly seek out Tenny's sister-in-law, then get his new address. Tenny had answered his short letter and they arranged to meet in the city.

Arthur was five weeks into his job at Melbourne's South Wharf goods shed. The series of sheds and warehouses lined the southern bank of the Yarra River, punctuated by narrow access points. Arthur's shift started at dawn and ended when the last cart, truck or trolley was loaded with goods. He had wanted a factory job, preferably one where he would work inside, protected from the weather. This had not happened. Eventually it was Elsie who confronted him with the reality of the situation. She was mixing flour in a chipped, duck-egg blue earthenware bowl, puffing at a tendril of hair which hung over her eyes.

'You're getting on a bit, Artie. The bosses are gonna give jobs to the fit young blokes first.' She pounded the dough. 'Then if they're decent coves, they might look after the veterans.' She lifted the dough out of the bowl and slapped it onto the floured table. 'If you have to go on the wharves again –' She punched the dough dead centre.

Arthur was on a two-day break from trundling his two-wheeled hand trolley from ship to truck or cart. The foreman, an Irishman known as The Judge, had given Arthur a trolley with a cracked wooden rail and a wonky wheel. Arthur never did discover if this was bad luck or maliciousness on the foreman's part, nor did he ever discover the man's real name. On his second day another worker called Stan explained one thing.

'Watch out for that bastard Irish foreman. Ya can't get nothin' past him. He sits there all shift with his beady eye on ya.' Stan spat on the ground. 'That's why he's called The Judge; he's always sitting on a case.' The story was told not expecting a laugh in response. The cargo they shifted could be anything; wooden slat boxes of Queensland bananas, puffed up and dusty bags of grain, or boxes of bicycle parts. On the final day of his last ten-day spell, he and his workmates moved nothing for several hours but heavy wooden crates of what Stan called 'fuck-me-back car parts.'

'Who knew there were so many cars in Melbourne these days?' said Stan as he slotted the base of his trolley under a wooden crate. He gripped the top edge of the crate and heaved mightily, bringing the heavyweight crate towards him until he arrested its drop by taking up the weight. 'An' if they are so bloody good,' he grunted, 'Why do they need spare-fucking parts?'

Arthur walked the twenty-minute journey from his South Melbourne home to the centre of Melbourne. He didn't even think of getting the tram or train. More money for a drink with Tenny. Checking the clock on the stone edifice of Melbourne's Town Hall, he confirmed that he was early to meet with his Ockwells mate. He crossed the town hall corner, making sure he obeyed the stop and go commands from the policeman. He didn't want to get bowled over by a cable tram or delivery van, but he also didn't want some stuck-up copper to give him an earful or worse. He put his hands in the pockets of his trousers and strolled up Collins Street. When he dressed for his outing, he had seen that the cuffs of his trousers were starting to wear through – no-one would notice. His white shirt was clean, the collar stiff from Elsie's starching and ironing. He eased a finger between his collar and neck. A thin, navy-blue jumper was visible between the lapels of his deep-grey jacket. Arthur's black shoes were in very good condition – they only came out for weddings and funerals and only needed a brush-up in the laundry. He sought his reflection in the window of the jewellery store. All-in-all, Arthur reckoned, he was as good as the next man to walk around the capital city of the state of Victoria.

He resumed walking, hands in pockets and head up. He had no intention of going into any store, let alone buying anything. A short way up the Collins Street hill he came to the Atheneum Theatre, one of Melbourne's live theatre venues. *Who knows, perhaps Elsie had performed there?* There was also an Atheneum art gallery. It sold works by Australian and overseas artists, holding regular exhibitions. The placard in the foyer of the Atheneum advertised its current exhibition. *What's this? Sir Arthur Bloody Streeton. The old fellow's been busy and done some paintings, has he?'* Arthur took his hands out his pockets, straightened his jacket lapels and went into the foyer. Off the foyer, the door to the exhibition was ajar. A lettered sign read:

Paintings of Victoria's magnificent Grampians
By Sir Arthur Streeton

Arthur went in, nodding to the man sitting on a chair at a card table set up inside the exhibition entrance. Arthur walked around the gallery room, tapping his hat against his leg, getting a feeling for the whole exhibition. The paintings were all landscapes of the Grampians area completed over the last two years. And as Arthur muttered to himself, they were all bloody good.

Sir Arthur Ernest Streeton was a senior figure in Australian art. These days he was part of the city's establishment, on first name terms with successful politicians, land developers, traders, manufacturers and bankers. He had made his name as a young artist who, through his painting, challenged the status quo of late 19th century Australian Art. With artist friends Tom Roberts, Walter Withers, Charles Conder, Fred McCubbin and others, he painted in an Australian idiom on the rural outskirts of Melbourne. Streeton was famous for being part of the artists' camps of this time. Arthur Norman had heard some of the stories about these camps, stories passed down over the years in art schools about how Conder was always too drunk to do any decent work. And stories of in-fighting which suggested the camps were nowhere near as matey as the artists later described. There was no argument that they did some excellent paintings though. Streeton's career as an artist took him to London, and while he didn't starve, he was never as successful there as he was in his homeland. He was appointed one of Australia's Official War Artists in the Great War. Norman had seen some of these paintings and thought them strangely sterile. Still, reasoned Arthur, Streeton got closer to the action than he had in the camouflage painting shed. After the war, Streeton had settled back into life in Melbourne, building a home at Olinda in the Dandenong Ranges.

Norman studied a wall of Streeton's recent paintings more closely. They were not exactly a series, but a thematic exhibition of his drawings and paintings. The Grampians rose out of flat farm land from all points of the compass. They were a sandstone range, an elongated escarpment running south from near Horsham in the Wimmera to the township of Dunkeld, not far from Hamilton in Western Victoria. In most of the works, Streeton had chosen to use the mountain range as a benign backdrop, his focus more on the pastoral landscapes. As much as the land and ranges, these paintings reflected national pride and prosperity. Norman analysed the compositions with his artist's eye. Streeton had used a two-thirds foreground formula, with a big mass of mountain range in the distance, as his standard approach.

This is the pick of them, thought Arthur, reading the title, *Land of the Golden Fleece.* From less than an arm's length away, Norman admired the painting of the dry, high-summer paddocks in the foreground. He could tell that Streeton had used a lot of titanium white oil paint, with a smudge of brown ochre to capture the sun-bleached grass. And that he had used a number four chisel-edge bristle brush to paint it, employing a terrazzo-like technique that stepped the viewer into the scene. Norman also saw where Streeton had used a flexible palette knife to apply the paint. The Grampians were shown as a grand back-drop, a theatrical prop to the eucalypt-dotted paddocks. In painting the mountains, the artist had used a delicate range of bluey greys and mauve, achieving the effect of both impact and distance. Again, Norman listed the oil colours in his head. He had turned his attention to the sheep, tiny pink-tinged profiles taking on the colour of the land, when his concentration was interrupted. A couple came into the gallery room, arm in arm.

'Good afternoon, Harold.' A man handed over his hat to the attendant, who accepted it as if it was an offering. The man entered the gallery, standing with one hand in his pocket, his chin angled at the paintings. 'We have to see these latest paintings by Sir Arthur. Don't we, Iris?' Arthur didn't wait to hear what Iris thought. He had spent much longer looking at the paintings than he intended and was heading out the door.

The exchange of short letters between the two men had established that they would meet at The Victoria Hotel in Little Collins Street. It was only a five-minute walk. Arthur was soon standing in the foyer of the recently renovated hotel. Built in the 1880s as a coffee palace, it had been a hotel for some years, having more recently undergone a further facelift and extension. It offered accommodation and hotel facilities which were an alternative to the rowdier hotels in the city.

'The public bar is at the back… sir.' Arthur had no time to get his bearings before a uniformed employee addressed him. The employee had a second thought, speaking quickly. 'Unless you want accommodation mate, and that's at the register counter there.'

'She's right,' said Arthur. He found the bar, which had only ten or so patrons, with space for four times as many.

'Tennyson, my old mate.' Arthur went to his friend who eased his backside off his stool.

'Geez Artie, don't call me that.' Tennyson Slater gave a haunted look over his shoulder. As if someone may have overhead Arthur using the name his mother gave him. Arthur grinned at Tenny's discomfort, shaking hands. Tenny's strong jawline, good teeth and immaculately-parted hair made him look more like a matinee idol than a truckie. He had a glass of beer on the bar and ordered the same for Arthur. Sitting side by side, knees not touching, they toasted each other's good health. Arthur scanned his surroundings.

'Why're we in this toffy hotel, Tenny?'

'I didn't want to go to Young & Jackson's, Artie. It's too busy. And there's always some bloke wants to push and shove. Then a fight's on again. Not only that.' Tenny became serious. 'Archie said a mate of his knows a bloke who works there, and they water the beer something terrible.' In his letter arranging their meeting, Tenny had explained why he was going to be in the city for a few days.

'Sorry to hear about your sister, Tenny.' Arthur's voice was barely above a whisper.

'I went to the hospital today and they are sending her home tomorrow. Can't do anything for her – she's coughing her guts up. She'll be going home and that's it.' There was nothing Arthur could say to that. He took a long pull on his drink.

'How's South Wharf these days?' asked Tenny. He had driven a truck around Melbourne long enough to know his way around the wharves and railway goods yards. He got his tobacco and cigarette papers out of his pocket.

'Ah, mate.' Arthur sighed and bought himself some time by buying more beers. He waited for the barman to move down the bar. 'I've got to get out of there. Fair dinkum, there's a big Irish prick in charge … and … you know what happens.' Arthur flicked his palm open, let it drop. He did not go into details, such as why The Judge told Arthur to always leave a certain padlock hanging, unlocked, and to not ask questions when two men would join the shift in the middle of the night, never clocking on or off with the rest of the workers. Security for the sheds was through a war veteran who had the shakes. One afternoon Arthur was talking with the nightwatchman.

'You got a good tool there, cobber.' Arthur indicated the hardwood club resting on the ground next to the man.

'This? You know what's this for? This is to let 'em know I'm comin' when I'm on me rounds. If I hear anythink, I belt the bloody fence good and proper. I've got a missus and kids at home who need feedin'. In the varnished wood bar of the Victoria Hotel, Arthur slowly shook his head.

'The thing is, after a while they try to rope you in,' he said, staring at his beer. Tenny nodded in complete understanding. He had personal knowledge of men, even youths, who had suffered bad accidents working on the wharves – a rope failing, a stack of cargo toppling over. By coincidence, the incidents happening not long after declining an invitation to do 'a special job.'

'I'm glad to be out of that, Artie. Me and the missus made a good call to take this job in the bush. Gets us and kids out of the city muck and away from trouble.' Tenny rolled another cigarette. Smoking was something Arthur never took up. He always said because he was drawing all the time, he didn't have enough hands to draw, drink and smoke. One of them had to go.

'You driving a truck for this farmer?' asked Arthur.

'He calls himself a grazier, Artie. Means you got more land and sheep than the next bloke. I'm driving a truck on the farm, carrying sheep and wool and feed and stuff, but I also drive a tractor and other bits of machinery. Lots of machines on a farm for me to fix and keep going.'

'And your missus is cooking?'

'Yeah, she's in the kitchen in the big house.' Tenny expelled steel blue cigarette smoke. 'Artie, you should see their bloody house. It's like a castle out of one of those English films.' Tenny lifted a forefinger to get the barman's attention. The two mates had eased into their session, their shoulders loosening up, faces becoming more elastic.

'What's the name of the place?' asked Arthur.

'Called *Wooreen,* whatever that means. Ya wouldn't credit how big it is, Artie. It's miles from anywhere so it's got its own butcher, baker, church, everything – even their own bloody cemetery.' Tenny's eyes got a remote look, lost in thought as he pictured the property. Or he may have been squinting to keep out cigarette smoke. 'It's on the Grange Burn, that's their river, big creek, one or the other.' Tenny had an inspiration. 'You oughta come and visit, Artie. Catch the train and stay in one of the huts. We could go rabbiting.' Arthur grinned, gave the idea some consideration.

'The owner wouldn't mind?'

'There's blokes coming and going doing all sorts of jobs. And you could do some of your drawing there too, Artie.' While Tenny was talking Arthur put his hand in his pocket, trying to estimate by feel if he had enough money for another pair of drinks. He took a gamble.

'My shout again, Tenny. Then I need to get off home. That rabbiting could be a goer. Have they got many at your farm?' Tenny pushed his empty towards the barman.

'You have to push the rabbits aside to put the ferrets down their burras.'

Arthur was preoccupied with his thoughts as he auto-navigated through the streets from the city to his home. The evening temperature was in the eighties; he carried his jacket over his shoulder. The heat was still warming the smells of horse manure, lingering smoke from the day's output from factories, and open drains of oily, sluggish liquid. He knew the city well, knowing which streets to take as a shortcut and which back lanes to avoid because of either rough types hanging about, or particularly rancid stenches. He could do these walks in his sleep. He thought about Tenny's poor sister. Then Tenny's enthusiasm for the rural life. *Tenny's fallen on his feet with that job in the bush.*

He stopped to have a piss at the rear gate of a closed factory, thinking how long it was since he had been in the bush. *Too long.* Last time was when a bunch of them from the Art School went to the Otway Ranges. He gave a shake and buttoned up his trousers. That was a week-long trip where a group of them stayed at a loggers' camp, tramping through the forest, picking off leeches and trying not to get lost. He resumed walking, skirting a dead cat. C*ertainly be better for Millie if she took up that domestic in Geelong.* Millie had shown that she had inherited some of his art ability. *Be really good if Millie could get some instruction in drawing as part of her new life. That was a bloody good painting by Streeton.* Arthur thought he should do more work himself. *You have to keep your hand in and it was too early for a man to give up.* Any sale would help bring money into the house. It might even mean he could give up the wharf job. *That would be good.* Arthur stopped for three cars to cross before he stepped off the footpath. *You have to watch it now, three cars in a row.* In the past, all you ever had to do was walk and the horses' hooves would warn you they were coming. *Perhaps it would be okay to go rabbiting. Try and get Elsie to cook it like those French cafes. Gee, that was something, being in those places. A noisy café, bunch of men and women, all drinking and smoking, arguing, kissing and cuddling, eating roast hare or rabbit stew.*

Arthur did not talk much about his time in France. It was something he could talk about with the Art School mob, when he was still in touch with them. They loved to rave on about which artist they had met, and who was the better painter, sculptor or whatever. A lot of that talk left Arthur cold – painting's painting when you get down to it. And there's good art and bad art. Among his co-workers on his other jobs there were returned soldiers who had fought in France and other countries. In their company he kept his pre-war experience to himself. The veterans, who he noticed would always sit next to each other at smoko, would lower their eyes and go quiet if anyone started yabbering on about Europe.

He had not forgotten though. It only took a funny smelling cigarette, going past a bakery at dawn, or a whiff of the Yarra at the right moment to bring back vivid memories. Elsie used to encourage him to talk about Paris, asking him to describe to her the Eiffel Tower or Notre Dame cathedral. She also liked to hear him talk about the ancient concierge of his rough accommodation, or what the young Frenchwomen wore to the markets on the banks of The Seine.

Arthur swung the gate aside at Dorcas Street. There were other things, people and places from that time. Things he had seen and done, which he didn't describe. He remembered those, too.

A few days later Arthur had an enforced break from work. He was not due for his two days off, but as he was pushing his trolley along the South Wharf, The Judge lifted his chin at him.

'Norman. You're goin' to be takin' a coupla days off.' The Irishman pushed his head forward on his neck, wanting a reaction. Arthur let his trolley rest on its prop legs. 'Starting tomorra.'

'What about the Norwegian ship coming in, then? asked Arthur.

'I'll be feckin' worryin' about that. You make yourself bloody scarce.'

After breakfast on the second day off, Elsie set up with a basket of mending from Williamsons. Millie was at the grocery shop and the boys had gone to school.

'You going to look for work, Artie?' asked Elsie.

'Yeah, going to see a bloke,' said Arthur, helping himself to a handful of change from a tin on a shelf in the kitchen. There would be no beer drinking today. Arthur was deliberately vague, hiding from Elsie that he was going to visit his brother Walter at *Conquest*. This was the home and property that Walter's flourishing stain and dye business had built. Arthur took the cable tram into the city, then the tram route that ran out to Kew Junction.

He sat on the varnished wooden slat seat in the tram, the breeze lifting his hair at the sides. The driver pulled his lever and the cable tram shuddered to a stop. Arthur had to resist an impulse to get off, cross the road, and catch the tram back to the city. Going to his brother

Walter's place was never a straightforward exercise. Over the last twenty years, Arthur had seen his brother on irregular occasions. He thought of the last time they had seen each other. It was for a double celebration. What should have been a pleasant outing.

Arthur and Elsie were surprised to receive the formal invitation in their Dorcas Street letterbox.

"The family of Arthur Norman is invited to an afternoon of entertainment at "*Conquest*", on 4th March 1923, to mark ten years service to the City of Kew by Councillor Walter Norman, and to celebrate the 15th birthday of his and Marigold's daughter Lydia."

Arthur had not spoken to his brother for months and his initial reaction was not to attend. In bed that night, he and Elsie talked it over.

'He's your only living relative, Artie.'

'Councillor Bloody Walter.'

'At least with guests, you and him won't have to say more than a word to each other.'

'I feel sorry for poor Lydia, you know. Having carrot-arse Walt as a father.' There was enough moonlight for Arthur to trace patterns in the ceiling cracks as he lay on his back. 'I'll give the boys a haircut the day before, if you do me and Millie.'

The two brothers disagreed on most things; politics, religion and football for starters. By many measures, Walter had done very well for himself. He had built his stain and dye business and lived in a tree-lined street in Kew. The home and garden of *Conquest* was far enough away from his factory, its smells, its noxious discharge, and its workers for the businessman and councillor to sleep in comfort.

Walter thought Arthur irresponsible to have pursued an art career. It was all very well as an interest, but his younger brother should have realised long ago that he was never going to make a go of it. Arthur's overseas travel had only made him more mis-guided, rather than working it out of his system. On return from Europe, the fool went back to that art school for more study, even a little teaching – which all led to nowhere. Walter had offered Arthur work in his factory.

'What, wearing a suit like you, in an office behind glass? Or on the factory floor with the other poor bastards breathing in those fumes?'

Arthur enjoyed the company of two-thirds of his brother's family. Marigold was quite good fun, he reckoned, if you could get her away from Walter. He sensed in their daughter Lydia an artistic soul which spoke to his own outlook on life. There was a turbulence in the young girl which appealed to Arthur as much as it exasperated her father. She was dark-haired and dark-eyed, could sing like a lark, and when she played the piano, it was an extension of her body. In what was a frustration and concern for Walter, Lydia was drawn to her uncle, aunt and cousins. On the few times when the brothers and their families mingled, Arthur delighted in seeing Lydia running on the lawn or playing games with Millie and the boys. After a game of hide and seek, Albert and William would find a bit of water to explore, or a ball to throw, while the two girls would be inseparable. They would have their heads together, eat shoulder to shoulder, whisper in each other's ears, and giggle uncontrollably at secret jokes. If they were at *Conquest,* Lydia would sit Millie next to her on the piano stool, showing her where to place her fingers and what keys to hit to produce a simple four-hander. Millie would spread out sheets of paper and show her cousin how to draw dogs and horses, or they would paint flower posies from the garden. But as the girls grew, invitations to *Conquest* and opportunities for the girls to be together became infrequent. Other girls, Lydia's schoolfriends or daughters of neighbouring families, received invitations to the Kew home.

The celebratory afternoon started poorly. Shortly after arriving at *Conquest*, William leant over the rim of the ornamental pond, pointing out the larger goldfish. He may have over-balanced, or Albert may have pushed him in – the result was he had to be hauled out of the cold water by one of the councillors. Half an hour later, the boys needed to be rounded up from the far corner of the gardens to pose for their family photograph. Their footwear indicated they had been in the chook shed, the sides of their boots oozing chicken shit. Then, it was just bad luck that Walter overheard Arthur saying to his and Marigold's neighbours (an eminent doctor and his wife), that Walter's factory workers could always be identified in the pubs around Abbotsford.

'There the ones with the running noses and stained hands. Easy to spot.'

Walter invited guests to sit on wooden chairs (borrowed from Kew Council) set out on the terrace, facing the folded-back doors of *Conquest's* music room. Elsie got a firm grip on the boys and sat them down on either side of her, their feet off the ground. Lydia introduced her two compositions.

'I will be playing *Chopin étude – Opus 10, number 3* and *Shepherd's Hey*, a composition by Percy Grainger, based on tunes he collected in rural England.' Millie sat next to Arthur. He could feel his daughter in subtle motion with the music. Looking sideways, he saw her rapt gaze as her cousin played with flair and sensitivity. Lydia sung two verses during the Grainger composition. Words that Lydia had herself written for the performance left her mouth and took off into the tree-tops.

As the applause ended, Millie bounced out of her seat to see Lydia. Arthur stood up, easing his stiff limbs, watching Millie skip across the flagstones between the terrace and music room. There was a tangle of guests, councillors and their wives, and young girls from Lydia's school gathering around the piano. Arthur saw his older brother come up to the group, lifting and spreading his dark-suited arms. Making space for Lydia, but more than that. By turning his body and sticking his backside in her direction, Walter kept Millie from being close to her cousin. Millie hovered, uncertain, on the edge of the group, then stepped away from Walter's back and walked slowly through the terrace doors into the garden.

'Artie … Artie! The boys need to go to the toilet. Can you take them?' asked Elsie.

On this mid-week visit, Arthur was aware the Kew Junction stop was next. Again, he wondered what he was doing. He had no firm plan. He was definitely not going to ask Walter for financial assistance – he would never bring himself to do that. Nor a job. He was not even sure he was going to see Walter. Going to *Conquest* was like picking a scab. His secret hope was that Walter would be on his civic duties and that he might have a cup of tea with Marigold, have a chat with her and Lydia.

He stepped down from the tram. There was a drinking fountain in the junction which he used before taking the route to his brother's home. It was a short walk, three streets to Highfield Grove. Arthur noticed a long string of cars parked along the street, almost as long as *Conquest*'s brick and hedge fence. Near the house a charabanc came down the street, then turned into the driveway of *Conquest*. It carried a full load of sixteen people, men and women dressed for an occasion. Arthur approached the man at the entrance gate. The gate was decorated with green and red ribbons, reminding Arthur that they were in the month of December. A gatekeeper was wearing a uniform Arthur did not recognise, until they were standing just apart.

'What's on, mate?' asked Arthur.

'What's it to you? A private function, an' I'm guessing you don't have an invite.' The man was leaning on one crutch. His pocket insignia told Arthur that he was an employee of the City of Kew. Arthur was tempted to say that this was his brother's place, and that he was going to have a cup of tea and a scone, to enjoy the reaction. But the man was probably a war veteran, doing his job. The gatekeeper adjusted his weight on the crutch. 'It's for the City of Kew. The mayor's garden party, I s'pose you'd call it.' The man decided Arthur was not a threat, his love of a chat coming to the fore. 'All the councillors and their missus are here, for the end of the year. There's gunna be music, they reckon.'

'Thanks mate.' Arthur walked away. The mayor! This bit of news didn't make it to Arthur's side of the Yarra. He turned for home, the rest of the day stretched out ahead of him. He walked at a saunter, the brick and hedge fence on his side. Before he rounded the corner of Highfield Grove, the first notes from a piano carried to him across the grounds.

The blazing sun was intensely, momentarily, on the horizon. Tenny squawked the klaxon horn on his truck as he drove away from the Hamilton Railway Station. Arthur had spent all day in a carriage drawn by a steam locomotive. He had a dawn start from Geelong and a change of Victorian Railways line at Warrnambool. The train did not miss a stop. It stopped for passengers to get on and off, to pick up or throw off parcels and small goods, to take on water and load fuel for the locomotive, and even for lunch for the train crew.

'Fair dinkum, complained a fellow passenger. 'Why couldn't they have their flaming lunch while they were filling up the loco?' Arthur sat and watched the endless farmland go by his window. He tried having it open once to clear the compartment of pipe and cigarette smoke, only for a coal cinder to fly into his eye.

He threw his small suitcase and Gladstone bag onto the boards of the tray behind Tenny's truck's cabin.

'Not far to the farm,' said Tenny, right elbow resting outside the driver's side open window. 'Had to bring the Morris half-tonner into town to pick up a coupla things. How's Elsie, Millie and the boys?'

The couple of days rabbiting had turned into much more than that for the Norman family. Elsie had listened to Arthur talk about his proposed adventure with Tenny as she sorted the family's washing in their backyard. Arthur sat on a box that had an Ockwells Sauce & Pickle label on the side. Elsie held up a pair of underpants to the sky.

'You could shoot peas through those, Else,' said Arthur.

'Yes, well they'll have to do for another wash at least.' Elsie had sorted the washing into several piles and set about transferring them to the laundry shed.

'You've missed a pile, love.' Arthur pointed to the collection of faded clothes left on the brickwork.

'That's the rag pile, Artie. That's all they're good for.' Elsie disappeared into the laundry, wielding a smooth, weathered pole which she got from behind the door. She tossed some shredded naphthalene flakes into a copper basin and gave it a stir. The copper contained hot water which had been heated on the kitchen wood stove. After throwing half the washing into the copper Elsie made herself a cup of tea, sorted out her sewing for the afternoon, swept the hallway and front porch, then stepped outside the front gate. She looked up and down Dorcas Street, wondering if she could see where the boys were playing.

After pegging out the washing on the cord strung across the backyard, Elsie sat down on the Ockwells box. She watched a magpie perch on the shoulder-high brick fence which was their boundary on one neighbour's side, daring the magpie to soil the line of washing.

'Don't you even think about it, maggie.' Elsie tilted an ear to the brick fence, thinking she could hear the boys playing with the neighbour's children. Might be them. She got up, going to get that parcel of peas she needed to shell for dinner. She had decided what the family would do. Arthur was sitting at the kitchen table with a newspaper in front of him.

‘Artie, I’ve got it worked out.’ She spoke from the lean-to kitchen.

‘Worked out what?’

‘The rabbiting. You know how Millie is going to live at Geelong. We should all go there first, take Millie to my aunt’s, then the boys and I can have a break at Ivy’s.’ Arthur closed the newspaper, folded it. ‘You can go on from Geelong, take the train to Hamilton, and meet up with Tenny.’ Elsie had looked at this plan from all angles and couldn’t find a flaw in it.

‘As long as we can pay for the train fares, I s’pose,’ said Arthur. He folded his arms across his chest. ‘I’d better get onto Tenny then.’

Tenny had driven Arthur to *Wooreen,* steering a smooth curve into the open-sided machinery shed. They stood and admired the bluestone homestead for only a few seconds, before Tenny took Arthur in the opposite direction of the home and paved courtyard. They went through an open farm gate, past a large timber building which smelt of horse, across a gravel area to an almost square weatherboard building with a door at one end.

‘You’re in the old schoolhouse. Dump ya gear inside; I’ll get rid of my load and catch up with ya.’ Arthur went up the stairs and into one large room with a three-quarter height partition at the end. It was bigger, but not much more, than his brick backyard at Dorcas Street. There was a dusty blackboard attached to one wall, but any other signs of schooling were not visible. Arthur checked out the hieroglyphics on the blackboard – a list of racehorses, someone’s betting card. On his right was a low, single bed. He dropped his suitcase next to it and put his Gladstone bag on a fruit box making do as a bedside table. His footsteps rapped on the bare floorboards as he walked to the partition. Behind it was a wash trough and wooden stool.

'This'll do me,' said Arthur.

In the afternoon of the following day, Tenny and Arthur sat on a rocky outcrop in one of *Wooreen's* paddocks. Both men were sweaty, their clothes scuffed, grass seeds filling their trouser cuffs. They were on a rise which gave them a view of the farming complex and small village which was *Wooreen.* The SummerHayes homestead with its central tower was guarded by lesser buildings scattered around the home and gardens. Tenny had explained that some of the buildings no longer served their function, which is why some were getting a bit run-down. Burials were now held in town, the butchery and baking had been brought into the kitchen, the kids went to the local school.

They were in the middle of summer, the grass in the paddocks brittle and straw-like. But the vegetation around the house and along the Grange Burn was verdant. On the other side of the Grange Burn, more grazing farmland stretched out to a band of silver haze which made the Grampians mountains quiver.

Tenny gave a mighty tug, pulling the last of the skin off the dead, warm rabbit. He dropped the length of skinned rabbit in a hessian bag with several others, adding the skin to a pile next to a tangle of nets, a blood-smeared knife, a hammer and short wooden stakes.

Behind them there was a rattle as one of the pair of ferrets scuttled around its wire cage.

'Settle down Ollie … or are you Stan? said Tenny. 'Stupid bloody names Ivo gave his ferrets anyway.' Arthur repositioned his notebook on his knees, moving his legs to ease his stiffness. He was drawing the view in front of them with a carpenter's stubby pencil.

'I can hear something coming inta the paddock I reckon.' Tenny got to his feet and squinted down the slope. 'It's the farm truck, prob'ly Ivo, or Alec the son drives too.'

'Come to give us a ride, save walking back.' Arthur said it deadpan, putting down his notebook and standing up.

'E's coming our way. Don't let him run over our bunnies,' said Tenny. The two men stood together as the truck chugged its way over the hard earth and short grass, following the line of a sheep trail. The driver steered towards them. Any farmer or farm manager would always check out what other blokes are up to on your property – even if only to say g'day.

'Shit,' Tenny said out of the corner of his mouth to Arthur. 'It's Alec, and he's got the boss with 'im, Mr SummerHayes. They're not a bad mob, but let me do the talking, Art.'

The truck rolled to a stop with a wheeze and a grinding noise as Alec SummerHayes pulled on the handbrake, leaving the motor running. He grinned out the driver's window, the point of his elbow facing Tenny and Arthur. His passenger and father, Samuel Alexander

SummerHayes, leant forward and tipped his hat at the two rabbiters.

'Get many?' asked Alec.

'Bagful,' said Tenny. 'Even dozen.'

'That won't make a dent in 'em, Tenny,' said Alec, his grin getting broader. He included Arthur in his comment. 'Need to do better than that.' Samuel called across the truck's cabin, looking at Arthur.

'I don't know you.' Tenny promptly answered.

'Artie's me mate from Melbourne. I told Ivo about 'im helping out with some rabbitin'. Tenny had a sudden impulse to impress the SummerHayes father and son. 'Artie's a painter, an' a top notch one, too.'

'No worries,' said Samuel. 'Better get those bunnies back to the kitchen.' Alec nodded in agreement, put the truck into gear and drove further into the paddock. A little exhaust smoke puffed towards Tenny and Arthur.

'They'd get to the kitchen fuckin' quicker on a truck ride,' said Tenny as he bent down to gather up their gear. In a couple of minutes, he and Arthur were walking through the paddock, back towards the homestead and out-buildings.

'You know what pest rabbits are?' Tenny's question was rhetorical. Most Australian adults, rural or city, were well aware that the introduction of rabbits in the mid-19th century was disastrous. They had bred so quickly that millions of rabbits competed with sheep and cattle for feed and hugely damaged the environment. 'It was a bloody Victorian grazier who brought 'em into the country, to hunt.' Tenny shook his head as he shifted his load of ferrets and hessian bag to his other shoulder.

'And you know who it was?' Tenny paused, waiting for effect. 'Old Man SummerHayes, the original, Ivo told me.'

Arthur had to wait until Tenny's next trip to town before he could do his return train journey to Geelong and Melbourne. He helped Tenny strip down a steam engine in the machinery shed. The inner workings of the engine was a mystery to Arthur, but he kept Tenny company; chatting, passing the 5/8th spanner, squirting machine oil where Tenny pointed, even rolling his mate a cigarette. Tenny's missus in the kitchen made sure Arthur had a plate of food each evening, also supplying bread, cereal and biscuits. He sat at their kitchen table and drank tea with them after dinner each evening. The food was different in a way Arthur couldn't put his finger on. He tried to explain to Tenny as they carried tins of paint from a storage shed to the garage.

'The potatoes taste different here Tenny. I dunno, they taste more potato-ey.'

'Potato-ey, they're bloody fresher, Artie. Ya city-slicker.'

The morning's task was repainting the paintwork on the shallow timber tray of the farm truck. This was something Arthur knew about. While Tenny had been learning about engines and machinery in the army, he knew little about painting. For this job, Arthur gave directions on scrubbing and scraping the old painted surface, sanding the boards smooth, then painting with undercoat and top coats. Tenny was painting on one side of the tray, cigarette in the corner of his mouth. Arthur was stroking the dark green paint along the tail-gate.

'Do you want to do the hinges on this tailgate a different colour Tenny?'

'That's a bit ... fancy ... isn't it? Have to open … another tin a paint … too.' The slow-speaking response came from Ivo, the long-term farm manager at *Wooreen*. 'Good to see a man … who takes ... pride in his work.' Ivo, light of tread, had come into the shed to get some tools. With brace and bit in hand he circled the almost-finished tray of the truck. 'You've done a good job there … mate.' The manager looked out of the machinery shed, as if something in the distance caught his interest.

'Do you want to stay on … do a bit more painting? We've got a few things ... need a lick of paint ... around here.' Arthur held his brush mid-stroke. Tenny had confirmed that he was able to give him a lift to the train station early in the morning. He rested his brush on the open tin – he had been thinking it would be good to see Elsie, Millie and the boys again. Ivo was comfortable with the silence. He walked off, talking at the same time.

'Think about it ... I'll have to talk to the boss ... you might come back ... next month.'

'Thanks Ivo.' Arthur remembered his manners. 'I'll let you know before I go.' Ivo nodded with his back to the painters, still talking in a slow drawl.

'Good to get some painting in ... before the weather … turns cold.'

On Arthur's last day at *Wooreen,* Tenny took his mate for an evening's fishing. The two men ambled away from Tenny's cottage, stomachs full from the missus's cooking. Dinner at Tenny's was a thick slice of salted beef, boiled pumpkin and stewed tomatoes – all produce from the property. They walked along a dusty path by the side of the tennis court's wire fence, the courts not occupied. The path led down to the tree line following the creek, to Tenny's preferred waterhole on the Grange Burn. Each man held a fishing rod made from lengths of bamboo. Tenny had shown off his workmanship on the fishing rods to Arthur, pointing out the fine wire which he had wound around the heavier gauge guides that took the fishing line. They had stopped at the gardener's shed, using a fork to turn over some compost and collect writhing red earthworms. Tenny cupped a handful of wriggling bait and placed the worms in an old tobacco tin which had a lid pierced by nail holes.

'We're set Artie. Let's catch a trout, eh?'

Two hours later the men were lying on their backs on an incline, feet pointed at the almost immobile inky water. Their arms were raised, hands behind their heads. Neither had spoken for twenty minutes. The massive gum trees shaded their spot on the creek bank, fishing rods propped at water's edge, reflections creating perfect triangles. Arthur could hear cockatoos squabbling along the creek line, more melodious bird calls drowned out by the cacophony. He was thinking that Tenny might have dropped off to sleep, when he heard voices.

'Be careful of rabbit holes down here.' It was a man's voice. 'Should get a man to rip up those warrens.' The answering voice was female, coming closer to the two men on the bank. Arthur nudged Tenny.

'I want to see the water, Alec. Before it gets too dark for me to take my picture.' Tenny and Arthur got to their feet as Alec came into view, a young woman holding his elbow. Alec stood with his weight on one foot, then the other, not knowing where to put his hands. The woman took charge of the chance meeting.

'Good evening to you gentlemen. Have you caught anything?' The woman was wearing a sleeved, cream coloured dress and ankle length brown leather boots. On a strap around her neck, she cradled a black, rectangular box with a circular eye at the front.

'Nah miss,' said Tenny, re-looping his braces over the shoulders of his shirt. 'Not a nibble.' He made to gather the rods, Arthur assisting. 'We was just packin' up anyways.'

'Very good,' said Alec.

'But I want to take my photograph of the pond from down there, Alec. The men can stay.' The young woman was looking down-creek where a bend in the Grange Burn made a small promontory.

'Be too muddy there, Matilda.' Alec held his hands awkwardly at his sides. They seemed too large for his suit. The two anglers picked up their gear, placed their hats on their heads and were on their way.

'Evenin', said Tenny and Arthur in unison.

'Mind that bank. There's rabbit holes that'll twist your ankle,' said Alec. After a few steps had put distance between them, Tenny muttered from the corner of his mouth.

'Mind the rabbit holes, Artie.'
'Bloke could do an ankle, Ten.'

The open newspaper was in the exact centre of Walter Norman's desk. After breakfast with Marigold, he poured another cup of tea from the sideboard and carried it into his study. His practice was to allocate one hour to read the news and plan his day. Using his fountain pen he wrote notes under headings; Clerk (council matters), Housekeeper (home), Gardener (grounds), Manager (business matters) and Marigold (family matters).

'My God!' Walter had no sooner sat down than he rose out of his seat. The newspaper did not usually get this reaction. He craned forward to read the front-page headline again – *Mad Rifleman Shoots with Murderous Accuracy.* Walter looked up to the diamond patterned leadlight window above his desk – the light outside would indicate a cataclysmic change in the universe. The garden and trees of *Conquest* were as usual. He looked back to the paper. The headline had not changed. He read the next few sentences. Then he lowered himself into his chair and read the whole account.

On the previous, unremarkable day at the Melbourne Botanical Gardens in South Yarra, a man had opened fire on innocent people. He had used his rifle to kill four people and seriously wound another. Walter read the news story, which told him that two women, one thirty-nine and one forty-seven, a thirty-seven year old man on a family picnic, and a seventy-five year old Englishman enjoying a moment of solitude, had been randomly targeted by the shooter and killed. A mother with her baby was wounded. The shooter left his rifle in the bushes and was seen running off down Anderson Street. Walter could not sit and read. The man had not been found – police were still hunting for him. He had to tell his family immediately. He scooped up the newspaper and stalked back into the dining room. He was already calling 'Marigold! Lydia!' before he had gone through his study doorway.

'What is it?' asked Marigold, coming into the dining room from the kitchen, along with housekeeper Mrs Maxwell.

'It's an …' Walter held up the newspaper. '… an abomination! In the Botanical Gardens! What *has* the world come to?' Her father's raised voice had succeeded in stirring Lydia from her music room where she had been leafing through volumes of sheet music.

'Look at this.' Walter spread the newspaper out on the dining room table where his wife and daughter could read the terrible story. Walter hovered at their shoulders.

'The details are in these paragraphs,' said Walter. He put his hands in his pockets for a few seconds, then used a wobbling forefinger to point to a section of the story. 'Read this bit … in the *Gardens* of all places.' Marigold and Lydia read in silence, Mrs Maxwell stood just apart from them. Walter composed himself.

'I'm sorry Marigold and Lydia, that you have to read such horror.' Walter put on his best council chambers voice. 'This means you will have to stay within the grounds of *Conquest* until this man is caught. Even then, if you are in the grounds, please make sure the gardener or Mrs Maxwell is with you.' No-one knew what to do following that statement. Mrs Maxwell took charge.

'I'm sure we will be quite safe here, in Kew,' she declared. As if their suburb provided some sort of innate protection. A change of subject was also called for. 'And here is your mail, Mr Norman.' A little deflated, Walter took a bundle of various sized envelopes from his housekeeper.

'I'll read these in the study.'

Less than an hour later Walter had cause to call his wife and daughter together again. At the City of Kew end of year mayoral function, held at *Conquest* a few weeks ago, Lydia's music teacher had been present to hear her pupil play and sing. Miss Bonnacci was accompanied by a male friend, Mr Jobling, who had listened to Lydia's playing and singing with a keen ear. He had since written to Lydia's father. Walter opened the letter and now stood with it in his hand in Lydia's music room. Marigold was summoned by Mrs Maxwell and his wife and daughter were an attentive audience as Walter read. The first paragraphs contained the usual introductions and an expression of pleasure in attending the mayoral function. Mr Jobling, it transpired, was part of the retinue of the Australian opera singer Dame Nellie Melba.

Dame Nellie Melba had returned to Australia, and Victoria, in 1920. Mr Jobling had assisted the singer in her very recent series of homecoming concerts. The *Concerts for the People* featured Dame Nellie and other performers and were a gesture of thanks to the Australian people who had supported her career. The concerts were put on with low ticket prices so that the common person could attend and hear the internationally regarded performer. Lydia and her mother were part of the 70,000 music lovers who had been to one of the concerts, held in Melbourne and Sydney. Walter now read pertinent paragraphs from Dame Nellie's assistant's letter:

"... and Sir, after listening to the piano-playing and vocal renditions of your daughter it is my personal opinion that the young woman possesses an exceptional talent. Your daughter plays with rare vitality, yet also with what I described to Dame Nellie as a winsome intensity. She sings with aplomb, and with professional guidance, I have no doubt would further develop her individual composure. If it is within your consideration, I believe that your daughter is capable of performing to larger and no less appreciative audiences. To this end Sir, I beg your indulgence to meet with you to discuss your daughter's participation in a forthcoming event. Dame Nellie Melba is to sponsor a cricket match, the proceeds of such going to the *Melba Appeal for Limbless Soldiers.* As part of the entertainments, I am authorised to invite –"

'Well! Lydia to play in a concert!' said Marigold.

'Dame Nellie Melba?' Lydia started to laugh. 'I'm to play at a cricket game?'

'Lydia! Don't be hysterical. It's a benefit event and jolly decent of them to invite you.'

'Oh, I'll play and sing father, it will –'

'It will be up to your mother and I to decide. And there are more things to consider than you laughing your way through life.' Lydia did a few gay dance steps to take her over to her piano. She sat down and without looking at any music played an exercise scale, causing her father to frown.

'I must practice father.' Walter turned and walked out of the music room, Lydia changing her melody to *The Sailors Hornpipe*. Marigold could not suppress a smile.

The staccato chitter and rhythmic swish of the lawn sprinkler contributed to Walter's pleasure in the evening. A muted chugging from the petrol generator in the garden shed in the far corner of the grounds reinforced the message of maintenance and good order. He and Marigold had completed their circumnavigation along the compacted gravel paths of *Conquest*, arriving at the garden seat facing the ornamental pond. The gardener had recently covered the water with chicken wire to try and prevent visiting birds from swooping down and helping themselves to a meal of goldfish. It was not clear if kookaburras or ibis were the culprit. From the house Mrs Maxwell could see Mr and Mrs Norman sit down at the pond, Walter taking his cigarettes from his jacket. She picked up the tray of refreshments – sherry and fish paste on thin toast, and took them out. Around their tour of the garden the conversation between the couple had been garden-focused. The salvias had done their best flowering and should be cut back. The fernery was in need of a good soaking, must tell the gardener, and so on. When they sat down Walter opened proceedings.

'This Melba concert. I'm not entirely in favour of our Lydia performing,' said Walter, tapping the end of his cigarette and lighting up.

'Walter, I –'

'It's a good cause; I'll grant you that.'

'Yes Walter, and it is a wonderful thing that Lydia's talent has been recognised.' Marigold sipped her sherry.

'Oh, I know she has talent. That's not the question.' Walter's cigarette hand waved away any contrary thought.

'It would be such an opportunity for Lydia's career,' said Marigold, realising as soon as she spoke that she had erred.

'Career, Lydia's career?' Walter pounced on the opening. 'That's the *very* thing Marigold. Is a life in the arts what we want for our Lydia?'

'I think she –'

'You see, the arts are such a tawdry environment. And is *that* what we want for our only child and daughter? Not everyone is going to be a Melba.' Marigold knew what was coming next. She picked up a dry toast and bit down on it. 'Take Arthur for example. What has the man done with his life? He had the same start in this world as I did, and he has wasted it – frittered it away. He insisted on going to Europe, pursuing his so-called art, and now where is he?' Marigold washed down the fish paste with the sherry, wondering why sherry glasses were always so tiny.

Walter leant forward, dropping his cigarette onto the path. He ground it out with the sole of his shoe, warming to his theme.

'He's still not holding down a proper job. Still lurking around the wharves and scratching out drawings.'

'Do you think we should ask Lydia her view on the matter of the concert performance?' Marigold added a smile to the suggestion. 'Walter?' Her husband was halted mid-stream and needed to re-gather.

'She may very well have an opinion, but she is still very young.'

'She also has a will, Walter. You can't deny that.' Walter sighed regrettably as if his wife had reminded him of Lydia's disability. Marigold felt her husband was momentarily on the back foot.

'The concert is one thing. It may lead to who-knows-what?'

'What do you mean?' asked Walter.

'Miss Bonnacci has talked about Lydia studying music in Europe. She and Mr Jobling may be able to assist in the arrangements for furthering her career –'

'Her career, again. Why didn't you tell me about this Europe suggestion? I don't appreciate you and Miss Bonnacci going behind my back.' Walter stood up, adopting his best mayoral stance. 'I'll talk to Attwood on the council and see what he thinks about this concert. Europe is out of the question.'

In his office above his Abbotsford factory, Walter heard the hooter signalling the end of the working day at the stain and dye works. At this point in his day, he once had the habit of turning around and face the window giving a view of the front gates of his factory. He would stand back from the window, observing the men and women stream through the wrought iron gates on their way to the railway station and their homes. They had earned an honest day's wage. Pity that half of it or more would see its way through the tills of the many pubs and gambling places in the surrounding suburbs.

Today he remained seated, leaning back in his padded leather chair. He was not used to working in his office as much lately. Since elected mayor he divided his time between the mayoral office at the town hall and his study at *Conquest*. Besides, the business here was going very well without him having to walk the factory floor, or distribute orders to his foremen from this very office. Which he must tell his secretary was looking a bit dusty. Should have thought to have mentioned it when she came in ten minutes ago, delivering the evening newspaper to his desk.

'They've found that madman, Mr Norman,' said Hilda. 'The one that shot those poor people in the gardens.'

'I didn't think we had a procession of madman on the loose, Hilda.' The gunman from the Botanical Gardens massacre had been on the run for two weeks. The newspapers were finding it increasingly difficult to maintain a high level of drama with each day that he was missing.

'But he was dead, Mr Norman.' Hilda pointed to the front-page article. 'Slit his wrists and bled to death in the bush.'

'Thank you, Hilda. That'll be all for today.' Walter eyed the newspaper and several other papers on his desk without enthusiasm. His desk, with the window behind him, faced the door through which Hilda left. On that same wall, where it was half-obscured when the door was left open, was one of Arthur Norman's paintings. Walter scowled at the *Evening at Beech Forest* landscape, as if it was responsible for his out-of-sorts mood.

Walter's closest confidante on the Kew City Council had been excited to hear that Lydia was invited to perform at one of Dame Nellie Melba's soldier benefit concerts.

'You and your good wife must be so proud,' said Councillor Attwood. The trouble was, Walter found it impossible to find a high level of joy in his daughter's musical talents. He looked at Arthur's painting as a case in point. He remembered acquiring the painting from his brother in 1908, or was it 1905?

Arthur had returned from his travel and study in Europe (wearing a dreadful pair of linen trousers, with paint stains). The would-be artist was allocated some teaching classes at that art school, and hung out with a group of staff and students who went off for days, weeks at a time on their art excursions. It was after one such week that Arthur returned from the Otway Ranges with a pile of canvasses and a full sketch pad. That Fritz man at the art school had raved about Arthur's painting, going on about the light, as if Arthur would have been able to paint anything if there wasn't any light. Anyway, at that time Walter was quite prepared to help his younger brother make his way in life, though suggesting Arthur join him in business was a rash offer. The painting was the pick of the bunch, according to Fritz, so Walter acquired it from Arthur – in exchange for payment of Arthur's next order of art supplies. Quite a canny purchase, really. Except Walter did feel that Arthur was excessive in his order of art materials. He thought Arthur must have ordered enough materials to set himself up in paint and paper for the next ten years.

Which brought Walter back to Lydia. Music was a satisfactory pursuit for a girl, and a young woman. And women did indeed make a success of musical careers, even if not always at the upper echelons as had Dame Nellie. But a creative streak is a … it's a *curse*, decided Walter. It destroys more people than it makes. What has Arthur done with himself after painting Fritz's masterpiece which Walter now looked at on his office wall?

Walter sighed as he put his arms on his desk. An opened letter brought to his attention faced him accusingly. He picked up the letter from the proprietor of the Fairfield Boathouse. The establishment was on the Yarra River, providing rowing boats and punts for lazy Sunday afternoon couples and families. Walter's factory backed onto the Yarra, which after rising in the ranges north east of Melbourne, had to make its way through the industrial suburbs of Collingwood, Abbotsford and Richmond before it got to the city. Rising as a fresh and exuberant river, it became a foul, stinking drain through the suburbs, in stretches moving fast, at other times sluggishly, through heavy industrial precincts before it formed part of Melbourne's port, finally merging defeated into Port Philip Bay.

The letter writer was complaining, again, about the water quality of the Yarra, drawing attention to Walter's factory which backed onto the river. Well, so did the much bigger Carlton & United Brewery, which was almost next door to the stain and dye business. Walter dropped the letter back to the desk. Did he really have to answer the letter to explain the obvious? That Walter's business and factory, and CUB for that matter, were *downstream* from his damned boathouse? And that businesses such as Walter's, and the brewery, provided essential products and employed hundreds of people, precisely because they could use the river as a convenient depository for side products?

'Ridiculous,' said Walter to the empty room. The boathouse owner would have us stay in the 19th century in row boats. As Walter never tired of telling his councillors, business acquaintances, and Marigold – chemicals were the way of the future. Natural dyes have already given way to chemical treatments and scientific solutions were going to lead the way in the twentieth century.

And that was the other issue in relation to Lydia. She wanted to live in a gay world of singing and dancing, like Arthur's make-believe world, rather than face reality in a modern world. Walter had difficulty levering himself up from his chair. As he left his office he thought he must get Hilda to get it re-upholstered.

*

Archie sat on a wooden bench, one of several rows. He bent at the waist, reaching down with his hand.

'Bugger it!'

'Language Archie!'

'Sorry love. I had an itch on me ankle, but it was me wooden leg. Bloody phantom pains.'

'Watch your language!' his wife remonstrated. She looked over her shoulder as if they were being monitored and would be ejected from their seats in the audience. They were part of a crowd who had been shepherded onto temporary bench seats set out on the grass of the oval, close to the white picket boundary fence. Over the fence of the Albert Park Cricket Ground, in the stand where the public would usually be, a performance platform was set up. Archie and his wife were attending Dame Nellie Melba's benefit concert to raise funds for limbless soldiers from the Great War. The cricket match was completed, having been played in light-hearted spirit with lots of big-hitting, chiacking, broad grins and pats on the back. The guest on Archie's side, a man with wooden crutches tucked under his seat and his trouser leg folded back at the thigh with a safety pin, had been grumbling in a low voice.

'Bet the bloody cricketers are having a few jolly beers in the clubhouse now. Drinks on Dame Nellie while we sit with splinters up our arse listening to the pianna.'

Archie shrugged, the man needed no encouragement. 'Couldn't she drum up a comedy act for us?' Archie wondered why the man had bothered to accept the invitation to be a guest at the concert.

Dame Nellie had opened the entertainment and would return for a final *God Save the King*. There had been a pause in the program as arrangements were set up for the current performer. The pretty young woman had played a very lively piece on the piano, causing Archie's wife to tell him to keep his good leg still. The young woman had then asked for two volunteers to join her on the stage to help her with the next piece. Two ex-soldiers, an older man with one arm and a younger fellow who appeared to be all there as far as Archie could tell, stood next to the piano. From her piano seat, Miss Lydia Bonnacci announced that she would be playing and singing a new song by the American composer Mr Irving Berlin. Helping her sing *Always*, she told the audience were 'Harold and Tommy.' Archie's neighbour was unimpressed.

'An' if they're volunteers I'm a monkey's bloody uncle.' The first of the piano's notes sounded, as Archie muttered.

'Give it a rest.' Lydia sang the opening lines.

I'll be loving you
Always
Where the love that's true
Always

Lydia's words soared high and out across the oval, ringing like peals from a chapel bell. From her first words, the audience went completely quiet. All shuffling ceased, lips fell apart in awe and eyes glazed over. Lydia's hands moved over the piano keys like water over river stones. Her chin pointed up, her back rod-straight, her singing effortless. As if Lydia and her piano were magnetic, much of the audience bent at the waist, leaning towards the stage. When the chorus of the song came, the two returned soldiers stepped close to the piano, singing in harmony with Lydia. Archie was not the only person who had tears in his eyes. The hard soul sitting next to him sniffed audibly, never taking his eyes off Lydia.

Behind the dark curtains in the wings of the makeshift stage, Jock Jobling looked on with gratification. His few weeks coaching had paid off handsomely. Lydia was a willing pupil, taking on Jock's recommendations about the selection of music, playing techniques and choice of costume. In a pure white dress buttoned to the neck, the bodice subtly embroidered, she sang the next verse of *Always.* Her dark hair was gathered up to expose her neck, wound into a floral tiara, with several tendrils left out to respond to her body's movement at the keyboard.

'*Norman*, that name won't do for the theatre, Lydia.' Jock had the authority of Dame Nellie behind him. They were taking a break during one of her private rehearsals. Jock had found her to be full of energy, prepared to work hard but also not afraid of speaking out when she thought it necessary.

'What do you suggest, something more exotic?' Lydia ran her hand through her hair and raised her head, presenting a three-quarter profile to her mentor.

‘I’ll think of it, don’t worry. It’ll be something European.’ In the end he had borrowed Lydia’s music teacher’s surname ‘She won’t mind – it’s a compliment.’ But it had been Lydia’s suggestion that she recruit two ‘volunteers’ to sing with her. The two men now walked off stage, the young man limping, while the audience stood and applauded Lydia’s performance. There were whistles and calls from some of the men in the audience, carrying over the enthusiastic applause. Lydia stood next to the piano, a small bow of thank you and a face alight with pleasure.

Jock’s off-stage vantage point, as always, made sure it included a view of Dame Nellie. She sat in the wings on a padded chair, her attendant never leaving her side. He had checked during the performance how Lydia’s item had been received by the great Australian soprano. His employer’s professional smile was firmly in place, but he did think Dame Nellie gave the signal to the stage manager a little early. She may have accidently cut short the reception for Lydia.

Arthur travelled back to *Wooreen* to take up his farm painting job with Elsie's blessing. She had been pleased with how quickly Millie had taken to working and living in Geelong, and assured Arthur she would be able to look after the boys on her own for a few weeks. The chance for Arthur to get away from the unsettling wharf environment was a big part of their reasoning.

'Perhaps I could even ask around and see if there is any work in the town out there?' said Arthur. 'We could go bush like Tenny.'

'What, in Hamilton? What would you do, they don't have any wharves or sauce and pickles factories, Artie.'

In Western Victoria Arthur found Tenny remained the same – a picture of rude, good health. He and his family continued to flourish in their lives on the farm. When they shook hands, Arthur thought his old Ockwell's mate should have been on an advertising poster for the rural life. Tenny's forearms were mahogany brown and his Akubra hat sat like a permanent fixture. Arthur had bunked down in the old schoolhouse again, having space to himself but also not far from Tenny's cottage and kitchen table. By late summer the land was feeling the effect of the long, sun-drenched days. The pasture that remained in the paddocks was bleached of all colour. The water table was so low, any shower of rain made the dry grass release a heady perfume, but there was no run-off. The Grange Burn was flowing, just. If the district didn't get any rain before Easter, it would become a series of waterpools.

Arthur had no problems picking up the work for his job as a farm painter, nor falling into a rural rhythm. He woke with the sun, aided by sleeping in a bed under an east-facing window. It suited him to wake early. As he lugged buckets of brushes, tucked long wooden planks under his arms, stirred full tins of paint and climbed up and down ladders, Arthur was pleased to find his forty-five year old body was holding up well. Any time he needed an extra pair of hands for a few minutes, there was always Tenny, Ivo or another farm worker to call on.

The early morning light pierced the buggy room at *Wooreen.* White-hot beams came through myriad nail holes in the corrugated iron walls. Ivo, the manager, walked with Arthur into the shed shortly after Arthur's breakfast – a slab of bread and butter and two cups of tea. The buggy room was a shed housing a disused horse buggy, a timber dray and a variety of farm implements and tools. The flatbed dray could be hooked up for either horses or the tractor. With the entrance doors behind them, Arthur had to squint at first to see the shapes of the farm vehicles. Arthur was listening to Ivo's instructions – the manager measured out his thoughts in four-word deliveries. It meant that Arthur could simultaneously listen and be fascinated by the solid rays of whiteness which punctuated the interior. The nail holes, randomly distributed in the iron walls, were enlarged by the savage sunlight as it forced its way into the shed. Golden dust motes bigger than flies hung in the air.

'We'll get you started ... on this shed … the buggy shed ... needs a touch-up. You can't do too much damage here.' Ivo had shown Arthur the paints, brushes, and other painting materials that were stored in a lean-to next to the machinery shed. 'Don't know what this shed was for ... coulda been a dunny ... though don't smell like it.' Ivo left to attend to other farm business while Arthur went to the exterior of the buggy shed and started to patch up the holes. He used an old brush, left to go stiff, to dab the black, bituminous paint into the nail holes. There was a ladder for the high spots and to get onto the roof. After he had done only a few holes, Arthur thought he could get himself better organised for the job – he would do the roof before the day heated up, then work around on the shaded side of the shed. Good to have a plan.

The next day Ivo came round the corner of the buggy room, leaning to one side to compensate for the weight of the ten-gallon tin of paint he held by its wire handle.

'Oi, Artie. Here's your paint ... full tin of *Reddo* ... that oughta do the job.' The paint, with its red oxide base, was a popular choice for modest weatherboard homes, as well as sheds or outbuildings on rural properties like *Wooreen*.

Arthur graduated from the now russet-brown buggy room ('Still looks like a shed to me,' said Tenny) to painting two weatherboard walls, the exterior of a series of utility rooms attached to the rear of the homestead. These spaces were called the Laundry Room, built onto the main bluestone building and accessed by an L-shaped covered way and well-worn brick paving. It contained a woodstove, two large boilers and built-in shelves holding large, cane wicker baskets to cater for *Wooreen's* laundry needs. The long rectangular building had stone walls on two sides. The Laundry Room also housed the Mud Room, where the SummerHayes family washed up from their labours before entering the house. They also used this room to bang and scrape mud off their boots in the winter, or take off their gaiters and shake out the dry seeds in warm months. There was also a drying room, set up with timber racks and cords strung across low rafters, and a general storage room where the house staff put their cleaning equipment. The weatherboards needed to be repainted white, the exterior of the stone walls had to be painted with slaked lime.

On the farm, the midday break was long enough to eat a chunky sandwich and, if Arthur was painting near enough to Tenny's cottage, a quick cuppa with Tenny and the missus.

'Any longer break an' a bloke would go to sleep,' reckoned Tenny. Arthur wanted a short break as well so that he only had to pack up and wash up his painting gear the one time. Arthur had worked his way along the Laundry Room weatherboards, using a punch and hammering the nail heads below the surface. Next, he scraped pea-sized bits of putty onto a stiff knife and worked it into the nail holes, thinking how much time farm-painting allowed for a bloke's thoughts to ramble. *Not like art-painting, where you have to be thinking about each brushstroke, adjusting your colours, always watching your technique, stepping back to assess progress, taking more time for thinking than brushing time.*

Arthur thought of Millie and her new life in Geelong. He pictured her in a smart summer dress and soft leather boots, under a shady tree on Eastern Beach. Some young men hovered nearby, out of his picture. He wiped sweat off his forehead. *Is it this hot in South Melbourne? How were Elsie and the boys coping? Albert and William might at this moment be walking down to the bay to jump off the pier at Kerford Road. If Albert got a tailor's apprenticeship he would be doing okay. Don't know about Willy though. That one's a mystery.* Arthur took a folded piece of sandpaper from his overall pocket. He wrapped it around a palm sized wood off-cut as he walked along the weatherboards to where he had started filling the cracks and nail holes with putty. He started to sand off the first patches that had now dried, still ruminating.

Arthur brought his sketch pad and some painting materials to *Wooreen*. At the end of his days of scraping, filling, sanding, priming, painting and cleaning up, he would have a sleep on his bunk in the schoolroom. After an evening meal with Tenny and his family, he found there were usually still hours of daylight in the day. He had got into the habit of doing drawings in his sketch pad – scenes from around the farm; a cart in the courtyard, a corner of the machinery shed, staked plants in the gardens. He preferred the vegetable garden to the flower garden, to the amusement of Tenny's missus.

'Don't you be drawin' me pickin' tomatoes, Artie. Draw some of them pretty flowers over that fence.' On the farm's rest day, Sundays for the workers were for extra sleeping or lying around, fixing up clothes and mending gear, having a smoke and a good yarn with a mate or two, perhaps reading the paper, and perhaps having a sly look at the SummerHayes family. Sunday was their visiting day. They would either pile into the big car in the morning and go to another property, play tennis on the court behind the house, or else another family would arrive all dressed up for a roast lunch and a walk in the gardens. Not a bad life.

The courtyard at the rear of thc house was the hub of farm operations. It was where the domestic routines and the rural jobs originated and diverged. The courtyard provided access to the machinery shed, buggy room, laundry and wash-house, dairy store, toolshed and woodshed. Arthur was often crossing the courtyard to pick up or store his painting materials. With his art-trained eye, the courtyard was a rich source of material. At midday on this Sunday, he noticed a carload of visitors arrive and flock into the house. By late in the afternoon, the courtyard was quiet enough for him to set up his easel and select his subject matter. He propped his lightweight easel on the cobbled pavestones, facing a corner of the courtyard where red-brick buildings and heavy timber uprights abutted. On the other side of the courtyard there was a flatbed dray, which Arthur was going to place in one corner of his canvas. He only wanted to do an oil sketch this afternoon, finish it off another day. He set himself up, then felt stiffness in the muscles of his back. It was all that bending up and down.

He went into the machinery shed and found what he wanted – an empty ten-gallon drum. He inverted the drum to make an artist's stool.

Arthur was pleased with his sketch. He felt he had captured the solid, functional honesty of the buildings. He arched his back and wiped his hands on a rag, movement behind him and to his right surprising him. It was Matilda, daughter of friends of the SummerHayes family, and object of Alec's affection. She was with Alec who was dressed in his Sunday best. His hands still protruded disproportionately from his jacket cuffs.

'Let's walk around the garden Matilda. You can take pictures of the flowers.' Matilda walked towards Arthur. 'Leave the man, Matilda.' She ignored Alec and he had to follow.

'I hope you don't mind, but I took your photograph.' Matilda held her camera towards Arthur.

'I don't mind miss. Is that a box brownie?' asked Arthur, standing. The young woman, in her early twenties, was scrutinising Arthur's oil sketch.

'It is. You were so absorbed in your painting. That's coming on nicely, don't you think, Alec?' The owner's son wanted to continue their walk.

'It might be alright when it's finished.'

'I like the spontaneity, the freshness an artist gets in preliminary studies. That's what I want to capture in my photographs.' Matilda's smile at Arthur caused dimples in her cheeks.

'Come on Matilda. I'll pick some flowers for you from the garden.'

Sometimes Arthur liked to take himself away from the homestead and outbuildings, to vary his subject matter. On the next Sunday, a still, hot day, he got his pencil and drawing pad, oil paints and some small boards and took off across the paddocks. There was plenty of landscape potential around *Wooreen.* It was hilly and the homestead was in a gentle valley with the Grange Burn beyond. Further away, the Grampians Ranges were a permanent backdrop. He walked across the straw-dry paddock, carrying an old fruit box modified by adding a broad, leather shoulder strap. He was gauging the view for an oil sketch, remembering to check the ground for snakes. Tenny, thumbs pulling his trouser braces away from his chest, had told him most snakes were down the creek, they loved water and a feed of frogs, but they did like to bake on low rocky ledges in the heat of the day.

'Still, when they're like that, they're too dopey from the sun to get angry. You'll be right, Artie.' Arthur was not sure if Tenny was pulling his leg. Since he arrived at *Wooreen* he had been on the alert for the playing of rustic practical jokes. So far, he had not betrayed a city slicker ignorance.

Arthur chose his position and set up the fruit box as an easel. After doing a couple of landscapes on other Sundays he particularly wanted to do a painting of the two-storey towered homestead. He wanted to take it home as a souvenir for Elsie. The vantage point he had chosen was among a few exposed boulders, positioning *Wooreen*, the Grange Burn and the Grampians exactly as he wanted. He did some preliminary pencil drawings – eventually completing an oil sketch in a couple of hours.

Ivo's next painting task was another promotion. This time Arthur was being allowed to paint the grand homestead itself, or at least the timber framed west-facing windows. With the homestead and its many functional outbuildings, cottages and sheds, there was ample work for a full-time painter. Arthur was directed to use a deep, rich green colour which was the match for the windows. There was enough to get him started, but Tenny would have to pick up some more when he was next in town. In the meantime, Arthur could do the preparatory work. He talked to Ivo like a professional housepainter now.

'It's all in the prep, Ivo. Skip on the prep and the job will never be any good.'

'Righto, Artie ... leave you ... to it.' The manager left Arthur scraping the old peeling paint off the ledge of the lounge room window. Arthur's mind started to stray again. He thought how much he had enjoyed the drawing and painting opportunities at *Wooreen*. *Quite pleased with the results too, even if I do say so myself. That one from Sunday of the homestead is still on the schoolroom's outside window ledge to dry. Never able to do that in France, some bugger would have nicked it before you could say* d'accord. *Gee, if a bloke could get some money together, it would be good to go back to France. What else am I going to do with myself? Work on the wharves with an eye out for the smart-boys all the time? I could do some good paintings down the wharves though – all those industrial shapes and colours.*

Arthur placed a ladder against the bluestone wall to reach the upper parts of the window frame. He was still at the scraping and sanding stage, but made a note to himself to be careful not to get any of the green paint on the stonework. *Wouldn't be so bloody clever then. What's this?* Arthur could see straight into the lounge room, the curtains allowing daylight to spread across the walls. *Paintings, photos, drawings, looks like some prints too. Tenny said the SummerHayes family had a real art collection. Wonder what they've got?* Arthur concentrated on the window frame, noting where the wood had split and where he would put some beige putty. *Let the family have their privacy. They've been good to me, and to Tenny too.*

When Arthur had packed up, cleaned his painting materials and washed at the workers' trough in the machinery shed, he went to the schoolroom looking forward to his afternoon kip. As he rounded the corner from the courtyard, he saw Tenny and two men outside his building. One was the owner, Samuel Alexander SummerHayes and the other his son Alec. Arthur had come across the two SummerHayes men on his first visit to *Wooreen* when he went rabbiting with Tenny. Alec spoke first to his father.

'It's the rabbiter, come back to do some painting for us. Hope you're a better painter than rabbiter.' Tenny shifted his weight from one foot to the other. The two older men ignored the comment.

'We were telling Tenny about the paint he needs to get in Ballarat for the house,' said SummerHayes senior. *Wooreen*'s heir and current owner was a few years older than Arthur, but where Arthur was wiry, Samuel was beefy. Where Arthur was fair-skinned, Samuel had gone beyond tanned to having extensive black and purple patches of sun damage. He turned to indicate the small study on the window ledge. 'That's yours, then?' When Samuel used his forefinger to tilt his broad-brimmed hat back from his forehead, it revealed contrasting pale skin to a non-existent hairline.

'Yes, I've been doing a few drawings in the evening and some stuff on Sundays.' Arthur thought surely, he wasn't in trouble for breaking the Sabbath or some farm-based rule. The older man peered at the sketch, his son tongue-tied and uncertain.

'I know the spot where you did this from. Probably the best view of the homestead in the whole farm.' He included his son in an explanation. 'There's a rise in that paddock that gives you a good view of the homestead, and the garden and other buildings.' Samuel SummerHayes turned back to Arthur. 'Would you show me your drawings and other sketches?'

'Sure, no worries,' said Arthur. Five minutes later *Wooreen*'s owner was turning over the drawing sheets from Arthur's sketch pad. Arthur and Samuel were sitting on the schoolhouse steps. Alec had lost interest and departed for the homestead, Tenny was hovering. Samuel also asked to see Arthur's oil sketches, propping them against a terracotta pot whose plant had long ago dried out.

'We've got some fair paintings in the house. Some old stuff from England and some newer Australian stuff. Where did you train, Arthur?' Over the next few minutes Arthur's story came out. He relaxed when he realised he was not going to get into trouble for impersonating a house-painter, nor for painting on a Sunday. Tenny grinned encouragement as if Arthur was his protégé.

'This one.' Samuel pointed a blunt finger at the oil sketch which had been drying and had first attracted his attention. 'Would you like to do a proper painting of that scene for me. A commission, as they say?'

'Sure, but when.'

'While you're here, take your time and do a real canvas, for historical purposes – the homestead in 1924.' The corners of Samuel's eyes crinkled like accordion bellows. 'I'd pay you a fair sum for it.'

‘I would have to order a canvas and a couple of brushes, some extra oil colours –’

‘Tenny can pick up what you want in Ballarat. He’ll be going there tomorrow anyway.’

‘And could you post a letter to Elsie for me?’

*

Arthur dipped his paint into a diluted solution of burnt sienna. He was back on the small rise, his painting gear spread out on the low, lichen-covered rocks, after ensuring no snakes were sunbaking. Using a pointed tip brush like a drawing instrument, he stroked lines on his primed canvas. At the schoolhouse Arthur had prepared the 24 by 36 inch canvas with a white primer. When he saw it drying in the sun, he had decided it was far too bright, too ‘high key’ to be his starting point. He needed to bring down the whole canvas, but not with any colour from his tubes of oil paint. Pleased with his rural inventiveness, he marched over to the farm paint store and stole an ointment jar of the russet-brown paint he used on the buggy room. He then mixed this into another coat of primer – exactly the depth of tone he wanted.

In the paddock he painted precise lines on his background colour to position the homestead, the tree line of the Grange Burn and the profile shape of the Grampians Ranges in the distance. He added a diagonal line tracing the path of the road to the homestead. He had to shake himself to get rid of an ‘out-of-school’ feeling, that he should have been painting around the farm or its buildings. But Tenny had returned from Ballarat with the supplies he had written down and the deal had been done with Mr SummerHayes. Arthur looked away from his easel, searing the view in his mind while he mixed some weak oil paint. His palette had a big squirt of titanium white, with smidges of other colours. He selected the larger of the new flat edge brushes and mixed pale solutions of colour. He then blocked in large areas of paint on the canvas; for the foreground paddocks, the mountain range, the homestead and the Grange Burn.

Arthur took his time over the painting. He imagined his finished work, framed and hanging in the bluestone house alongside paintings by established English and Australian artists. The thought made him smile as he put the road leading to the homestead coming in from the lower left of the painting. He next roughed in some clouds in the upper right, not worrying about the types of clouds yet. He would decide that later, using their shape to balance the composition. They also led the viewer's eye to the homestead.

'All eyes lead to home,' muttered Arthur. Arthur charged his brush with a mid-tone ochre colour, decided it was too dark, so worked in some titanium white. He had started humming to himself. Around the shape of the homestead, Arthur used this colour to block in the farm's outbuildings, taking care to get the size relationships right. Buildings in view ranged from a small outhouse to the schoolhouse and butchers, on to the chapel and large stables. Getting the sizes right would assist in giving the painting its perspective. Later he would modify each building, with more attention to light and shade than colour and detail. When the outbuildings were 'roughed in' he stopped painting, wiping his hands with a rag, all the while looking from view to canvas, canvas to view. This was not something to rush.

Two weeks later, on the Saturday evening after dinner, Tenny helped Arthur drag the two schoolhouse benches outside. They had arranged them a short distance away, facing the schoolhouse steps. On the little landing at the top of the steps, Arthur had set up his artist's easel and his finished painting. The sun had set, leaving a soft even light at *Wooreen*. The finest of the day's dust hung in the air. Most of the farm's flies had gone for the day, night insects not yet taken their place. The viewing party comprised Samuel SummerHayes, Ivo and Tenny. Alec SummerHayes had arrived with his father, looked briefly at Arthur's painting, shook his head without comment, then departed.

'Alec's no art-lover,' said Samuel, inspecting the artwork then sitting down with legs spread and a rolled-up magazine in his fist. 'You've done a mighty job, Arthur.' He slapped the magazine into the palm of his hand. 'That's a beauty. You've got the dry paddocks, the Grampians out the back, the home looks top notch in that setting. It's so *proper* the way it sits in the countryside.' Arthur sat down and Tenny slapped him on the back.

'This calls for a beer, Ivo. Didn't you bring a couple with you?' Samuel looked at his manager who silently got up and walked to the rear of the homestead. He was soon back with two brown bottles and four pewter mugs. Beers were poured and the men toasted 'the painting'.

'I brought this art magazine, Arthur.' Samuel opened *ART in Australia* and began flicking through pages. 'There was a story in here … somewhere … about Sir Arthur Streeton painting at a property in the Western District.'

'Awh …' Ivo looked very dubious. 'Heard about that ... that was over ... awhh ... near Willaura, boss.' He shook his head and gazed at his empty beer mug. 'That's miles from here ... or anywhere.' Samuel gave up looking for the article ('Must have been in the previous month') and levered his body off the bench to get closer to the painting on the easel.

'See this bit, Ivo?' Samuel had his nose close to the painting's surface.

'Yes ... those paddocks need ... a good rain, boss.'

'True enough, Ivo, but Artie's painted those paddocks with a little bladed trowel. See that.'

'Yes ... terribly dry.'

'Well, so am I Ivo. A couple more bottles I reckon. And bring the cheque book back from the office too.' It was now dark but still warm and breezeless. The men had settled into a cosy group, sitting like over-sized schoolboys on pews. The number of discarded empty beer bottles grew.

'Well before I forget let me write you a cheque, Artie.' Samuel pressed back the cover of his cheque book, holding his pen.

'Hang on!' said Tenny. He was flushed from several mugs of beer. His face was less matinee idol, more Sunday comic supplement. 'Artie hasn't signed his painting.' He pointed at the painting, where the others now looked.

'That's right,' said Ivo. 'He hasn't.' Samuel was used to finding solutions to problems and giving orders. 'Get your paints out and do it now Artie. I'll sign this cheque. Ivo, your shout again.' Arthur took the steps into his schoolhouse accommodation, selecting a brush and mixing up a small solution of thin paint. He thought deep, yellow ochre would go with the grass in the paddocks at the lower right of the painting.

The other three men watched with beered-up concentration as Arthur slurried a small amount of paint on a scrap of wood.

'Our painting's as good as a Streeton, Ivo. It's only right that Artie should sign it.' Samuel gestured with his magazine. Arthur was about to touch canvas with brush when Tenny burst out again.

'Eh Artie, you should write Streeton's name on it, 'stead of your own. How's that for a lark?' Tenny laughed at his own joke, the others also appreciating the humour. Arthur again moved to add his signature in the lower right, when Samuel interrupted this time.

'Why don't we? Eh? It would be a good rise, Artie.' Arthur did not know what to do. He could picture Streeton's signature on the paintings in the Atheneum exhibition. 'Go on,' urged Samuel. Ivo and Tenny's faces were like primary school kids playing with fireworks. Arthur's brush made a capital A. He collected more paint, allowed a space then brushed in the characteristic zig–zag capitol S, emphatic and spikey, followed by the other letters of the artist's name. The three men laughed in chorus, poured more beer into their mugs and toasted 'to Artie.'

The following morning Arthur discovered several things. He had, not unexpectedly, a hangover. Not the worst one he had ever had, but in the top ten. An empty easel stood on the landing at the top of the schoolhouse stairs. It was from here that Samuel and Ivo had waddled off with skinfuls of booze, a painting of *Wooreen* homestead and property tucked under the arm of the owner. The steps smelt of rank weeds and the school seating had a metallic, stale beer tang – the source an untidy stack of empty brown beer bottles. And in Arthur's shirt pocket was a *Wooreen Pastoral Company* cheque. The amount was enough to make Arthur think he may not have had his last trip to Paris after all.

PART THREE

The rear yard of Rosemary and Evan's 1970s home in the eastern Melbourne suburb of Heathmont showed the onset of autumn. The liquid amber, apricot, plum and ornamental pear trees were shedding yellow and red, brown and black leaves onto the patchy grass. Stuart stood next to his sister Alex, watching Declan kick a football in the air, then mark it above his head.

'Did you see me mark it, Dad?'

'I did, Decs. Has Tarquin been coaching you?'

'Yeah, you've got to mark it with your fingers spread out wide as you can.'

Alex half-turned to see into the house. Tempered by over four decades, the wire-cut bricks had weathered from their original orange to a colour less harsh to the eye than the original. Fragments of conversations carried to the back verandah from the relatives, friends, neighbours and ex-work colleagues brought together for post-funeral refreshments.

'We should have had this at the crematorium. They cater for these things,' said Alex.

'But Mum wanted it here. She said it was too impersonal and this is where she feels Dad is more …'

Stuart searched for the word he wanted '… evident.' His sister sipped her white wine.

'I thought it went well,' she said. 'The funeral.' As if Stuart may have been thinking about anything else.

'Yeah, although I had some nervous moments when Ron and Jeff did their tennis mates double-act talk.'

The day of his father's funeral had been warm enough to tempt Stuart to remove his jacket outside the funeral parlour. Immediate family, extended family and friends assembled in the foyer, then trickled into the reception room where the coffin held centre stage. Mourners were compelled to look at the coffin – that's why they were there, yet they also wanted to avoid staring at it. As the service proceeded Stuart felt all the warmth of the day leak away. By the time Ron and Jeff had told their weak anecdotes Stuart was buttoning up his jacket to better enclose his shoulders. Outside the funeral parlour, Stuart made small talk with Aunt Gillian and her friend Patsy, who said 'I've come to support Gilly.' Stuart felt cold. The small talk felt even smaller due to the occasion. And now, back at the family home with the other mourners, he was colder still.

Stuart's soon-to-be-ex-wife Leah joined him and Alex. She had sat with her husband and son during the service. From the verandah she called Declan in from the yard, needing to take him home.

'We're off. Declan and I will find Rosemary and Gareth inside to say goodbye.' Leah smiled a farewell and Declan hitched his football tighter under his arm.

'Bye Dad, Auntie Alex.' Alex allowed until the two were out of hearing before hissing to Stuart.

'Bloody Gareth.'

'What's he done?' The youngest sibling had been very distressed during his father's funeral. Not even the musical interlude, which usually pierced defences, had brought more than a sniff from Stuart.

Alex had set a tone for them all when she arrived for the funeral. She had chosen a navy pants suit from her corporate wardrobe, throwing a harlequin patterned silk scarf around her neck. She marched up to her mother and brothers. By way of chat, she managed to make a statement.

'This is sad for us all. But it's just that, isn't it, a sad occasion, not a tragic one.' Stuart wondered if Alex had made her comment as some type of warning, or attempt to set the parameters of the family's grief. Now back at the house she referred to the copious tears, nose blowing and tissue use that Gareth had displayed before, during and after the service. 'You'd think he was an only child, the way he's carrying on. Or as if Dad had died suddenly in a plane crash. He's not the only person whose father has ever died.' Even now, back at the family home, Gareth was intermittently breaking down in fresh bouts of tears. Alex looked into the house again. 'And he's the one who's hardly been home since he left school. Travelling around the world without a care. Well, at least no care for his parents.'

'Perhaps that's why he's so upset,' said Stuart. 'I should go inside and do some more mingling.' He and Alex put on the tight, half-smile of the recently bereaved but-coping-as-you-might-expect. As they went in the house, the mourners had let loose some of the reins and were noticeably noisier.

When he said goodbye, Stuart hugged his mother and held on to her, even after she made to pull away. She felt thinner, more fragile, than he ever experienced. Gareth was red-eyed, nose congested and about two-thirds drunk when he embraced Stuart.

'Man, this has been so heavy. You've been brilliant, Stu.'

'Take care, Gareth.'

'Bro, we gotta do the drinks again. That was so good to talk with you and –'

'We will, definitely.' Stuart extricated himself and left the Heathmont house. He turned his phone back on as he got into his car.

'How are you? Hope it was not too hard. Call me if you like? Alison'

Alison opened the door of her townhouse, Stuart took three steps inside and they hugged. From nowhere, Stuart cried. Holding Alison all the while, streams of tears ran silently out of him. His breathing stayed even, there was no sobbing – it was like a membrane had broken. He broke their embrace when he feared his tears were making her top wet.

'Sorry,' said Stuart, finding tissues stashed for the funeral service in his jacket pocket. 'Sorry.'

'Don't apologise, Stuart. Have you been holding yourself in all day?' She led the way through to her kitchen, pointing to her post-work glass of wine on the bench.

'I don't think I've been trying to hold myself in, not … consciously.' He shook his head as he deposited soggy tissues in the under-sink bin. 'We reckon it's good for Declan to see its okay for men to cry, but that came from somewhere … I don't know where.' He accepted a glass of wine. 'Gareth was a real mess.'

'And that's okay, too. Everyone processes grief in their own way,' said Alison. They had arranged to meet with no plans for anything else, other than seeing each other. 'How was Declan?'

'All wide-eyed. But he was okay. I think he was sort of prepared for it because Dad had been sick and in the home. Decs did say it was weird sitting between his mum and dad again.'

'That's nothing but a good sign. That he can talk about it feeling weird.' Alison had prepared some marinated olives and giardiniera, which she took into the lounge room. 'And your mum?' Stuart sat down and had some wine before answering.

'Finding it tough of course. They had a marriage and relationship better than most I suppose.' Stuart rotated his neck and rolled his shoulders. 'Mum seems to have aged ten years all of sudden. Or are us kids just perceiving her differently?' Alison didn't say anything. They were sitting on a sofa, both facing a wall on which hung a large painting. It was painted by Matt, their NAGA colleague. Alison had purchased it in Ballarat at Matt's last exhibition. Their eyes were drawn to the blue, green and purple swirls and swathes of the painting.

'Do you still like it? Get enjoyment from it?'

'I do,' said Alison. 'All the time, and more so over time – which must be an indication of a good painting, don't you think?'

'As long as it keeps meaning something to you. And me.' Stuart held his wine glass but didn't drink from it. 'Mum *was* different. She has been since dad had his stroke. When a couple have been together for so long you would expect them to become co-dependant, to a lesser or greater extent. When one is no longer there, it's like one half of an A-frame is removed. The other angled piece looks odd, or out of place.'

'And vulnerable.'

*

Alison insisted on ordering a delivery of Thai food. Stuart said he was not hungry, but when the basil chicken and lemon grass vermicelli was put on the kitchen bench, he found an appetite. To stop from rushing his food, he put his fork down and asked about Alison's day at work.

'Interesting. I'm trying to find out more about Michael's painting. We know Streeton was painting in the Western District in the 1920s and had an exhibition of his Grampians paintings at the Atheneum Gallery. It must have been quite a big deal to have Australia's senior artist paint your property. Michael is gearing up to make the public announcement and appeal for funds.'

'Has he set a date for that?' asked Stuart.

'Not yet, thank goodness. I need to fit in another trip to *Wooreen* to look through more of their documentation.'

'Michael must be busting to make his announcement.'

'He's like a kid before Christmas. And Jane is ready to go all out on publicity for the Streeton. You won't be able to get her to do anything else.'

'And I will need her to work on promotion around the Rodin drawings. Jean Lehni's visit is next week.' Stuart pointed with his fork. 'Can I finish that?'

'Of course – bloke who wasn't hungry. Hey, Melanie from *Conquest* sent me an email too. Wanting to know how we were going with their find.'

'I've had to concentrate on Rodin. I would have liked to have more time to go through Norman's stuff.'

'Mel wants me to give her a call, as she has to talk to me about something. She mentioned the Sorrento home.'

'They said they had some Heidelberg School paintings down there, didn't they? Or Netty did.'

'I'll get back to Mel,' said Alison. She watched Stuart pack up the remains of the Thai food, commencing with a sigh. 'You're tired from an exhausting day. I don't think you should be by yourself tonight. You need a warm and breathing body next to you. Don't go home – stay here tonight.'

In the Boardroom at NAGA, Jane Hollingway was in full flight. She was bouncing from one foot to the other, touching her hair, talking rapidly, pointing to images on the screen.

'This is going to be massive everyone. Announcing a newly discovered Australian masterpiece is a classic, rolled-gold PR opportunity. We're going to milk this puppy, team.' The NAGA Audience Activation Manager was talking at the gallery's senior management group weekly meeting. Stuart looked at the two slides each taking a half of the large screen – the *Wooreen* painting by Streeton and a list of dot points to which Jane was talking.

'First, we will be mining our NAGA donor and member database. They will be a prime source of funds to help us reach our financial target. The Sodaspring Beverages Group will be one of our key partners, spearheading a corporate partner strategy. We have a special appeal package which we will direct mail, respond to online leads.' Jane was wearing black pants and a smock-like top with an animal mix pattern. Stuart could see colourful representations of tigers, elephants, giraffes and … were they leopards or panthers, randomly cut and placed to make a montage on the fabric. She had reapplied her livid red lipstick prior to the meeting, where she now addressed the in-house audience.

'However. We have to get the public onside with this appeal. I'm thrilled to say that Michael and I have negotiated a media arrangement for this, with *AuscoMedia*. We've got a fabulous deal from them, people. They are giving us a four-page newspaper wraparound, radio comment on their morning *and* evening programs, and a television spot.' Jane rubbed her hands. 'I'll let Michael tell you about that.' Jane changed the slide to reveal more dot points, leaving Streeton's landscape on half the screen.

'Social media. We have a fantastic social media strategy ready to roll, using several platforms. We have negotiated with this list of key influencers. My team will be working very closely with these people to help us get the chatter about our new Streeton.' Jane beamed at the names on her screen. Stuart thought he could put a face to half of the people on the list; a celebrity chef, a singer who won the last *Voice of Australia* (he thought), a couple who presented a morning television program, an ex-Australian test cricketer and an actress who he believed was in Hollywood. Jane scanned the faces of her fellow managers, most of whom, like Stuart, were going through the list looking to recognise individuals. Michael thanked Jane and nodded to her.

'I haven't quite finished Michael –'

'Oh, we get the drift Jane. It looks great. You've put together such a strong strategy.' Jane sat down. 'Even if half this bunch wouldn't know a PR opportunity if it popped up in their pasta.' Michael mock-glared at his group of twenty managers.

'Thanks, Michael. Tell us about the initial launch of the public appeal?'

'Sure. People, a key part of the fund-raising strategy that Jane has put together is timing. Everything is integrated and scheduled to roll out over a six-month concentrated period. The chairman and I will be doing a media event at a special location –'

'Whereabouts? Not here in the gallery?' asked Kelly.

'No. Jane and I wanted to make an announcement in an appropriate place, getting away from the confines of NAGA. We thought about *Wooreen* itself, but it's so bloody far from anything. It might be at the old site of the Athenaeum Gallery where Streeton exhibited. Jane spoke up.

'I also thought we could go to Heidelberg and set up a media event. The Yarra River there still has some sort-of rural spots, we could even do a re-creation of the old Heidelberg School artists with their little tent, a camp fire –'

'Well, we haven't got a decision on that,' said Michael. 'The chairman needs to be consulted and we'll thrash it out with him.'

'And there's the morning TV slot we've arranged, Michael?' Jane was referring to *AuscoMedia's* flagship morning program *What's Doin'*, hosted by the husband and wife team Aaron Watts and Sophie Duyen. This was the influencer couple from Jane's list. They had won a sequence of Australian television awards and were active across several media platforms. The running joke on their morning program was to play up their couple status, pretending that viewers had dropped into their home for breakfast, even indulging in some coy bickering. It rated highly and the program boasted a huge audience share.

'Yeah, the morning after the chairman and I do the media event, wherever it is, I will be with the Watts-

Duyens at some ungodly hour.' Stuart believed Michael actually puffed out his chest. 'Christina-Rose and Karsten, a heads-up for you two that the Watts-Duyen will need the Streeton in the studio that morning.'

'In the studio, under lights?'

'Yep. You and Karsten can work out how to do it. Get it there safely and set it up. Don't let some studio lackey put their elbow through it. Jane will give you the name of the studio contact.' Michael made his last statement at the weekly management meeting. 'Team, this doesn't need saying. All this is confidential and not to go any further.'

'Except for the teasers. Which I will be coordinating,' said Jane.

Stuart spent the afternoon preparing for the visit from Jean Lehni of the Rodin Institute. He read over the draft program of activities; a full-day seminar, a curatorial exchange, an exhibition of the drawings with supplementary material from the Rodin Museum. Michael as Acting Director signed off on Stuart's program, giving him the okay to go through it with M. Lehni. Stuart had images of Rodin's NAGA drawings for *The Cathedrals of France* on his computer screen. He moved his mouse and brought up a new screen, this one a document listing the Arthur Norman artworks he and Alison had found at *Conquest.* Stuart was saved from having to make a decision about which of the two subjects he would work on by his phone.

'Is that the gallery?' The man's voice was coarse and raspy, possibly through smoking or half-strangulation.

'Yes, this is Stuart Williams, Senior Curator Australian Art.'

'You've been trying to get me.' The voice accusative, but not menacing. 'It's Julian Hillier here.'

'Oh, thank you Mr Hillier. I came across your phone number in a file here on one of our works of art. Are you related to –'

'Yeah, what did Uncle Herbert do now?'

'You are related to the antique dealer Herbert Hillier?'

'Yeah, he's my uncle. Was my uncle.'

'Mr Hillier, I wonder if we could arrange to meet?'

*

The address given to Stuart was in the inner south suburb of Armadale. Not as well-known as its famous neighbours South Yarra or Toorak, but in real estate terms the difference was only a camembert or two. Julian Hillier was eager to talk to someone from NAGA.

'This evening's as good as any.' When Alison heard that Stuart was following up a Hillier phone call after work, she was excited on their behalf and offered to go with him. He thought it best that he does the first meeting himself – he had no idea who or what to expect.

Stuart also had a football commitment that night. Tarquin had given Declan tickets to the first game of the season. The arrangement was, for Leah to take Declan to the club's training facility, Tarquin to show Declan around, 'introduce him to the coach and players', and then Leah would look after Declan while Tarquin prepared for his first game with his new club. Stuart would meet up and complete the handover outside the football ground.

Stuart stepped off the tram remembering, as he did fifty percent of the time, to look for cars or cyclists not stopping as he alighted. On the footpath he dodged a café owner swinging a round table back into the building, closing up for the day. He walked past a women's clothing store, then a red and silver themed hairdresser. Inside, a customer sat getting a Friday night treatment involving aluminium foils tied into her hair. The street number belonged to an Edwardian-era home, just after the shops ran out. The red bricks and cream-trimmed concrete had not been cleaned since men smoked pipes. Julian had said to ignore the front door and walk down the side of the single-fronted home. Stuart saw why – the area between the wire-looped fence and house-front was thrown into deep shade by two oversized oleanders and a woody cotoneaster. A narrow concrete path ran between rank agapanthus and rampant salvias. Stuart went down the path, the front door made ineffective by boxes and cartons taking up all the concrete porch. The stack was covered by a blue tarpaulin weighted down with terracotta roof tiles.

Down the sideway of the house more plant growth encroached from the fence side across the path, leaving a track like that of a furtive bush animal. Stuart rounded the corner of the home, giving a view of a predictably overgrown backyard. A mulberry tree created a dome of darkness across most of the yard. Underneath the tree there were several sets of outdoor furniture, none entire, and all being used as foundations for more stacks of boxes, garden implements, rusted wrought iron gates, two wheelbarrows, plastic and terracotta planters, and to one side an enormous cast iron street light. The light was on a lean, light fitting missing, a trumpet shaped shade giving the street furniture an art nouveau appearance.

'You found me, then?' A shock of white hair surrounded the pink face of a man in a black crew neck jumper, ill-fitting jeans and sneakers from the seventies. He came out the back door of the house while Stuart was still mentally sifting the treasures from the junk.

'Mr Hillier?' Stuart and the man shook hands.

'Julian. Do come in. Thanks for coming, I don't get out much these days.' Julian Hillier had a slight stoop and tilted his head to one side, as if one ear heard better than the other. He led the way into what once could have been a sunroom, an enclosed back verandah area which was, like the outside of the home, cluttered with objects. He invited Stuart to sit on one of two chairs at a round wooden table on one side of the room. The other side had a sink and taps, microwave oven, caravan-scale refrigerator and an ancient set of floor to ceiling wooden cupboards, once varnished and now peeling. Without asking Julian busied himself with kettle, water, cups, teapot and biscuit tin. Stuart sat and watched while the man, who he put in his seventies, told him about the house.

'This was my uncle and aunt's house. Not his shop, that was in South Yarra – or the showy one was. He also had a storeroom he used to sell things out of as well. That was in the industrial part of Prahran, forget the street name.' Julian moved some books and magazines across the table. 'But Uncle Herb, he liked to say he sold more expensive stuff from the storeroom than the High Street shop.' Julian chuckled at the memory. 'Someone would come into the showroom, he'd find out what they were interested in, then make up a story. He'd say, you know madam, sir, I believe I may have something in the storeroom you'd like. Then he'd take them there and talk down his stock, say I don't suppose it would be smart enough for your needs, or good enough for your grand house, or whatever, and bingo, he reckons it worked all the time. He would invariably get not only that sale, but he would say I've got these two old things in the storeroom somewhere, pretend that he didn't know exactly where every item was – it would be an antique washstand and a dining table setting say, if you had space for them …'

Julian put a carton of milk on the table next to the tea and biscuits. 'You don't have sugar? Good-o. And of course, Uncle Herbert would have marked everything up 300%, without even having to wipe the stuff over with a rag.'

'I'd like to talk to you about the Rodin drawings that your uncle left to NAGA.'

'He didn't give them, Aunty did, after he died. She organised the auctioning off of all the stock from the shop and storeroom. She always said to Uncle Herb that the drawings were the only valuable thing he had. What didn't sell is still in this house.' Stuart could sense from the space where they were having tea that the rooms of the house were as crammed as the outside. There was next to no light coming down the hallway that presumably led to the main rooms of the house. There was also no noise coming from the street or anywhere in the house; no traffic outside, passing pedestrians, background television, not even a ticking clock. The objects in the house had absorbed all light and sound.

'That was in 2009, then?' Stuart asked.

'Was it that long ago? Anyway, Aunty sold up the shop, gave those drawings to the gallery, took herself off on a round-the-world cruise and died on the ship in Hong Kong.'

'Were you involved with the business, Julian?'

'Me?' He laughed. His voice was getting smoother the more he talked. Perhaps he had been out of practice or perhaps it was the tea. 'I was just a nuisance nephew. I would get sent up here from Mount Martha, where my parents lived. They would expect me to help out Uncle Herbert however I could; dusting this, cleaning that. I did learn a few tricks of the trade, and also picked up the collecting bug.' Julian looked around him to demonstrate the point. He made to straighten the pile of books and magazines on the table at their side. They began to teeter, in danger of spilling over, but he was quick to arrest them. Stuart helped pat the pile back into stability.

'To be correct, I'm a hoarder Stuart, not a collector. There's a difference you know. But I don't mind. The council sends a person around every now and again, as if I'm not well. Half the time I'm happier in myself than the miserable bugger they send here.' Stuart grinned at the honest assessment. Julian Hillier did indeed look healthy and content. 'A collector has a plan, and organises their stuff. That's not me. I like having stuff around me, all the time. I can relax, I feel more comfortable. I might need something at any time too. I know where everything is. And it all means something to me.' Julian pointed to several pairs of similar sized salt and pepper shakers on a shelf above his kettle. 'See those, there's a story behind them, like there is for everything. They came from the old Coles Cafeteria in Bourke Street when they closed up. Lots of people remember going into the city, doing some shopping then dropping in to Coles Cafeteria for lunch.'

'My grandparents have spoken about it.'

'That's right. And have a look at this.' Julian got up and took one small step up into the hallway, Stuart following. They had to turn sideways to walk down the hallway. Both walls were lined with stacks of cartons and piles of books from the floor to shoulder height. There were two hall-stands and a long, shallow hall table, discernible by their shape, but also loaded and obscured by books, magazines, bronze domestic sculptures, mantle clocks and paintings propped against the wall. Three hallway doors were closed. Through an open door Stuart saw into one room. The dim light illuminated what may have been a dining room. The floor space was taken up with bulky, once polished but now dusty furniture pieces, together with six or more display cabinets. They were full of small-scale items; the tops covered in more. Julian took Stuart to the next room, which was at the front of the house. He went straight to an arm chair with thick arm rests and sat down. It faced a television, new but modest in size, and some built-in shelves which may have been constructed in the 1900s when the house was built. It contained a 1980s music system. On the other corner of the room was a desk with computer and screen, not new but not old. This room was less cluttered than the rest of the house. Julian chuckled as he saw Stuart's eyes roaming the room.

'You're looking at the paintings on the walls, aren't you?'

Stuart checked the time on his phone, explaining to Julian that he had to pick up his son. He was on his feet to leave and had made his way to the rear of the house from where he had entered.

'There's still one question I need to ask, Julian. Do you know how your uncle came to possess the Rodin drawings? Did he buy them at auction or –'

'No.' Julian waved away that notion. 'He got them from his maiden Aunt Tilly. She lived in Greensborough when it was miles out in the sticks. She was ancient even in the 60s and Uncle Herbert was nice enough to take them off her, to look after them. Although he never talked about those drawings with any confidence, as if he never fully believed in them. Which says something coming from him. It was Aunty who had the better eye and did recognise their true worth.'

'And where did his aunt get the drawings. Do you know?'

'Well, according to uncle, Aunt Tilly got them from her lover. A woman she never lived with but they were inseparable, always holidayed together, that sort of thing. Forget her name but she brought them for Aunt

Tilly, somewhere in France.' Stuart had to leave to meet Declan. He arranged to talk again with Julian Hillier.

Outside the football ground, a throng of supporters were going in the entrance gates of the colossal stadium. Stuart read Leah 's message again to check the meeting point.

We will be under statue of Bill Ponsford, a man with a cricket bat, at 7pm

Stuart found the stone plinth and bronze statue of the Bradman-era batsman, then circled it to find Leah and Declan. He was surprised to register that Declan was taller than his mother's shoulder and would soon exceed her height. When did that happen?

'Dad, Tarqs took me into the clubrooms – I saw the premiership cup – the coach said hello to me and they've got a swimming pool – just for themselves – next to their own gym.' Leah left the father and son to their evening of football.

'That's exciting Declan. I've never been in the clubrooms.' A group of supporters whooped and chanted as they went past.

'Devils! The deadly Devils' They were in the colours of the newest team to take part in the Australian football competition. The main colour of the Tasmania Devils was forest green, with yellow and black as secondary colours. They were only in their second year since joining the competition and in tonight's season opener were playing Tarquin's new club. His club was one of the founding members of the competition when it arose out of its Melbourne suburban origins, taking on its tribal affiliations and rivalries. The supporters of his club still saw the world in black and white.

They found their seats in the stand, giving them a high view, straight down the ground.

'What number is Tarquin, Decs?'

'Twenty-two, that's him doing run-throughs with the other backs.' Declan indicated a group of about eight players doing their warm-up routine on the perfect grass of the oval.

'He doesn't look as tall as he does at home. Not when he's surrounded with other people his size, or larger.' Stuart did not follow the game very closely, but having an Australian football player as a housemate, and friend of his son, added a special level of interest. 'Hope he doesn't get injured.'

'I hope he kicks a goal, dad.'

At the half time break, Tarquin's team had a four-goal lead. The players left the oval for recuperation, injury treatment and interim coaching. The supporters around Stuart and Declan stood up, started conversations, reached into their bags for drinks or left their seats to find refreshments.

'Can we get some chips, dad?'

'Sure, in a minute.' Stuart was opening his phone to talk to Alison about his visit to Julian Hillier's home. While Tarquin had run kilometres across the oval in his 'run-with' role, Stuart's mind kept going back to the Armadale house and its contents. He thought that Alison would expect a brief report but he was not sure how much to say. The visit had been fascinating. Hillier was entertaining and told a good story. Stuart had learnt a little more of the background of the Rodin drawings.

Then there were those paintings. That was unexpected. And potentially … well, Stuart would have to do some curatorial work there, but. Normally, Stuart would have enjoyed instantly sharing a description of his experience, but something was holding him back. He wouldn't call Alison; he would send her a message.

Hi Alison – at the football with Declan. Visit to Julian Hillier was –

'Dad! Can we get chips now?' The person sitting next to Declan had come back to his seat, torturing the ten-year old with the smell of takeaway chips.

'Okay, two seconds.'

– interesting. House full of antique/old furniture, crammed with lots of junk. Learnt a bit more about Rodin drawings. Talk soon, Stuart

During the second half of the game there was a passage of play involving Tarquin right in front of his two greatest supporters. The bouncing ball came towards Tarquin and his opponent, the Tasmanian Devil player nudged Tarquin's body, shifting his opponent's weight under the trajectory of the ball. This gave the player a metre of separation from Tarquin, who had to stop, turn, and chase his opponent who ran on with the ball and goaled. There were cheers from the green, yellow and black scarf-waving supporters, groans from the black and white ones. Some supporter comments carried to father and son.

'That's the new fellow, Tarquin Power from WA.'

'He can go back there if that's the best he could do.' Stuart saw Declan's eyes widen and the ten-year old tuck his bottom lip into his teeth.

'Don't worry, Decs. They can say whatever they like.' Declan sneered by way of response.

When the game was in its dying moments, his team maintaining their four-goal margin, the ball came to Tarquin in the middle of the field. He met the ball at a run, gathered it cleanly, his momentum helping him break a tackle from two Devils. Tarquin was within reach of the goals, a long, straight kick required. He steadied, his peripheral vision and spatial awareness telling him he was clear of opponents, and kicked towards the tall posts. As it sailed high towards the goal, Declan could not keep his seat, grabbing his father's arm, standing up and shouting 'Yes, yes!' The ball veered from its path and faded to the right, making a minor score. Declan sat down.

'It was good play though, Dad.'

At Stuart and Tarquin's shared townhouse, Declan was disappointed that he wouldn't see Tarquin that night.

'He has to do exercises and wind-down with the players, so he won't be home till late,' said Stuart. He made them both a warm drink and asked Declan what he wanted to do the next day.

'Will I see Tarqs in the morning?'

'I think so. Though you must let him have a rest. And don't the players do a day-after swim or something? We'll see.'

After Declan had settled in The Dude's Room, as all three males called it, Stuart checked his phone.

Stuart Thanks for report. Sounds intriguing: weren't there any paintings? Saw a bit of the football at Ben's. Number 22 is a good–looking boy. Alison

Stuart thought again of the paintings Julian had shown him. He fetched his laptop, typing the name of an Australian artist into the search engine. He read as much as he could find about the artist for the next hour. He didn't answer Alison's message. And he would keep this bit of research to himself.

*

The two sons were in the main bedroom of the Heathmont house. Rosemary had left them to the task of sorting out their father's clothing. She had already taken everything out of the drawers and wardrobes – they had to make decisions about which pile things belonged; donation to charity, throw away, or reserving something of their father's wardrobe for themselves.

'How about this Hawaiian shirt, Stu?' Gareth held up a shirt by its shoulders.

'He never wore that, surely,' said Stuart.

'You don't know, Stu. You don't know what dad got up to. I reckon he could be a real party animal as a lad.'

'Bullshit.' Gareth was finding the clothes sorting quite energising. He had reserved two bulky knit jumpers for himself.

'They'll go well on Lake Como,' said Stuart, his arm draped with never-worn polo shirts.

'It does get cold there,' replied Gareth. 'Hey, look at these.' They had flopped two suits on hangers onto the bed. Gareth pulled the waistcoats from each suit off the hangers and eased each of them out from under the suit jacket. He put one of them on over his t-shirt. 'Now this is a look. This *will* kill them at Como.'

'You can't do that, Gareth. You can't rip the vest part out of the suit. It makes it useless for re-selling by the charity. It breaks the … integrity of the –'

'Integrity!' Gareth laughed. 'What a load a crap. How would someone in an op shop know –'

'Fine.' Stuart threw the polo shirts down on the bed. He noticed Declan standing at the door to the bedroom.

'What are you arguing about?' Declan asked, then bit into a chocolate coated biscuit.

'We're not arguing. Uncle Gareth's being a goose. I'm going to take some stuff to the charity bin.'

Alison had company on the long drive west from Melbourne to *Wooreen*. A young research assistant, Levelle, had jumped at the chance to get out of the research team office and help with field work. Levelle was born in Mauritius and educated in Melbourne. This time, Alison could only devote one day to the visit, so her colleague was also to help with the driving. It was important that Alison go to *Wooreen* before Michael's media-heavy Streeton announcement. Michael had again stressed to her the importance of finding more material in relation to Streeton's painting adventures in Western Victoria.

'You need to find a photo of Streeton painting the homestead, or a local news report. Surely Alison, it would have been big news at the time? There must be something if you look in the right place.'

Alison wanted to catch up with Stuart on a break from their work at NAGA, but that had not worked out. Stuart cancelled one coffee break at the last minute, then said he was too busy with work for his French visitor to reschedule before she left for *Wooreen*.

By the half-way point on their drive to the heritage property, Alison and Levelle had covered the polite topics and Alison had gone over the background to today's research task. The young researcher was good company, yet Alison was not fully engaged with their conversation. She thought she would risk a call to Stuart from the car, knowing with Levelle's presence it would not be private.

'Stuart. Hi, it's Alison here with Levelle on the road. On our way to *Wooreen*.'

'Er, hi. To you both.'

'You've been a hard man to pin down. I wanted to talk to you about the Norman family. And want to hear more about what you learnt at Hillier's, about the Rodin drawings.'

'Oh … it was not a lot really. Except that Herbert Hillier got the drawings from an aunt of his, who got them from a friend in Paris. I'll put it all in the file.'

'That's more than we knew. What about Hillier's nephew?' Alison caught Levelle's eye and raised her eyebrows, acknowledging the drawing out of information.

'He's what you'd call a mild eccentric, I suppose. Harmless.' The road hum continued, the silence long enough to query the connection.

'Stuart?'

'Yeah, I'm here.'

'Thought we'd lost you. I rang Melanie Norman back. And guess what?' Alison allowed a shorter pause this time. 'She says they have had another find. This time at the Sorrento home, *Fairwind*. You know, where Edward, grandson of Arthur Norman, retired to. Edward was Netty's older brother. Either Netty or Melanie has got his family stirred up, digging into cupboards and attics.'

'Is Edward still alive?'

'No, he died in 2000 something. Melanie mentioned a Francis down here, Edward's son I guess.'

'So did they find something?' asked Stuart.

'They did. Mel sounded excited, but again wants us to look at it first. She mentioned paintings and drawings. They were not hidden, they were sort-of taken for granted apparently. She wants us to go to the Sorrento home. Doesn't want to risk transporting the artworks. What do you think?'

'No harm, I suppose.' Alison pulled a so-so face at Stuart's lukewarm enthusiasm, making Levelle grin.

'I can go with our star young researcher Levelle. She'd love to do some work down on the Mornington Peninsula.' Levelle nodded at Alison's open teasing.

'No, that's okay. You set it up and we'll drive down.'

Annabel and Charlotte formed a *Wooreen* welcoming party for the NAGA visitors. Annabel greeted them, stayed for a cup of tea and lemon slice, then left on unspecified matters. Charlotte was more animated in her mother's absence, eager to work with Alison and make the most of their hours of collaboration. Charlotte assisted their work by updating the spreadsheet of *Wooreen*'s art collection. As well as the works of art, she listed the art-related ephemera; magazine articles, newspaper stories, photographs, letters and even receipts. She took them to the lounge room, again using the polished wood dining table as a workspace. She had pre-arranged orderly piles of black and white photographs, cardboard boxes and folders containing records.

*

Stuart had met Jean Lehni, Director of the Rodin Institute, when he and Michael were in Paris preparing for the *Masterpieces from the Musée d'Orsay* exhibition. They had attended an exhibition at the Rodin Museum and established a connection between the two galleries. Stuart had been mostly a spectator as Michael and Jean had a red-wine fuelled discussion long into the evening. Today's visit was the follow up to the initial meeting between the two art bureaucrats. Now, Michael was NAGA's Acting Director, in the director's office with M. Lehni and Stuart. They sat on lounge chairs with a low table at knee level. They had exchanged greetings, commented on how well they all looked, commiserated about the long flight from Europe to Australia, admired the view of Melbourne's skyline, asked after colleagues, and had tea and biscuits.

'Jean, I know you want to get down to conservation to see our Rodin drawings, so I won't hold you up. Stu will take you there in a minute.' Michael reached around and took a document from his desk. The cover reproduced a detail of one of NAGA's Rodin drawings of Reims Cathedral. 'This is our proposed program. I have put into it some elements that I am sure you will find attractive.'

'I'm sure. I will read with interest.'

'Let's go over that later. First priority, Stu will take you to conservation to see our drawings. Then, Stu, you make sure Jean has a lift to his hotel room to freshen up, so that Jean can do that and get back here for the board dinner tonight. Jean, I'll leave you in Stuart's hands. We have a huge announcement for the gallery in a few days and I have some things to do.'

'D'accord.' Jean shook hands with Michael. 'A plus tard, pour le diner.'

Astrid left her work and Christina-Rose came out of her office when Stuart arrived with the French visitor. The Rodin drawings were in a storage box on one of the conservation workshop tables. Astrid took each of the six drawings out and arranged them on sheets of clean paper. M.Lehni stood back a short distance, hands behind his back, his posture accentuating his nineteenth century persona. Stuart told Alison that the portly man, with salt and pepper, tapered beard, rimless glasses and tweed-heavy suits, had walked out of a late nineteenth century Parisian studio photograph. M.Lehni walked to the table and bent over the drawings. The three NAGA people waited. He worked his way along all six drawings. It was like a doctor inspecting a patient, the relatives waiting for a medical prognostication.

'Mais ce sont très jolis, Stuart. M.Lehni was still bent over. 'I am astonished. I have never seen these before and did not know they exist.' He straightened up but still directed his gaze at Rodin's drawings. 'Stuart, you must tell me the story to how they got to the other side of the world. I want to look at the drawings with a glass, s'il vous plait?' Christina-Rose passed over a magnifying headset which the Frenchman fitted.

'Ah, a watercolour wash on these ones at Notre Dame de Chartres.' M.Lehni waved a finger as he spoke. 'Rodin did not do that many sketches for his cathedral series. There are not many in existence. He said that too many preparatory sketches killed his drawing, ruined his fresh vision.' No-one was going to disagree with the Frenchman. M.Lehni went back to the drawings. 'Incroyable.'

M.Lehni continued his inspection of the Rodin drawings while Astrid stood next to him. Stuart was with Christina-Rose.

'How's the Streeton looking? asked Stuart. 'All set for Michael's big announcement?

'We're all ready. We're only waiting on Michael and Jane's grand plan to kick off. The painting is in good condition as you know. We've got all our tests done, the canvas and stretcher are from the 1920s, pigments also of course, though there is one –'

'Stuart, on peut passer par les toilettes avant de quitter le musée the gallery, s'il vous plait? please.'

'Bien sur.' As Stuart took M. Lehni to the bathroom Christina-Rose went back to her office.

*

In the middle of the afternoon the three researchers in the *Wooreen* homestead were tiring. It had been a long day and they had waded through hundreds of dusty records. Alison had found herself thinking more about afternoon tea than finding contextual material for the Streeton painting. She wondered how Levelle's concentration was holding up.

'Anything in that box of photos, Levelle?'

'Not really. Loads of Charlotte's family pics.'

Charlotte looked up from where she had taken herself – a padded leather armchair in the corner of the lounge room. She was picking up tightly bound ledger books, checking their date span, then setting them aside, until she had found one to review more closely. Levelle blew upwards through her lips to dislodge a corkscrew of hair from her face, her hands lifting the next carton in front of her.

'Photographic records are funny, aren't they? There are heaps of the property. Lots of photographs of the homestead. This last lot look to be from the 1950s. They look professional, may have been done for a magazine feature article.' Levelle put her head on the side. 'And lots of occasions – birthdays, Christmas dinners, weddings, but very few of people doing their daily stuff. The gardening, preparing food in the kitchen, mustering stock, selling sheep.' She stood up straight. 'In fact, for a farm that has been a sheep run for so many years, you know what there is not here? The shearing of any sheep. Such an integral part of *Wooreen*'s life, a regular in the farm schedule and …' Levelle gestured to the dining room spread with papers and images, 'Not one image of sheep shearing.'

'Probably because it is exactly that, regular and seasonal. It would be like taking a photo of grass growing in a paddock,' said Alison. She looked towards Charlotte, who had been very quiet during Levelle and Alison's musings. Charlotte was holding the ledger book open. She was bent forward, a V in the middle of her forehead.

'I've got something,' she said. 'At *last*. Look at this.' Charlotte kept her place with a finger, not reading but fixing the other two with a face transformed. Her expression was enough to draw Alison and Levelle to her corner. Charlotte waited until they perched on the broad arms of the armchair.

'This is *Wooreen*'s farm journal for 1924. There are boxes of them but I put off going through them because I thought they would be full of sheep sales, costs of building materials, staff comings and goings, and they are. But I found this!' Alison and Levelle had been trying to read over Charlotte's shoulders. The looping handwriting in ink was strong in some entries, faded in others. The ledger was part diary, part fortnightly planner. The ledger book was produced by Elders Stock & Station Agents, Hamilton, Victoria. It would have been given to valued clients as an annual goodwill gesture. Alison's neck was stiff from trying to read at an angle. She stood up.

'You read it Charlotte.'

'Okay: *2nd March 1924. Overnight rainfall nil, Grange Burn not running at bridge over lower paddocks. Ivo will take Alec to next Hamilton Sheep sales* … bit more about sheep numbers, ah ... *The painter chap who's been staying here did a good picture of the homestead and land. It shows the manor with the Grange Burn and Grampians most stately.*'

Levelle squealed and Alison put her arm around Charlotte's shoulder. Charlotte got to her feet and started pacing around the dining room.

'The painting chap has to be Arthur Streeton. And it says he's stayed here. In those days all the important guests stayed upstairs in guest rooms.'

'Who would have made this entry, Charlotte?'

'It would've been Samuel SummerHayes. The journal wouldn't have been written up by farm workers or housekeepers, even if they could. It was too important for that.'

'And it describes the painting exactly,' said Levelle. 'The manor – I suppose that's the homestead, the land, the Grange Burn and Grampians. Brilliant.' The rise in volume from the three seekers and their sudden animation had attracted Annabel into the room. Before she could say anything, Charlotte linked arms with the other two.

'We've earnt afternoon tea.'

A celebratory treat was organised for the band of researchers. Charlotte put the afternoon tea things she and her mother prepared on a tray and set off from the kitchen, telling Alison and Levelle to follow her. She took them into the lounge room where they had been working, but only for her to pick up a set of black and white photographs. Annabel and Charlotte conferred mysteriously, then the four women went into the hallway which led to other rooms on the ground floor and the timber staircase. They took the stairs, then on the next level Charlotte took them along the bedroom corridor, to a flat door flush with the wall. It was painted the same sage green colour as the corridor. Annabel produced a single key and put it into the standard yale type lock. The door opened inwards. Annabel reached through and flicked a light switch to turn on bare light bulbs illuminating some unpainted stairs.

'We're going up the tower!' Levelle clapped her hands. The double flight of dusty stairs ended at another door, Annabel stopping, the other three concertina-ing, gently bumping into each other. This door was more like a largish cupboard. They stooped to go through it and emerged onto the open-air platform of the homestead's turret. Harsh daylight hit the group. They blinked as they stepped to the sides of the platform, irresistibly drawn to the view over the turret walls.

'Wow, how wonderful,' said Levelle.

'It's stunning,' said Alison. 'I want to look in every direction at once.' The viewing platform had a low-roof side in which the access door was set. The other three sides had built in bench seating. Charlotte put the afternoon tea tray down on a bench seat.

'Didn't spill a drop. You look; I'll pour.' From the vantage point they could see all parts of *Wooreen*. Alison felt the aerial view even more accentuated the toy-town feel created by the sheds and outbuildings. She half expected to see figurines strategically planted going into the schoolhouse, queued at the old bakery, and riders on horses coming out of the stables.

Charlotte had hold of the photographs she had picked up. She now held one of the photographs at arm's length, moving it to her right, pausing, then slightly lowering the image.

'This is it, I reckon. The Grange Burn, with the tennis court in the bottom.'

'That's clever,' said Levelle.

'Pick up one yourself. When I saw these, I knew they had to be taken from here.'

'When were they taken, do you think?' asked Alison.

'1930s I guess,' said Charlotte.

'Or earlier,' said Annabel. 'Charlotte, I didn't even know we had these.' Alison sorted through the twenty or so photographs, all about small notebook size.

'This one is lovely.' She held it so the others could see. By style it was one of the same set, though it was not taken from the tower, but from the bank of a creek.

'That would have to be the Grange Burn,' said Annabel. The photograph showed a fallen tree and small bank or promontory, framing a still, black waterhole. The water was flat, reflecting the canopy of eucalypts from both banks.

'This is beautiful. Timeless,' said Alison. 'You don't know who took these?' Charlotte and Annabel both shook their heads.

*

Jean Lehni was a guest at the monthly NAGA board dinner. The board meeting finished in the late afternoon. Michael had included an agenda item on the Streeton acquisition, taking the board through his and Jane's plans for an extensive promotional and fund-raising strategy. Michael had then chaperoned chairman Russell Dalton-Smith and the other board members down to see the Rodin drawings with Christina-Rose and Astrid.

The group had now reassembled in the gallery's restaurant for pre-dinner drinks. Stuart was with Jean, Michael, Dalton-Smith and two other board members while the gallery's restaurateur topped up their glasses of wine. Everyone agreed that the Rodin drawings were a superb acquisition and that a curatorial program was very much required.

NAGA's café and restaurant business was put to tender nine years ago. Patrick Riordan was the owner and operator of NAGA's *Pat's Palette* café, and the up-market *Patrices* restaurant. Each month, Patrick made sure he was on hand to supervise the evening's food and wine. The dinner was always a four-course delight.

'Looking forward to another Elise extravaganza tonight, Patrick.' Michael then spoke to Jean.

'Our gallery chef is fantastic Jean.' He was referring to the fair and skilled hand of Elise O'Loughlin, recruited by Patrick from Ireland. Patrick poured more sparkling wine.

'Gentleman, we may have a problem in keeping our chef,' said Patrick. 'A television production company has been in touch to see if she would be interested in a cooking program.'

'I would have thought we had reached saturation point with cooking shows,' said the male board member. Michael put out his hand to stop Patrick moving on.

'Hold that thought, Patrick. We need to talk about that. I can see an opening for NAGA here.' Michael was suppressing his agitation as an idea formed. 'I can see why a production company would want Elise, she's blonde, bright and cooks like an angel. But we need to get a pitch together that puts her into a package.'

'What do you mean?'

'An art and food package. The pitch is they can have Elise as talent, *and,* fucking access to the NAGA collection. I'm serious, Patrick. We'll do it.' Jean's very good English was not quite able to match Michael's inspiration.

'Qu'est-ce qu'il veut Michael, Stuart?'

'He's suggesting a food and art cooking program.' Jean tilted his head. 'Pourquoi pas?'

Stuart reflected, not for the first time, that for all his faults, and he had many, Michael did have an ability to generate original ideas. A television show bringing together art works from the NAGA collection and the culinary talents of Elise O'Loughlin was something Stuart could envisage.

During the dinner Stuart had Jean to one side of him and the NAGA board artists' representative on the other. On the nine-person board, one position was reserved for a 'contemporary practising artist'. This position was currently filled by Brittany, a Brisbane artist who worked across media producing films, video works and online material. Stuart noticed she was doing a good job of matching Jean in the wine consumption stakes, whereas he had switched to mineral water. Stuart told Brittany a short version of the explanation he had given Jean earlier about how the Rodin drawings had got to NAGA.

'So, they were owned by a Melbourne woman, this dealer's aunt, who was given them as a gift?' Stuart and Jean both nodded in confirmation.

'And it was a close friend of the aunt who purchased them in Paris, or France at least.' Stuart wondered if Brittany was filing this information away for future artistic endeavours. He nodded again. Brittany addressed Jean.

'Then where would they have come from in France, Jean?'

'It's possible they could have been bought from a dealer.'

'Or picked up in a flea market in Paris?'

'At the moment, what we know stops with the friend of the dealer's aunt in Melbourne.,' said Stuart.

'The lover of the woman who lived on the fringes of the city,' said Brittany. 'Let's put some poetry into the story, hey.'

Elise's dessert this month was, according to the menu card, 'fruit salad'. Which was like saying that Leonardo da Vinci's *Mona Lisa* was a 'family snap'. Next to Stuart, Brittany moaned in anticipation as she split the glazed concoction of fruit and berries. Her dessert spoon scooped up some of the fruit salad with a curl of homemade ice-cream and a shard of chocolate. Stuart couldn't resist watching as Brittany placed the dessert in her mouth, audible sounds of appreciation coming from deep within the artist.

'This is heavenly,' said the artist. Stuart smiled in response. He put a spoonful of dessert in his mouth, holding onto the flavours as they dissolved in his mouth. He found his mind going back to his visit to Julian Hiller's place, recalling crystal clear images of the paintings in the lounge room.

Not long after dessert, Michael brought his chair next to Jean, asking Patrick for a new bottle of red wine. It was clear that the two men were settling in for more drinking. Stuart did not ask if Michael needed him for French translation purposes – he had seen in Paris how with every glass of red wine Michael and Jean were able to surmount the language limitation on both sides. They did so through expansive gestures and vigorous English or French words or phrases. Stuart offered to get a glass so that Brittany could share the wine. He brought the glass but didn't resume his seat, leaving the gallery soon after.

Saying goodnight to Brittany, he thought if Alison had been at the dinner he would now be telling her about the paintings at Hilliers, probably.

The Mornington Peninsula is one of several coastal destinations within a reasonable drive for Melbournians. Its coastline ranges from safe, sheltered beaches to wild stretches of churning ocean. Sorrento is almost as far down the peninsula as you can go. The narrowing land mass of the peninsula means that greater Sorrento spans from a shallow paddling pool for toddlers to an ocean rip braved by only the strongest swimmers.

Stuart and Alison travelled down the highway, the city skyline receding in the rear vision mirror. Alison told Stuart about her second trip to *Wooreen*. While it was great that Charlotte had found the journal entry, Alison was equally excited by the anonymous black and white photographs. She added the task of doing more research into the mystery photographer to her one-day projects. The people and scenes were more than family snaps – they had been taken by someone with an interest and knowledge of photography.

It had been sunny when Stuart picked up Alison, however the sky clouded over to a gentle grey cloak. The mist was almost microscopic, and immobile. It kept the temperature down and softened the landscape by blurring all edges. When Stuart and Alison got out of the car at *Fairwind*, they both reached into the back seat for an additional layer of clothing. Stuart admired the Sorrento home of the Norman family. Alison crammed a fuchsia beret onto her head and zipped up a sleeveless puffer jacket.

'Cute,' said Stuart.

'The house?'

'No, you in that beret.' Stuart leant in and kissed her on the cheek. Over the last few kilometres, they had gone over what they knew about *Fairwind*. Most of their information was gleaned from Netty's comments when they visited *Conquest* in Kew. Netty told them that her brother Edward was *Fairwind's* longest term resident. It was Albert, Arthur Norman's eldest son, who had established the Sorrento place as a holiday home in the 1930s. In that era, it was still an option to arrive for the summer by boat from Melbourne, disembarking at the Sorrento Pier with luggage for the month. Stuart and Alison walked to the entrance across raked gravel, the dampness lessening their scrunch. Stuart looked up at the large home. He could make out at least three phases of building.

'Albert did well out of his menswear business.'

'He did,' said Alison. 'Then his son Edward, as well as continuing Normans Menswear, had a couple of newsagencies, one of them down here on the peninsula.' Stuart pressed the door bell, listened, turned his mouth down.

'Mel is expecting us.' Alison surveyed the front garden. 'Sorrento was popular back in Albert and Edward's time, but nowhere near the sky-high real estate it is today.'

It was not Melanie but Francis Norman, son of Edward and grandson of Albert who answered the door. Stuart was taken aback by the man's appearance and had to gather his thoughts during introductions. From the couple of photographs he had seen of Arthur Norman, the early twentieth century artist was now taking them into the warm stone cottage. Melanie stood up from a tartan fabric lounge setting, her back to a wood combustion heater that had been going since early morning.

'Apologies for the clothes,' said Francis. 'I've been tidying up in the garden.' Stuart figured it was the V-shaped jawline and receding hair which made the forty-something man most resemble his great-grandfather. He had Arthur's nose too. The effect was enhanced by dried paint stains on the gardening jumper, worn with baggy corduroy pants.

'This old place has seen some changes.' Francis was stating the obvious as he and Melanie took Stuart and Alison through a rear extension to the house. The multi-purpose family room had one wall of tinted glass. On one side of the room was a lounge, bar and entertainment centre, the other side had a table draped with a white sheet. The lathe-turned, stout legs were the giveaway that it was a billiard table. Mel and Francis had displayed the art works on a clean sheet spread over the table. Francis stood in the middle of the room. 'We know this place was bought by my grandfather Albert in 1938. The oldest part of the building, the stone cottage, dates back to the nineteenth century.' Francis and Melanie were both looking towards the covered billiard table as he spoke. 'Mel tells me you've been to *Conquest,* of course. I lived there till I was eight, then my father came down here. Been a Sorrento local ever since.' Stuart and Alison went to the table. 'We've had these around for years. Never thought anything of them, until Mel mentioned that you had been to *Conquest* and were interested in old Arthur's work.' Francis and Mel joined them at the table, making a line of four.

'We're so keen to see what you have,' said Alison.

'They've had a hard life.' The pencil drawings on paper were significantly damaged. Corners were rounded, bitten off by insects and moisture had got to the surface, leaving them mottled and spotty. One drawing had been torn decades ago, the tear left un-repaired.

'I put the drawings into two groups,' said Mel. 'I don't know if that's correct chronologically, but you can see there's an inner urban theme and a rural theme.' Alison and Stuart shuffled small steps to position themselves in line with a separate arrangement of small paintings.

'Mel, these are delightful.' Alison referred to four paintings on thick paper or card, two more were on irregular rectangles of plywood. They were each painted with a limited range of colours, either browns, ochres and pale orange, or either very muted greens and washed-out blues. The monotone effect gave them a coherency. The paintings had weathered their rough treatment better than the drawings.

'How did these come to be at Sorrento?' asked Stuart.

'Don't know,' said Francis. "My father may have brought them down here with a whole pile of stuff when he moved from Kew. That concrete garage was built onto a coach-house out the back. I hunted through our junk rooms to find these.'

'Stuart.' Alison put her hand in the small of his back. 'Netty mentioned about some Heidelberg School paintings –'

'She did.' Stuart leant closer, peering at the painting of a corner of an orchard. A similar painting showed a grove of trees in blossom. The other paintings were two beach scenes and some figures dancing as if in a reverie. All the studies were carefully composed and delicately handled.

'The paintings, Stuart –'

'Yes, hold on a minute.' Stuart moved around Alison to be in front of the rural drawings. 'I wonder if these were done at the same time as our Beech Forest painting? It would be interesting to compare the fields in each … they're not exactly the same.'

'No,' said Alison, who had now registered Norman's signature in the corner of each painting. 'Each of the paintings is signed A. Norman. But they are so Heidelberg School.' Mel stepped forward and picked up the nearest painting to her. It depicted fruit trees in deep pink blossom.

'Look at this.' Mel reversed the thin wooden panel and pointed to some writing in pencil on the back.

Pte A.E. Norman
VX 764881
A.I.F

'Francis and I were saying that Netty always said Arthur was a war artist. Is this what he did?'

'I'm not sure,' said Stuart. 'But I would definitely like to do some more research on these. Would you mind if we took them on a study loan basis, like the others?'

'Of course. We thought they may be too bashed around –'

'As part of our study we will do a condition report, and with your permission our conservation team may do some stabilising.'

The nineteen drawings were inserted between the pages of a drawing pad Stuart had in his car. The six paintings were wrapped in the clean sheet from the billiard table. As Stuart put the latest Arthur Norman find on the back seat of the car Alison checked her phone and closed it. She slid her phone into her bag on the floorwell as Stuart got behind the wheel. It took all her energy to force a polite small for Francis and Melanie as they left. Even when they were on the road back to Melbourne, she remained looking out the passenger side window.

'What do you think about our new Normans?' asked Stuart.

'Mmm.' Alison was sitting still and looking at the scenery.

'Those paintings are fascinating, aren't they?' Stuart snatched a quick look at Alison, but her face was averted. She had been so enthusiastic in the house, delightful in her response to the artworks.

'Are you okay?'

'I'm okay.' But she didn't stop looking out her window until they were half-way back to Melbourne. She turned sharply, looked ahead through the windscreen and spoke to Stuart. 'I want to stop for coffee please. The Mordialloc Hotel is in five minutes.'

'Sure.'

The hotel was on the beach side of the highway, where the oily-black Mordialloc Creek ran into Port Phillip Bay. Tables were set out on a broad deck overlooking the creek, where bobbed a bunch of tethered blue and white hire-boats. Stuart came back with their coffees. After five minutes Alison had not said anything, her gaze fixed on the boats at their pilings.

'You haven't touched your coffee,' said Stuart.

'I got a phone message, Stuart. From Julian Hillier.'

'What did he want?'

'He had both our numbers. Said he has misplaced yours –'

'That's not hard to imagine,' Stuart grinned.

'He asked if we had decided what we were going to do about his paintings. He mentioned some names.' Alison now sipped her coffee. Stuart's grin dissolved.

'What paintings, Stuart?' Stuart frowned but didn't speak. 'Would these be paintings that were in Julian Hillier's home that you didn't tell me about?' Stuart had a flashback to himself standing in the Hillier front room.

'I thought I –'

'Thought what? That you would give me the impression there were no paintings of interest? Because that's what you did. Despite Julian Hillier feeling they were important enough for you to follow up?' Alison pushed her coffee cup away. "When were you going to tell me? Never?' She pushed her chair back from the table. 'Obviously I'm only a research person and you're the big deal curator. And our friendship, such as it is, apparently counts for fuck-all in your eyes.' She stood up, picked up her bag.

'I'll catch the train home from here.'

'Alison, don't do that. Alison, let me –' But he was talking to her back.

Tarquin had added another exercise option to the garage gym. Stuart, in shorts and t-shirt, stood up to the red bag. Left-left, right. Right-right, left. Left-left, right. Right-right, left. *How many times can I do this? Couple more.* Stuart was blowing heavily after only a few minutes of pounding into the suspended punching bag. He reset his stance. Left, right, left, right, left, right – *Whooo! This takes it out of you.* He steadied the bag with his left hand, then punched repeatedly with his right. Swapping stance and punching hands, he caught movement at the door of the garage. *How long had Tarquin been standing there?* His housemate offered Stuart a metre-long length of chunky timber that he had picked up from against the brick wall.

'Here Stu, it's still breathing.'

'Is that ... what it … looked like?' laughed Stuart. 'How're you, Tarquin?'

'I'm good, you're the one who's not been yourself.'

'You could tell? Sorry if I … haven't been great company.' Stuart was still getting his breath back to normal. He sat down on the bench press seat. Tarquin pulled up a plastic garden chair and sat with legs splayed.

'Don't apologise, Stu.' Neither man spoke. Stuart used his t-shirt to mop sweat from his forehead. He slowly shook his head, his face pained.

'I've done something stupid.'

'At work?'

'No. It's sort-of work related but I've done poorly by someone.'

'That someone would be … Alison, I'm guessing.' Tarquin was searching Stuart's face.

'Yeah,' said Stuart, a little surprised.

'Mate, I can tell you think a lot of her. The way you talk with her, the way you walk when you're off to see her … even a footballer could read you.' Tarquin drew his feet in. 'Stu, if you want to talk some more about it, let's go to the cafe and grab a coffee.'

'Don't you have to be at the club?'

'That can wait if you want to have a coffee with me.'

'I'll be okay, but thanks.' Stuart and Tarquin stood up.

'I'd give you a hug but you're too fucking sweaty,' said Tarquin. 'Just think though. If you're feeling shit, really deep, bad shit because of something you've said or done to Alison, that in itself has to mean something.' Tarquin picked up the plastic chair. 'It's saying you care. A lot.'

Stuart drove to his mother's house with Tarquin's words fresh in his mind. *How bad is it when you have to be counselled in relationships by an AFL footballer?* Since Alison had left him on their way home from Sorrento, he had been beyond miserable. He was disappointed in himself, wishing he could wind the days back.

Alex and Gareth were also at the Heathmont house, Gareth in residence and Alex visiting. His mother was at the kitchen table which was covered with manila folders and papers.

'Your dad still liked to keep a paper record of everything,' said Rosemary. 'He has all our stuff on the computer as well but this was his back-up, he used to say.'

'Stuart,' said Alex. 'I'm trying to talk mum into tidying up the records online and getting rid of all these papers.'

'Mum may want to keep both going, like dad,' said Stuart. His mother looked washed out and reduced, like a faded version of herself. 'As executor, it's your choice anyway, Mum.' Gareth was in one of the bedrooms, judging by the bumps and thumps coming up the short hallway. Rosemary, still scanning the spread-out paperwork, anticipated Stuart's question.

'Gareth's sorting out your dad's sporting equipment. How many tennis racquets has he found now? Five? Seven? There's a set of hardly-used golf clubs for the taking Stuart. He never did get into that game.'

'It's a bourgeoise pastime anyway,' said Stuart as he circled the kitchen to make tea.

'I've been taking lessons from a pro,' said Alex. 'It's a very challenging game and not as easy as it looks Stuart.'

'Anyone else want a cuppa?' asked Stuart.

Stuart was sorting through more of his father's clothes when Alex came into the room.

'Mum's in the garage with Gareth. They've found a box of about a hundred tennis balls if you want to take some for Declan.'

'I might, thanks.'

'Mum really needs help, you know.'

'She's exhausted. As you'd expect. But the will's straightforward, isn't it?'

'Stu, you'll need to give her more support now. We all will. Though Gareth seems to have regressed to being a sixteen-year old in this house.' Alex left the room as Stuart's phone beeped with an alert.

Stuart – Declan needs to stay here at Kalorama for a couple of days more. Will give you a call but he has homework to do and is bugged by something on social media. Leah

He closed his phone, incomprehension on his face.

'Stu, bro!' Gareth had entered via the back door shouting. 'You still in here. Let's pack up man and go to that wine bar for a couple.'

'Can't Gareth. Have to –'

'Ar come on! Have one. Or two.'

'I need to talk to Declan. Perhaps Alex will go with you?'

'Yeah, that'll be fun,' said Gareth. 'Get another free lecture.'

'Why not take Mum and Alex for a drink then?'

'All right! Good idea, bro.' He walked away calling out to the rest of the house.

'Mum! Alex!'

*

In the Director's office at NAGA, Michael looked up from his computer. He had arranged to meet with Alison to discuss her emailed report on the Streeton painting. Alison had summarised her visit to *Wooreen* and the results of her research. Her report included the spreadsheet on the SummerHayes Collection which she had compiled with the help of Charlotte. Her notes said that more work was needed for the list of artworks to be comprehensive. Alison sat and waited while Michael scanned her report. Although his assistant Huong had set up the meeting, it was apparent that Michael had not read the report until Alison arrived at his office.

'So, it's not a bad collection, you'd say?' Michael raised his head towards Alison.

'Its strength is in the Australian artists of the first half of the twentieth century; Hampel, Blamire Young, Nora Heysen, R.W. Sturgess, Norman Lindsay –'

'R.W who?'

'Sturgess. They have some watercolours by him.' Michael referred back to his screen.

'The main point of your visit was to get some context for our Streeton announcement.' He gave the screen a disapproving glance. 'You couldn't find a photo of the old bloke? If not painting, posing with the owners, walking in the gardens, something like that? You went through the Hamilton Bugle or whatever for contemporary reports?'

'The Hamilton Spectator,' said Alison. 'We did go through their archives.'

'Who's we?'

'Charlotte SummerHayes has been a great help at *Wooreen*, and I've also had Levelle from the team searching records.' Michael scrolled down his screen, then closed Alison's report with a stab.

'But all you've got to show for six days work is a diary entry – that the old boy did a painting of the place.' He shook his head.

'Michael, we can't find something if it's not there. We have gone through years of correspondence, family photographs, scrapbooks and documents. It's not an academic record or anywhere near a curated collection.'

'Yeah, yeah.' Alison wanted to say more but Michael had moved from behind his desk. 'We'll have to work with what we have. But it's not enough.' Michael went to his door. 'Huong, get Jane for me, will you?' And after Alison had gone through the door. 'Keep digging Alison.'

*

Stuart collected his coffee from the pod machine, hearing the familiar noises of his housemate coming home. Tarquin was in jeans and hoody, a promotional beanie for *Bluegum Beer* covering his head and ears.

'Coffee with milk and sugar, thanks Stuart.' Tarquin carried a duffle bag which he slung down the short hallway to his room, ten-pin bowling style.

'Training okay?'

'Yeah. We finished with our down-the-ground vision review from the game.' My defence group had a couple of issues.' Tarquin sat at the circular pine table in the eating area, taking a banana from the fruit bowl. 'There was one good comment at the review.' He grinned at the memory. 'Robbo, the defence coach asked Jai why he was over here, on this side, and then why was he running there, at that time – the usual stuff. And Jai spits the dummy and says "I dunno Robbo, excuse me for trying to get the fuckin' football." Some guys are easily over-analysed.'

'Declan has been reading some of the online stuff –'

'Oh no.' Tarquin ate the banana in two bites. 'Kids have to be on social media. But there's so much rubbish.'

'That's what's upset him. He wants to get on to one of the fan forums and answer some of the comments posted – about you.'

'Why did we recruit this has-been? Tarquin Power is a flog. How much is Power paid for that shit game?' Tarquin picked up an apple from the fruit bowl.

'Have you read them too?' asked Stuart.

'No! I learnt in my second year of football to not go there. I know that's what to expect from the keyboard warriors.' Tarquin tossed the apple from hand to hand. 'I'll send Decs a message telling him I'm not worried, nor should he. You don't mind?'

'I think that would be good.' Tarquin was about to set off for his room.

'But I can't send a message to smooth out your love life, Stu. You need to do that.'

The next morning, Stuart sent a message to Alison suggesting a shared coffee break.

Sorry, can't do today. Alison.

Did that mean she really was busy all day, or that she didn't want to see him? And did it mean that she didn't want to see him today, or any other day for that matter? Stuart closed up the work on his laptop, finding it difficult to concentrate on the *Cathedrals of France* program. The last time he had spoken to Jean he discovered that the Frenchman planned a visit to Canberra, with a side trip to Sydney. As part of his study tour, he would talk to the major galleries in each city. The Canberra gallery had an edition of one of Rodin's best-known sculptures, *The Burghers of Calais*, so it made sense.

Stuart took the stairs down to the conservation area. The workshop was its usual quiet and efficient workplace. There was no sign of the Streeton painting. He waved to Christina-Rose behind a glass wall in her office, greeting Astrid at her work cubicle.

'Hi, I wanted to check on the two sets of Arthur Norman stuff I brought in.' Astrid was pairing a lime green dress with elastic-sided boots.

'Your junk finds? No worries.' Astrid hummed to herself as she led the way to the storage room. 'Actually, your discoveries are quite interesting, conservation-wise.' A few minutes later the two of them spread out the artworks that Stuart and Alison had retrieved from the Kew home of Walter Norman and *Fairwind* at Sorrento.

'Which ones did you want to look at?' asked Astrid.

'I wanted to see them all, or a few together. Leave them with me.' Astrid took only one step. 'Actually, Astrid. You've stored an image of all these works, haven't you? Could you send them to me in a file? Thanks.'

Stuart went to a vacant workbench and tapped out a list on his laptop. NAGA had Arthur Norman's *Evening at Beech Forest* painting. There were the two other paintings held by regional galleries. One was the farm courtyard painting, held by Ballarat, and the other was of South Melbourne market, which was in the Gippsland Gallery. Then there were the two paintings in the study at *Conquest*. All the works in front of him were in addition to these paintings.

In total, they had borrowed thirty-seven drawings from *Conquest* and nineteen drawings from *Fairwind,* making fifty-six drawings, in pencil mostly, some in crayon or pen. The drawings ranged from brief five-minute sketches to finished studies which would have taken several hours. The subject matter also ranged across people and places, urban and rural environments.

There were also twenty-five watercolours and twenty-one prints, etchings or lithographs, all retrieved from *Conquest*. Their subject matter focussed on the domestic – interior studies or modest working-class homes. There was a box for the French reproductions and ephemera, all worthy of closer inspection and study. Stuart spread the canvasses from *Conquest* on the table, then arranged the four watercolours and two other paintings from Sorrento alongside them.

Stuart lifted out each drawing and print, inspecting every item for several minutes. He then leant in close to each painting, a couple of times using a magnifying glass. He could now appreciate the artist's hand more fully. Norman's works were strong and assured. They reflected his training at the start of the twentieth century, but he had also developed a delicacy of touch in his handling of drawing materials and paints. His work was restrained and poised. The longer he looked at them, the more Stuart liked the works. Norman had a way of depicting simple scenes and imbuing them with honesty and dignity. There was an invitation in his works, to pause in your daily routine and share a moment of reflection. His work offered a view or snapshot of another person's world. He wanted Alison to be with him now, a want with a fierceness that jolted. He felt their broken closeness like a cracked rib – if he moved any way, it hurt.

Stuart looked again at one of Arthur Norman's paintings on canvas showing an inner-city grocery shop. He leant forward to see if he could decipher an advertisement in the shop window when Christina-Rose appeared at his elbow.

'It says … Ockwell's.'

'You reckon?'

'Think so. They were a brand of sauce or something.' The conservation manager turned to Stuart. 'Stu, I meant to tell you something else about the Streeton painting the other day.'

'When I was with M. Lehni?'

'I said that the tests showed the Streeton canvas and pigments were of their time, but there was something else. The canvas had been primed with a gesso base, as an artist would do for a major study. Streeton had then tinted the primer to reduce or mute the tone. That's not uncommon.'

'Yes, go on.'

'But in the primer, there was an additive I hadn't come across before. I've checked with the other galleries and conservation teams but they hadn't seen it before in a Streeton painting, or anywhere else for that matter. It sems to be a common house paint, widely used on weatherboard homes.'

'I've never heard of it. Have you told Michael?'

'Of course.' Christina-Rose looked down at the Arthur Normans. 'It's an anomaly.'

Stuart watched Christina-Rose return to her office, then returned to the spread of work on the conservation table. He lifted and moved the storage boxes containing all the drawings and prints to one side, rearranging the two sets of paintings in front of him. He thought of the Sorrento ones as the Heidelberg School paintings. He tried to imagine the circumstances that had led to Arthur Norman being a war artist, not serving outside Victoria, and painting these … Conder rip-offs. Of course, that's exactly what they are! They're knocked up Conders. Norman has made a point of signing them with his name, and for good measure written his name, rank and serial number on the back. He definitely didn't want anyone to think these were actually valuable Conder paintings. But that is exactly who he is paying homage to in the paintings before him.

Stuart retrieved one from the table. He barely registered the breezy beach scene at low tide. He focused on the signature, A. Norman, and went very still. The N was done in a leaning, zig-zag style which he had seen before, and very recently. He looked at Christina-Rose but she was talking on her phone. He went from one of the Conder rip-offs to the other, noting the consistency of Arthur Norman's signature in every painting. He had a way of extending the horizontal bar of the A by a fraction. The bar carried over the two slanting lines of the letter A. Stuart quickly checked the artist's signature on the seven *Conquest* paintings – the over-reaching horizontal bar was in every one.

Christina-Rose was still talking so Stuart went to Astrid's cubicle.

'Is the Streeton down here?'

'It's in Michael's office.'

'I want to look at something. Could you bring the image up on your screen?'

'Sure.' Astrid tapped into the conservation team's database and brought up multiple images of Streeton's *Wooreen on the Grange Burn*. Stuart peered over her shoulder to select a detail that included the lower right corner.

'Could you send me that one, plus this one of the whole painting?' Stuart went back to the conservation table. By the time he had taken four steps his phone alerted him to Astrid's email. He waved towards Astrid, opening the Streeton detail on his phone. He zoomed in, then with his open palm placed the painting's signature next to Arthur Norman's signature on the Conder rip-off. Could it be?

Astrid had resumed her work and Christina-Rose was still engaged with her call. He had to think this through before he said anything to anyone else.

'Cheers Astrid,' he called out, signalling his thanks. His departure was almost at a run.

Stuart went to the research team work area but Alison was not there. Her colleague told him that she was in meetings all day. He sent her a message.

Alison, need to see you urgently. When is good? Stuart

Back in his own office Stuart could not sit still. He was picking books up, opening them, putting them down without seeing anything. He sat at his computer but had no sooner opened it than he had to stand again. His phone beeped.

Said I can't do today. Come round tonight?

Definitely, Stu

Champagne was not appropriate for Stuart's visit. They were hardly celebrating. He was very aware he had some making up to do. As nervous as he was excited, he arrived at Alison's townhouse with a chilled French rosé.

'Stuart, is everything okay?'

'Yes and no. Thanks so much for seeing me tonight.'

'That's what good friends do, I believe.' Stuart detected the dryness of the comment but Alison had been welcoming enough at her door. She had removed whatever makeup she applied for work hours and tied her hair back with a headscarf. She accepted the offer to share a glass of wine. Stuart had to curb his impaticnce as Alison sat down, then rose again to get some nibbles to go with the wine. *Where should he start?*

'Now, what is so urgent?' Stuart took a breath.

'I'm sorry, Alison. I am so sorry. I've been a dickhead.' He was searching her face, sitting a person-width apart.

'You were, Stuart.' Alison fixed her gaze on her glass of wine. 'I was so disappointed in you. I felt you genuinely didn't trust me. And that hurts.' Stuart spoke softly, his voice intense.

'And that was absolutely my stupid fault. I don't why I didn't mention Hillier's paintings to you. But I couldn't go another day feeling like this.'

'Now we're sounding like teenagers,' said Alison with a smile.

'That's how I feel. Like a dumb teenager who did a dumb thing.' They talked for a bit longer but Stuart had said his hardest words. Alison could see the humour when he conceded he was so emotionally inept that he had to take relationship advice from a footballer. They spoke about the paintings at the Hillier home, but already some of the gloss surrounding them was tarnished. They were less earth-shattering now.

Pouring out a second glass of wine, Stuart gathered his thoughts again.

'There is something else I want to tell you.'

'Uh oh, is this the *but*?'

'No, no, no. It's about work and I don't want you excluded. I think I know what needs to be done but I don't want to make a dickhead decision again.'

'Okay,' Alison drew out the word as an invitation. Stuart sat closer to Alison and on an impulse, held her hand.

'Our Arthur Norman … was a forger. I think he did forgeries of Charles Conder paintings.'

'The ones from Sorrento? But he signed them and put his name on the back.'

'He did, but how do we know he didn't do others? I agree in this case he did sign them, but that was so they would not be confused with real Conders. Because he knew he was good enough to get away with it.'

'But he didn't. We've no evidence at all of him trying to sell or pass of fake Conders or anyone else.' Alison was puzzled, Stuart still excited.

'True. But put that aside for a minute – there's something else about Norman. This is bigger so prepare yourself.' He tightened his grip on her hand. 'I reckon Arthur Norman did that painting for the SummerHayes family at *Wooreen*. The Streeton.' Alison laughed, then stopped when she saw Stuart was serious.

'Here's why, we know –'

'Streeton signed the painting, Stuart.'

'Agreed, it is signed A. Streeton. I'll get to that. First, we know that Arthur Norman is a more than competent artist, and that he had the ability, and inclination, to do fake Conders. Perhaps just for his own amusement, we don't know. We do know that Arthur painted in Western Victoria in the early twentieth century. We have his Beech Forest painting in NAGA, and remember something Francis said down at Sorrento?'

'Remind me, I've been trying to forget that day.'

'His grandfather, Albert, died in 1989 or 1990. Francis remembered his grandfather saying how his father was an unappreciated artist, and that he had a strong affinity for rural scenes. And Netty said in her research into Walter that there was a reference to Arthur having a job on a farm. Okay? Now. One of the drawings I looked at today. I reckon it's a pencil sketch of the *Wooreen* homestead.'

'I'll have to have another look at it.'

'Yes, please do! That's why I need your help. You've been there and I haven't.'

'And remember, Charlotte's journal entry only said 'the painting chap staying here'. Surely if you had Sir Arthur Streeton staying as a house guest you would use his name in the journal entry. I would, anyone would,' said Stuart.

'And Alison, two things from today. Christina-Rose told me there is an anomaly in the canvas preparation of the SummerHayes Streeton. There's a stray pigment used to tint the primer – a house paint.'

'She told Michael?'

'Apparently. And the other thing from today.' Stuart opened his phone, flicking from one image to a second. They were close ups of the two signatures, A. Streeton and A. Norman. Alison peered closely at the screen.

'Could be a coincidence –'

'No. I can see it now. I can see Arthur Norman's hand in that so-called Streeton. Have a look at this detail in the capital A.' There were a few minutes when neither spoke. Stuart drank his wine, clamping his mouth to stay silent while Alison absorbed his information. She picked up his phone and flicked through the series of images which Stuart had gone through.

'What are we going to do?' asked Alison.

'You're convinced too, then.'

'As a good researcher I want to go back and check all your evidence, but yes. I definitely want to ask Netty about that reference to Arthur staying on a farm. And I think the dates are about right, for Arthur to have been in Western Victoria in the 1920s.' Alison and Stuart spent the next hour going over their plans. They had things they wanted to double check, agreeing that they would work on each bit of what they now called evidence, together.

'Oh hell,' said Alison. 'Michael will be making his announcement and public appeal any day now.'

'Right, that's why we have to move quickly.' Alison put aside her glass of wine and opened her laptop. They drafted a document setting out the evidence to support their argument. Against each point they made actions to follow up. Alison sat back, heaving a sigh at the list of tasks. Stuart was still on a high, but could see she was very tired.

'I had better let you go,' he said.

'Yes. My head is reeling a bit. I'm also fading fast.' Alison sorted out scraps of paper next to the laptop, held them in her hands. 'It's been an interesting evening.' She now spoke with deliberation, in a low voice.

'Stuart, when you said you needed to see me about something urgent, did you intend to say you were sorry, or to tell me about Norman and the Streeton?' Stuart covered her clasped hands with his, like nurturing a fire to make it start.

'I only today worked out that I think the Streeton is not a Streeton. But when I got here and saw you, the only thing I had to do was apologise.'

'Not a bad answer.' She kissed him on the cheek. 'Goodnight.'

Stuart and Alison worked like conspirators on their research. The word around NAGA was that a media event and Michael's morning television promotion were going to happen at the end of the week. The rumour was given further strength by the especially manic behaviour of Jane over the last few days. Kelly Bertolucci reported that she had seen Jane, walking at pace down the administration corridor, mobile phones held to both ears.

In the morning Stuart and Alison met downstairs in the conservation workshop. Stuart explained their visit to Astrid.

'I want to show Alison our haul of Arthur Normans.'

'God, you sound so false,' whispered Alison as they arranged the artworks from the two Norman homes. 'You'd never make a master-criminal.'

'Can you see the drawing I mean?' Stuart tilted his head without indicating a particular Norman sketch.

'Of course, that pencil drawing there. That must be the homestead, nestled in the slight valley of the Grange Burn.' Alison leaned in closer. 'Remember, I've been to the spot and stood where this was drawn.' She furrowed her brow. 'I don't know why I missed it before. Is it dated?'

'No. If we have to, we could ask Christina-Rose to do some dating.'

'The other thing to check is the signature.' Alison brought one of the small painting sketches towards her. 'You've got that detail of Streeton's signature?' Stuart opened the image on his phone and held it next to Arthur Norman's name. 'Wow, this is unbelievable.' Alison looked at other paintings' signatures, in every case seeing the angular, zig-zag letters and the tell-tale lengthened cross bar in the capital A. 'You've checked Streeton's signature on his other paintings? He didn't by chance do an A like that, and Norman copied it from him?'

'No, I checked. No chance.'

'Stuart, I'll give Melanie a call and see if Francis, or the magnificent Netty, can tell us anything else about Arthur painting on a farm. We know he did paint at Beech Forest but that's in the Otway Ranges. We need to know about that farm job.' They were talking very quietly, but Alison had let a sense of urgency, as well as the thrill of the hunt, into her voice. Stuart loved having her as an ally.

'Before we put these away, look at the totality of Norman's work. Can you see what I saw – that Norman had the ability to copy at a high level, and that he did that *Wooreen* painting?'

'I can. But can we convince Michael?'

Stuart did not want to hover while Alison contacted the Norman family. In his office he pulled up the document they had put together the previous night, setting out their reasoning and evidence. He read through their summary again, tightening up the wording, not wanting to overstate or downplay the observations. He decided to add a number, or score, at the end of each point. The ratings varied as to the extent that particular point supported the possibility of Norman being the painter and not Streeton.

Norman possessed the high level of professional expertise to complete a painting equivalent to Streeton
7/10

The primer on the Wooreen canvas used a house paint additive that is not found on any other Streeton paintings
8/10

There were other points, but he saved his highest rating for the distinctive capital As in the signatures. He hesitated, a ten would have been unprofessional, but nine was not adequate.

Norman signed his paintings with an A, always with a lengthened cross-bar. This letter is painted as part of the SummerHayes 'A. Streeton' signature

He typed 9.5/10. He was ready to send the document to Alison when she contacted him.

Stuart, Spoke to Mel. Meet in cafe in ten. That's an order! A

*

Stuart picked up his coffee. It had gone cold but he had a sip anyway. He and Alison had been talking, heads almost touching, for the last twenty minutes.

'Well, that's it then,' said Stuart. He sat back as Alison held their document setting out their reasoning and evidence about the painting. The painting they now called, under their breath, 'the fake Streeton'. It now resided upstairs in the Acting Director's office ahead of a public unveiling and appeal for funds.

Alison's conversation with Melanie had been guarded, but instructive. Mel said that the recent find at her home

in Kew, and the interest shown by NAGA, had prompted a lot of chats between the older members of the family about both of the Norman brothers. Mel had told Alison that after their visit to Sorrento, Francis had recalled more of his grandfather Albert's stories about Arthur. Albert used to talk about fancy garden parties at *Conquest* that he attended as a boy, and remembered his father being absent for weeks at a time when he went off painting in the bush.

Then, at Alison's request, Mel had sat down with Netty and asked what she knew or could remember. Netty said that in writing her history of Walter Norman and *Conquest* there were definitely several references in letters to Arthur going bush, disappearing for weeks at a time (which Walter found irresponsible), and some photographs which showed Arthur with drawings or paintings he had done on farms. Netty then went to her room and dragged out a box of papers which she had kept from when she wrote the brochure about Walter. Mel reported that Netty selected a large envelope without hesitation, pulling out several letters. One from Walter to Elsie at 38 Dorcas Street contained some sentences which Mel read over the phone. Alison read the words to Stuart in restrained excitement, keeping her voice to a whisper.

I would be pleased if you were to inform Arthur that I need to see him immediately on his return from his painting job at Wooreen. We need to talk about some personal matters which I am not at liberty to indulge at present.

The mention of *Wooreen* hit Stuart like one of Tarquin's football tackles. He could only stare at Alison. This time she put her hand over his.

'There's more.' Alison had also asked about any additional photos and again Netty had the answer – Ballarat Regional Gallery. 'They've got the farmyard scene, the courtyard painting by Arthur. And in their library material they have a photo of him doing the sketch.' The Ballarat Gallery curator had been very cooperative, being familiar with the Norman oil sketch and locating the two photographs which she had emailed to Alison and were now on her laptop. The photographs, by an unknown photographer, were two different perspectives, both shots of the artist at work, using a tin as a seat. In one, Norman was totally absorbed in his painting, in the other he was looking back over his shoulder at the camera, palette in one hand, paint brush in the other. The artist's spindly easel was in front of him, and on the easel was a canvas of the courtyard painting in progress. The upturned ten-gallon tin had the product name on it, upside down. Alison rotated the photo on her screen, then used her thumb and forefinger to enlarge the lettering – the painter was sitting on an old tin of *Reddo*.

Stuart recognised the artist in the photograph as Arthur Norman. Alison recognised the courtyard as the one at *Wooreen* homestead. They would talk to Christina-Rose about *Reddo*.

'Alison, I'm going to see Michael.' Alison nodded, wearily.

'We have to,' she said.

'I'll do it though. I'll talk to him and set out what we have found,' said Stuart.

'It's very persuasive,' said Alison. 'Our evidence at least raises serious doubts and we can't let Michael go ahead with the announcement.'

'I'm certain it's a fake. Imagine the fallout from this, the potential embarrassment.' Stuart gathered up their notes. They had some extra points to add, coming from Mel's latest information. 'I think it's best if we continue to keep it quiet, not tell anyone else in the gallery. I'll talk with Michael and he can un-wind things as best he can. No need for both of us to tackle Michael, we don't want to appear to be ganging up on him.'

*

The National Art Gallery of Australia had closed to the public. Behind the exhibitions and displays, gallery staff were finishing their day's work. The building was gradually emptying, leaving out of hours security staff to guard the treasures in the collection. At the building's highest level, in the director's office and informal meeting room, Michael and Jane were enjoying the company of M. Jean Lehni and Andrew SummerHayes.

'Bon voyage, Jean!' said Michael as he clapped the Frenchman on his back. 'Jane will help you get a taxi downstairs to the airport. Enjoy Canberra.' Jane slid her handbag up her arm and farewelled Michael and Andrew with potent white-wine kisses. Andrew stood up as the two left.

'I better be off too. Supposed to meet Annabel in the city …' Andrew checked his watch. 'Twenty minutes ago.' The two men shook hands.

'Great to see you, Andrew. We're ready to rock and roll with the Streeton. It'll be sensational.' Michael surveyed the empty wine bottles, assorted glassware, restaurant food platters and used napkins in the meeting room. 'Huong!' His assistant, following orders, had remained at his work station while Michael had entertained guests. He was sent down to see Patrick in the restaurant for extra wine an hour ago. The Vietnamese-Australian young man went into the meeting room.

'Huong, clean this up will you.' Michael went into his inner office – the Streeton was on an easel in one corner. Huong collected wine glasses and took them into the kitchenette, adjacent to the director's office.

Stuart had been waiting to see Michael since mid-afternoon. Alison had again offered to accompany him, but he had convinced her to go home. He reasoned that after he had spoken to Michael, that Michael would logically want Alison's opinion as a researcher. She would be able to reinforce their evidence after the shock had worn off for Michael. Huong said he would let Stuart know when Michael was available. Stuart stressed the importance that he speak to the Acting Director tonight. Huong put a stack of small plates on the sink in the kitchenette and sent Stuart the message.

Catch him now, quick.

'What is it, Stu?' Michael had food stains on his shirt.

'We need to talk. Best to sit down.' Michael was prowling his office, picking up papers.

'I haven't got time to –'

'I think that's a fake.' Stuart had not wanted to be so blunt and confrontational, but he needed to get Michael's attention. *That ought to do it.* Stuart nodded towards the Streeton as he sat down and put a folder on the desk. He opened his and Alison's document containing evidence for his claim. He had copies of the photograph of Norman from the Ballarat Gallery, screenshots from his phone and reproductions of NAGA database images of both Norman and Streeton artworks. Michael was stunned into silence. He looked around his office as if there was a hidden camera to record the prank. Stuart spoke carefully and clearly – he didn't underestimate what was at stake. Michael listened in annoyance to Stuart – unable to resist exclamations and interjections. His response went through the seven stages of bluster. He initially thought Stuart was making a joke 'in poor bloody taste', then he went to denial mixed with abuse, followed by anger and personal attacks.

'That's crap, Stuart. What a load of bullshit. This painting's been in the SummerHayes family for almost a hundred years. No-one has ever queried it.' Michael rose from his seat, stared at the Streeton, glared at Stuart.

'I don't know why you've been going behind my back, stirring up trouble. Are you jealous of me because I'm in the director's chair?' This was too ridiculous for Stuart.

'I'm saying things that are backed up with research into Norman's –'

'Ha! That Arthur fucking Norman. You're obsessed about him, Stu, always have been. And in this case, it has affected your judgement.'

'Look at our research –'

'Yeah, bloody research. I asked your Alison to research the Streeton background, and what did she come up with? One fucking diary entry! Piss poor effort. There must have been –'

'Michael. Abuse me if you have to, but don't talk like that about Alison.' Stuart shifted in his chair, locking his eyes on Michael's flushed face. 'She is the best research professional you'll ever know. She has more integrity than you could understand. Even if you knew the meaning of the word.' The discussion had escalated with every sentence, the voices of both men carrying into the kitchenette. Huong held the plates and glasses he was washing so as to not make a noise. As both men stood a metre apart, violence was one sentence away. Michael drew a large breath – his anger and abuse had over-rode his semi-drunkenness. After the initial shock Stuart thought Michael may have, by now, accepted some of the points about the fake Streeton. His director might be beginning to see things more clearly and be coming to a considered view. Michael had only gathered himself together for a statement.

'Stu.' He said it like a swear word. 'All you have said is that this Norman character might have painted *Wooreen*. Nothing in what you have said proves that Streeton did not.' Michael sniffed noisily. 'I can't believe you can come in here … and compare and confuse … the works of a great Australian artist in Sir

Arthur Streeton, with some two-bit nobody just because his name is also Arthur and your fucking obsessed with him.'

'Michael –'

'No, you've said your piece. I've listened to what you had to say, your so-called evidence, your co-research, and the accusations you have made about me. And, you've conveniently forgotten that I'm an expert on the Heidelberg School, something you've completely bloody ignored.' Stuart had made all the points he could, and now it was up to the other man. Michael looked at the painting in the corner of his office.

'To be crystal-fucking clear, Stuart. Are you, now you've had your say, going to drop this?' Stuart didn't hesitate.

'No.' Michael was ready with his comeback.

'Because I don't want a curator in my gallery who has such poor curatorial skills –'

'In what way?'

'This crap of yours shows poor judgement, it's totally unprofessional and disrespectful to me. And Jean from the Rodin Institute said the stuff you are doing with him is not up to scratch –'

'That's the first I've heard of it and it's not relevant here –'

'Oh, it's relevant, Stu.' Michael was more in control of his voice and emotions. 'Because I'm making the decision that your employment at NAGA is over –'

'What, that's not the issue –'

'– as from the end of the month. That's all I'm going to say. That's all I have to say.'

'You working from home Stu?' Tarquin had his duffle bag and was leaving for a training session at his football club.

'Sort of. What's on for you today?'

'Pilates and pool session. Catch you later.' It struck Stuart as Tarquin left how much his life had changed. His marriage of over ten years had finished, he was seeing his son only part of the week, he was sharing a home with an AFL footballer, and he was leaving his job at the nation's premier art institution. And talking of change, where did Alison fit into his changed life and whatever was ahead of him?

Stuart had been quite calm when he got home the previous night after confronting Michael. He had done his best to put his argument and it was up to Michael what actions he took. He was frustrated by Michael's response, red-angry at his criticism of Alison. If Michael followed through in ending his employment, it was neither here nor there to Stuart. In his mind, he had resigned anyway. He had worked with Michael for long enough, and had enough experiences, to have no respect for him. Stuart tested his own feelings several times. Each time he considered his current feelings, and his future, he felt comfortable and relaxed about no longer working for the gallery. He would miss many of his fellow curators and arts professionals, but he would not miss the petty politics and poor leadership at the top. Stuart's message to Alison last night had mentioned none of this.

Hi Alison – spoke to Michael. It's a strong argument but he reacted poorly, you might have guessed. Talk tomorrow. Take care, Stuart.

Stuart was checking his emails at the kitchen bench. He found himself bringing up the fake Streeton document, reading again the evidence points they had put together. He had confidence in their research and observations. Although he wouldn't change a thing, he made a decision. He was about to make a cup of tea and talk to Alison – he wanted them both to agree not to tell anyone else about the fake Streeton, but let Michael make his call. The kettle had boiled when his phone went off, Alison's name coming up.

'Hi, I was about to call you.'

'Stuart, you okay?'

'Sure, it was an ugly discussion as you can imagine.'

'I don't have to imagine. Huong came down to see me. He was in the kitchenette all the time and he told me everything he heard you and Michael say.' In the pause, Stuart could hear a currawong calling.

'Are you outdoors?'

'Don't worry about that. Huong was upset when he spoke to me. He told me that my name got shouted out last night, and what Michael said about your employment.' Alison waited for Stuart to talk. 'Has Michael followed up today?'

'Not yet, he may not but I –'

'Stuart, I'm around the corner at your local café. Come here and we'll talk.'

Stuart went to close his laptop. He stopped mid-action, noticing an alert for a new email in his inbox, from

Michael. It was short, confirming his employment cessation. Stuart closed the laptop and smiled, picking up his house keys and wallet.

Stuart saw Alison sitting with her distinctive straight back at an outside table. He had cut through a laneway, approaching from her side as she sat looking into the distance. The café umbrellas were furled. He loved her profile, her small and perfect nose. He stopped to avoid getting bowled over by a cyclist on the footpath. While halted, he felt the warmth of the sun on his face. It was everybody's favourite autumn day. On a day such as this, Melbourne was becalmed. Only the readiest of leaves would drift to the ground. The sky would stay metallic, brilliant blue until the sun was on the horizon. Then it would be a search for cardigans and jackets, a time to bring outdoor furniture cushions inside, think about what's for dinner.

Alison saw Stuart from three steps away. She stood up and they embraced. Still holding, he kissed her, inhaling her scent at the same time.

'Well,' she said when they broke. 'I did the right thing in coming here?'

'You did absolutely the right thing,' said Stuart, sitting down. Alison sat and faced Stuart, her eyes searching his face.

'I heard from Huong that you stood up for me with Michael. To quote Huong, you said I was the best researcher in the whole world, and Michael should know it.'

'Close enough.'

'It means a lot.'

'And did he actually sack you on the spot, as Huong said.' Alison's face was contorted with concern. 'He couldn't believe it. Huong had tears in his eyes, he said "but you're the best curator".' The café waiter came to take their orders.

'Let's have coffee. I've got plenty of time, you?' asked Stuart.

Stuart took Alison through last night's discussion with Michael. He went over the evidence which he and Alison had put together, trying to recall the exact wording of Michael's response. The tenor of his response was easier to convey – a spate of swearing and abuse. Alison was still worried about Stuart's dismissal.

'Michael sent me a brief email to confirm what he said last night, and you know what? I feel absolutely fine about it.'

'You don't look upset, I can see that,' said Alison. 'You're sure we shouldn't talk to the other curators, or Christina-Rose? Or should we go to the board – Michael's behaviour, about the Streeton but also to you, is beyond deplorable.'

'It is. However, I think we should leave it with him. He may change his ideas after last night. Perhaps not. But I reckon let him make the decision for himself, and face the consequences.' Stuart grinned. 'Making your choice and facing the consequences, that's what Leah and I have been trying to teach Declan.' Alison's phone beeped. It had been prompting her every few minutes. 'Why don't you check that? I'll have another coffee.'

When Stuart returned Alison was putting her phone into her jacket pocket.

'Stuart, I was upset when Huong spoke to me this morning. I had to speak to someone. I talked to Kelly about the fake Streeton, I hope that's okay.'

'Of course, she's your friend and she'll understand.'

'That was her sending messages, wanting to know where I was and if I was okay.' Alison smiled across the table. 'I told her I was with you and I was definitely okay.'

'As long as she gives Michael time to do the right thing,' said Stuart.

'I stressed that to her just then,' said Alison, indicating her phone. 'But Kelly wants to see our evidence too.'

'I don't suppose it will hurt to send it to her. And I'll remind her to keep it confidential too.' The sun was still splashing their table. Stuart had to hold his phone at an angle to see the screen. He sent the document and a couple of key images to Kelly, saying he and Alison would follow up soon and go over their findings.

'Let's walk through the park,' said Stuart, finishing his coffee. They strolled into the late nineteenth century municipal park. Its mature trees were glowing, their shadows monstrously long across the lawn. They chose a path at random, by unspoken agreement walking slowly arm in arm. Stuart's phone pinged. He paused on the asphalt path. Kelly was stirred up and wanted to know 'more, please, and everything else' but Stuart wanted to take this time with Alison. While checking his phone Alison leant into him. He returned the enfolding, about to close his phone, its screen showing the detailed photograph of Arthur Norman's signature.

'Alison?' She replied with a murmur. Stuart led them to the concrete steps of the park's rotunda. 'Sit down, here.' They sat side by side, oblivious to the dog-walkers, pram strollers and the rest of Melbourne. 'I know what I'm going to do.' His face lit up. In his boyish enthusiasm Alison saw a flash of an early teenage Stuart she never knew. 'I'm going to France to trace Arthur Norman's years in Paris. You know I found his grave from 1938, thanks to you. It raises so many questions. Just as him painting the fake Streeton does.' Stuart stood up, the idea so pulsating he had to move.

'It would be a good research area.' Alison was getting her head around Stuart's enthusiasm and plan. 'You could have a lot of fun chasing up his last years … and his missing years.'

When Stuart had got interested in NAGA's *Evening at Beech Forest* painting by Arthur Norman, he became intrigued about the modest career of the artist. When he was in Paris for his work on the Musée d'Orsay loan exhibition Alison, back at NAGA, had found a surprising fact. Norman had died and was buried in Paris. For reasons not known, even to Norman's descendants, Arthur had left his family in Melbourne and lived the last eight years of his life in France.

Stuart's mind was buzzing, but he knew some things with precision. He stood up.

'I'm going straight away. I just need a couple of days to make sure Mum is okay with her executor stuff –

anyway Alex and Gareth can look after her.' Stuart compressed his lips, taking small steps but not moving away from where Alison sat. He dropped beside her again.

'Alison, would you come with me? To Paris?'

At NAGA, Stuart set to with a sharp focus. Having made his decision, he wanted to finish at work and get on a plane to Europe immediately. Leaving his job at the gallery, while not in the circumstances of his choosing, was liberating. In his office he sorted out some loose ends in his workload, put aside a few personal items, then went to the conservation workshop. The news of his dismissal, or resignation (depending on who was telling it) had rapidly circulated amongst curatorial and professional staff. Stuart was not surprised when Christina-Rose shepherded him into her office, bypassing the work table where the Arthur Norman material had been put out again at his request.

'Stuart, I heard the news.' Christina-Rose peered at him over her bi-focal glasses. Even now, he felt like a schoolboy asked to explain himself. Before he spoke her face softened. 'I am very sorry to see you go.'

'It's okay, it's actually what I want.'

'That may be so.' Christina-Rose indicated the worktable outside her office. 'Astrid and I did a close inspection of your Norman material when she put it out this morning.' She used her principal-pause to full effect. 'There are some interesting things to see in the details.'

'There are. I'm handing over the ongoing liaison between the Norman family and NAGA to Alison.'

'Of course.' Another look over the rims of her glasses. 'Do you know what you're going to do?'

'I'll get another role, go freelance curating. Perhaps do a tree change and go to a regional gallery.' It was clear to Christina-Rose and Stuart that he was making this up on the spot. 'Christina-Rose, we found a photo of Arthur

Norman sitting on a tin of *Reddo*, the housepaint. Do you think …'

'I'll look into it. Kelly was down here earlier. Talking about you naturally,' said Christina-Rose.

'I'll catch some people while I'm here today, but come back and do a proper farewell later. Drinks at the Northern etcetera.' Stuart had a lot to do in a short time. He had room to worry about what Michael intended to do, or say. He was determined to follow through on the plan he told Alison. The idea of a break from work at NAGA, underlined by a trip to Paris and some personal research and relaxation, was what he must do. Alison was going to get back to him today with an answer to his invitation to accompany him.

Stuart did not seek out people at NAGA. Those he bumped into, he gave the same version and sentiment that he had with Christina-Rose. He had messaged his mother that he would be dropping in at the Heathmont house. There, he found her alone. He couldn't shake off a sense that his father was in another room, or would enter quietly through the back door in his gardening clothes. Alex was at work and Gareth was catching up with an old school mate. Rosemary prised the lid off a circular cake tin, lifted out a slice for each of them while Stuart made tea.

'It still feels odd to be in the house by myself,' said Rosemary. 'I expect your dad to come in and make an announcement about some result. Won the tennis! Or, no luck at Bunnings. They're all out of air filters.'

'It will take some getting used to,' said Stuart. He felt the triteness and inadequacy of the words as they left his mouth. They sat at the kitchen table. Insurance-looking papers and other documents were taking up one end. 'How are you going with the executor stuff?'

'It's all done mostly. Your dad set it all up for me, even leaving step by step instructions.' Rosemary used a spectacle cloth to clean her glasses.

'Are you needing your glasses more often?'

'Don't you start. I've always worn them. You've just started to notice. Alex thinks I'm a primary school student who needs tutoring, and Gareth is off in a world of his own as usual. Try this slice – date and almond.'

'Mum.' Stuart picked up the slice then put it back on his plate. 'I've finished up at the gallery. NAGA and I are parting company.' Rosemary's mouth opened, incomprehension on her face.

'What do you mean, parting company?'

'I've left, leaving. Finishing up.'

'That's sudden, isn't it? What are you going to live on?'

'It is sudden, but it's been coming for a while. I don't like the way things have been going lately and the acting director wanted to move me on, he –'

'What did you do?' A mother talking to her son.

'I didn't do anything, but we did have a professional disagreement.' Before his mother could ask, Stuart continued. 'It's actually what I want, mum. I'll be able to get by financially, don't worry about that.' They both drank some tea.

'I'm going to take a trip to France straight away. Like next week. Will you be okay if I'm not here for a little while?

'Of course I will. Are you going to see Juliette in Tours?' Rosemary's long term French friend was at the heart of a French obsession which mother had passed on to son. What started off as an old-fashioned pen-friend had turned into a life-long close friendship. Rosemary and Juliette had grown up, started families, visited each other, even staying in each other's homes. Stuart was the child who had most absorbed his mother's love for all things French. From the first trip with his parents and siblings, he had known that France was a special place to which he would always return. Stuart had maintained this interest into his own adult years, initially travelling by himself and then with his own family.

'Don't know if I'll get to Tours.'

'Are you going by yourself?' Rosemary gave her question a lightness and upward inflection.

'Alison may come with me. Depends.'

'You might never come back.' Stuart's mother smiled as she spoke, gathering up her plate, cup and saucer.

Stuart remained at the kitchen table, the memory of a million family conversations around that table crowding his thoughts. He opened his phone – there were several messages from NAGA colleagues.

Stu – so sad to see you go, talk soon Kelly (I have a lot to say)

Mate, let's have a few and you can tell me the story – Matt

There was more of the same, but nothing from Alison. A reminder message told him to pick up Declan from school and take him to Tarquin's club training facility.

At the black and white club, Tarquin had shown Declan and Stuart the training oval (like any other oval), the weights room (one or two players Stuart didn't know were there and weren't introduced), gym area (like any gym), team meeting room (infamous amongst players as the venue of too many, and too long meetings), kitchen (smelling of toasties), dining room (communal tables and chairs) and players' lounge. Pointing to the sign on the door of the last room, Tarquin told them how the 'players only' rule was strictly enforced – even the coach was not allowed in the lounge without being invited. He said the players need one area where they are not under constant scrutiny and can speak freely. Which they did. They were now standing at the side of the 25-metre pool.

'Jai,' called Tarquin. 'Can you do your walk for us? The big footballer was standing at the end of the pool, water up to his tattooed chest.

'Just for you, Tarqs.' He took a large breath, bent down at the knees to completely submerge himself, then starting walking under water. Declan and Stuart watched his progress. Jai could be seen under the clear, chlorinated water. He crouched, pumping his arms like pistons and steadily walking down the lane. Declan's mouth was open, hardly breathing, his eyes getting wider and wider. Jai walked until the end, touched the pool with his hand, then stood up, breaking the water with his hands on his hips, breathing deeply.

'Wow!' said Declan.

'Thanks Jai,' said Tarquin. Stuart's phone pinged – a short message from Alison.

'Yes!' said Stuart. He had been holding his breath too.

Alison stood in the middle of the lounge room of the Paris apartment. She let go of the extended handle of her suitcase and slowly turned a full circle. Stuart was in the bedroom with his luggage and she wanted this moment to herself – to fully experience her first Paris apartment. Looking up, she stifled a laugh, '*Chandeliers!' Are they kidding?* The room had aged, scarred and pitted, but polished floorboards. The floor was partly covered with rugs. The ceilings must be three metres high. *How had Stuart found this place?* Alison had travelled to New Zealand, and Thailand and Cambodia in Asia. She vaguely remembered a visit as a young girl to elderly relatives in England. It was wet and grey, the people ancient and musty. This place, a perfect one-bedroom apartment in the 7th arrondisement, was her introduction to France. Stuart joined her in the lounge room.

'There's a kitchen through there with a dining alcove.' Alison stopped him from exploring by grasping his hand.

'Stuart.'

'You alright?'

'We are in Paris. Everything is perfect.' There had been a flurry of activity for them to get to Europe. Stuart had booked flights and accommodation. As a veteran of trips to France and a French speaker, she was happy to let him take the responsibility. She had been swept up in his eagerness to roll some Arthur Norman research into a Parisian holiday. They would also visit Marion and JP at the Musée d'Orsay. Even now, she felt a thrill from the spontaneity of their actions.

'Hey, you haven't moved. Look over here.' Still holding hands, Stuart led Alison to one of the room's two curtained windows. With the back of his hand, he moved the curtain to one side, then opened a long, casement window which was also a door onto a shallow balcony.

'It's …' Alison stepped through the space. 'The Eiffel Tower!' The apartment had been especially chosen by Stuart for this effect. It was in a different arrondisement than he would normally have stayed. On other visits he had preferred to seek out a more neighbourhood feel – and he knew a view of the Eiffel Tower was a cliché. He reasoned if there is one time in your life when you can indulge a cliché it should be on your first visit to Paris. They stood on the narrow, second storey balcony, lime-green tops of boulevard trees below them. The buildings opposite took up half their view, the Eiffel Tower and the landscaped gardens of the Champ de Mars the other. It was late in the afternoon, the blue sky dotted with still, white clouds daubed by a street painter.

'Do you want to go for a walk in our neighbourhood?' asked Stuart.

'Stuart, I want to do everything. I want to take a boat on the Seine, see the Louvre, eat crepes, walk in every garden, go down the Catacombs, drink wine in every corner bar –'

'And so we shall.' Alison turned from the view.

'Stuart.' Their kiss was also in the realm of cliché, but neither cared.

On the flight to Europe, Stuart and Alison had talked for more hours than they slept. They went over and over the discoveries they had made about Arthur Norman and the fake Streeton. They talked about Michael's response and the implications of what might happen. In Stuart's trips to NAGA, colleagues had told him that Michael had all but locked himself away. Huong had caught up with Stuart in the curators' offices, dissolving into tears. Jane was the only person who was in and out of Michael's office, frequently with an uncharacteristically concerned expression. Nobody knew if Michael still intended to go public about the gallery's planned announcement about the Streeton.

Alison and Stuart discussed some ideas about how, during their time in Paris, they would see if they could get some leads into what Norman did, and how he lived – those last years of his life that were presently a mystery. Stuart promised that the first step in their research was to take Alison to Montparnasse Cemetery to visit Arthur Norman's grave. At the end of their flight, as the crew made the in-flight announcement and directions for landing, Alison held Stuart's forearm on the seat rest.

'You nervous?'

'No. I need to tell you something,' said Alison. They leant towards each other, shoulders pressing together as Alison spoke. 'Before I left NAGA, Kelly told me that the managers have gone to the Board about the fake Streeton.'

'Who?'

'Kelly, Christina-Rose. They've got Matt and others behind them. They have lodged a formal protest with the Chairman.' Stuart absorbed the information as the plane touched French ground.

In the apartment Stuart looked at the pedestrians on the street below. It was difficult to tell from the balcony but he thought that Parisian workers outnumbered tourists. He had been testing the internet connection, reading the Melbourne news. Tarquin Power had kicked two goals for the black and white in their win on the weekend. Team-mate Jai had injured his hamstring. He stepped inside, closed the casement window, pulled the curtain across and put his phone in his jacket. They were ready to go out into the Paris evening. Alison picked up her cardigan, Stuart held it for her to put her arms through. He smelt the barest suggestion of perfume, closing his eyes for a milli-second. As he closed the door on their apartment, he did not register his phone's news alert.

ABC News Melbourne: Lost masterpiece unveiled by gallery

A rare Heidelberg School painting, done in 1924 by Sir Arthur Streeton, has been found by Melbourne's National Art Gallery of Australia. NAGA Acting Director Michael Maher yesterday presented the iconic landscape to art lovers and the media. The painting of *Wooreen on the Grange Burn* has been languishing for almost a hundred years in the heritage listed Western District home it depicted.

Maher said, while launching a public appeal for funds to buy the Streeton, that ...

THE END

AUTHOR'S NOTE

The National Gallery of Australia in Canberra houses a magnificent collection of art works from Australia and overseas. It employs many highly dedicated and professional staff. There is also a National Gallery of Victoria, which is an older institution and is in Melbourne, south of the central business district and the Yarra River. For The Art Curator series, I have created the National Art Gallery of Australia, or NAGA, and located this fictitious institution in Melbourne, on the city's northern edge.

Following Blockbuster, this is the second book of The Art Curator series. In the third novel of The Art Curator series, Stuart has moved to central Victoria and taken up a position as regional gallery director.

www.ingramcontent.com/pod-product-compliance
Lightning Source LLC
LaVergne TN
LVHW030917080826
845145LV00013B/2936